Beijinger in New York

by Glen Cao

(translated by Ted Wang)

Cypress Book Company

San Francisco

 Address inquiries to China Books, 2929 Twenty-fourth Street, San Francisco, CA 94110.

Library of Congress Catalog Card Number: 93-073062
ISBN 0-8351-2526-2

Publishers' Note

When first published in China in October 1991, *Beijinger in New York* instantly became the country's No. 1 bestseller of that year. More than 120,000 copies were sold in one week. The serialization of the novel in the *Beijing Evening News* increased the newspaper's circulation from 500,000 to 2,500,000. It was broadcast as a radio play, and at last report the novel was on its eighth printing having sold no less than twenty million copies.

The book has been made into a twenty-episode television series, which aired on China's CCTV network to an audience estimated at 900 million. Directed by famed director Zheng Xiaolong, it was the first full-length Chinese drama to be filmed in the U.S. Subtitled versions will also be broadcast over Western Chinese-language TV stations, and a dubbed and edited version is in preparation for English-language viewers.

The novel tells the immigrant experience of Wang Qiming, a Chinese who in 1981 came to New York with hopes of searching for the fabled bounty and dreams of making his fortune, knowing little more than tall-tales and rumors, myths that coalesced from a lifetime of hearsay and opinion. It took him nine years of hardship and pain to find the line between the fable and reality.

For Americans, *Beijinger in New York* provides a rare opportunity to see themselves in the eyes of a Chinese immigrant in America's greatest city. Reading it is just like reading *Gulliver's Travels* from the point of view of the

Lilliputians; they never saw themselves until someone truly different came along.

Beijinger in New York provides students of Chinese culture with a thought-provoking introduction to some of the problems of cross-cultural understanding. Knowing Chinese attitudes in this book can help explain the obstacles of communication between Chinese and Americans.

Special thanks go to Bob Schildgen, Foster Stockwell, David Chachere, and James Wang for their editorial assistance in making this book possible.

About the Author

Glen Cao (Cao Guilin) was born in Beijing in 1947. After graduating from the Central Conservatory of Music he became a cellist with the Central Broadcasting Symphony Orchestra. He left China and immigrated to the United States in 1980. In the same year he founded the C & J Knitwear Company. *Beijinger in New York* is his first novel. His second book *Green Card--Beijing Girls in New York*, published in China in 1993, is the nation's No. 1 bestseller. Now he is working on his third novel *New Yorker in Beijing*.

Beijinger in New York

- 1 -

Beijing in early February was really cold. Daylight hadn't quite arrived yet, and a northwest wind whistled in the sky. Perennially hardworking Beijingers had already had their breakfasts and were leaving home to go to work.

They wore thick green army overcoats and blue cotton-padded parkas, or what might have been defined as "modish" down-filled windbreakers. Thus securely bundled up against the cutting wind, they hurried on their respective ways.

Cyclists and pedestrians, bicycle bells and the scrape and shuffle of footsteps—merged in streams of motion and noise. These streams were steady and even-flowing, but they nonetheless raised a considerable racket as they moved along. The clamor and commotion announced the beginning of another day for the ancient city of Beijing. Amid the flow of cyclists was a young couple. There was nothing especially remarkable about them.

The man, Wang Qiming, was thirty-five years old and a cellist with one of Beijing's symphony ensembles; the woman, Guo Yan, was his colleague as well as his wife.

They were dressed no differently from the rest of the people, nor did their bicycles stand out in any way from those around them. Submerged as they were in the flow of commuters, a casual spectator would hardly have singled them out.

A discerning observer, however, would have noticed that they rode somewhat faster than the other cyclists and were putting more effort into their pedaling. Now and then they also exchanged cryptic smiles which only they themselves were able to read.

Actually, the biggest difference wasn't on the surface; it was inside them. Most of the people on this street were going either to work or to school and were following their own mundane everyday paths. But Wang Qiming and Guo Yan had set out on a road they'd never taken before, one which they felt might lead them to an unknown and mysterious land.

Qiming rode with one hand on the handlebar. The other was on Yan's shoulder, helping her to put on a bit more speed. "Don't you get tired, pushing me like this?" asked Yan.

"Not at all," grinned Qiming. "Baby, I could push you like this all the way to the United States."

A shadow of anxiety flitted across Yan's forehead. "Do you think they'll give them to us?"

"Sure they will," replied Qiming. "I've got this hunch." That was what he said, but deep inside he felt much less confident than he'd let on.

Early as it was in the day, a long line had already formed in front of the American embassy. The sight of so many people took some of the wind out of Qiming's sails.

"Get a load of that! I told you to ride faster," he reproached Yan as he looked for a space to park their bicycles. "Now we're late!"

"If you knew we might be late," retorted Yan derisively, "why couldn't you get out of bed earlier?"

"A fat lot of good that would've done!" Qiming locked their bikes and then dragged Yan toward the end of the queue. "In any case you'd insist on serving Ningning her breakfast and seeing her off to school."

The mention of their daughter reminded Yan of another of her worries.

"What say we call the whole thing off," she said. "I'm scared to leave her here all by herself." Qiming got on the end of the line. He evidently thought his wife's last remark quite ridiculous.

"Call it off?! When we've already come so far? How can you talk like that? You've got to look at it this way—it's for Ningning's sake that we're busting a gut to get these visas."

"What kind of visas?" A skinny youth had sauntered over from the head of the queue and unabashedly inserted himself into their conversation.

Qiming took an instant disliking for this little slicker with a face the color of a cabbage leaf. "American visas," he drawled.

"As if I needed you to tell me that!" The skinny youth's expression was a study in scorn. "You wouldn't be lining up here for visas to the army labor battalions up in Heilongjiang province!"

"Then what do you want to know?"

"I'm asking whether you're applying for family visit visas or self-sponsored student visas."

"Family visit."

"Who're you visiting?"

"An aunt."

The skinny youth pointed at Yan. "Both together?" he asked.

Qiming nodded.

"Do you *have* to go together?"

"Why?" countered Qiming. "It makes getting our visas more difficult, is that it?"

"Difficult?! Worse than that, buddy," the skinny youth declared emphatically. "You don't stand a chance."

Qiming felt his heart tighten. Yan's hand, which was clutching his arm, twitched involuntarily and gave him a painful pinch. "Why is that?" Qiming didn't want to believe what he'd just heard.

The skinny youth was obviously pleased by the effect produced by his statement. He at once assumed the attitude of a visa applications specialist whose authority cannot be questioned.

"Let me put it this way," he said, striking an explanatory stance. "My pa and my ma were going to visit my uncle. Put together, they're a hundred and twenty years old. But the Yanks insisted they had immigrant intent.

They've sent in applications three times already, and they're still waiting. As for you guys, it's no dice. Take my word for it and go home. You've got better things to do."

Qiming said nothing. Not that he didn't want to say anything; he simply couldn't. The words got jammed in his throat.

"Don't listen to him," Yan whispered to Qiming. "What does he know! He isn't the American ambassador. Since we're here already, we ought at least to give it a try."

"Fair enough," said the skinny youth, catching Yan's last words. "Might as well have a bash at it, seeing as you're here and standing in line. One chick got an approval yesterday. Was it luck? Hell, no. She had this sweet little dial and a set of slinky curves and the Yank found her easy on the eyes, is all. They keep you guessing in this visa racket. You never can tell which cloud is going to make rain."

Just then, a Cadillac sedan flying an American flag rolled up to the embassy door.

"Make way! Make way!" called the guard.

The skinny youth edged forward and looked through the car's windows. "Hey, maybe you're in luck today. The Golden Monkey's here. It'd be no go for you if it was The Beard."

Mystified, Qiming turned to a boy who looked like a student. "Do they keep monkeys in the embassy," he asked.

"Not real monkeys. That's our moniker for one of their consuls," explained the boy. "She's a blonde, and they say she's nice to people. The Beard is one of the male consuls. I hear he's a tough cookie. You'd think the only thing he's ever learned is how to deny visas."

"You seem to be in the know here," remarked Qiming. "Got an inside line?"

"No. I've been here a few times, that's all."

"How many times?"

"Four, including this time."

Qiming felt his heart tighten again.

Half an hour later a man came out of the embassy building and handed each applicant a form. The line broke up into knots, each of three or four people who briefly conferred and then scattered to complete the forms. Qiming and Yan followed suit. Discussing between themselves and asking other people questions, they laboriously filled in the blanks on their forms. By the time they'd finished doing so, the man had come out again and was collecting the forms.

"Number one," called an embassy employee. "Zhang Mao!"

"O.K.! Yes, sirree!" The skinny youth scampered forward.

The name "Zhang Mao" drew a titter of laughter from the other applicants.

"Sounds like *sha mao*, blockhead," commented someone. "Why on earth did his mother give him such a name!"

"It's not so bad. Sounds respectable."

The northwest wind continued to whistle. The applicants waited, not saying much but all thinking about the same subject. Yan slipped her arm into Qiming's. She was shivering lightly, perhaps from the cold—or perhaps not. Within a few minutes the embassy door opened and Zhang Mao's skinny frame emerged.

"How did it go?" several people inquired.

"No dice!" Disappointment showed on Zhang Mao's face.

"The Golden Monkey is there today, isn't she?" asked someone.

"Yeah," replied Zhang, "but she's being bitchy. Maybe she caught a bug from The Beard."

There were chuckles and muted catcalls.

The embassy employee called in a few more people. Those outside peered in whenever the door opened, leaning forward and craning their necks as though they expected to see something. Every now and then one or two applicants would walk listlessly out of the building, wilted like vegetables hit by frost.

"Wang Qiming!" called the employee. "Guo Yan!"

"Think there's any hope?" Qiming asked his wife.

"We'll get them!" replied Yan.

Qiming knew now that women are stronger than men.

They hurried into the embassy building. To those standing outside, the couple were in the building only twenty minutes; to Wang Qiming and Guo Yan those twenty minutes seemed like a lifetime.

"It's no go for them," remarked Zhang Mao to a listener. "Visas for both of them at one go? No such luck! They can dream their American dreams, but that's not the way to do it. Ain't I right?"

The words had hardly left his lips when the door swung open and Qiming and Yan stepped out, arms wrapped around one another and tears glistening on their cheeks.

"Got them?" asked Zhang Mao.

Qiming nodded vigorously.

"Aiya!" exclaimed Zhang Mao, mortified. "That's real weird. It sure is!"

"Did we get our visas?" Qiming asked his wife, incredulously.

"Yes, we did."

"Really?"

"Really!" Oblivious of everything and everyone else, Qiming threw his arms around Yan and gave her a deep kiss.

"Hey! They're Americanized even before they've gotten to America!" commented Zhang Mao with more than a trace of envy. Ignoring him, Qiming and Yan continued to kiss each other in the windy street. Then, with a wave of the hand to the remaining applicants they walked away.

They had taken only a few steps when hand-clapping broke out behind them. Looking back, they saw that Zhang Mao had led a round of applause for them. Qiming cast about desperately for something to say, and finally managed to squeeze out: "See you in the United States, buddies!"

Bright lights illuminated the stage at the Beijing Music Hall; the hall was packed solid. Amid warm applause,

Qiming walked on-stage, followed by violinist Yan, Deng Wei who played the viola, and second fiddle Xiao Zhen. Qiming bowed to the audience, then swept his gaze over his colleagues. The audience looked better to him today than on any day in the past. He glanced again at Yan. Her complexion was pink with health and her dark eyes glistened.

"How beautiful she is!" he thought, suddenly as much in love with her as when they first started dating.

The four sat down and gave their instruments a final tuning. Qiming looked at the other three, then jerked his head in a sweeping nod. Music gushed forth like water from a fountain. They knew Mozart's string quartets better than any other item in their repertory. Their playing was flawlessly coordinated and each passage perfectly modulated.

Yan's glossy hair swayed with the pace and rhythm of the music. To Qiming, it seemed that her ineffably beautiful hair added a most fitting footnote to the ineffably beautiful melodies. Deng Wei and Xiao Zhen, too, played faultlessly, superbly. At the end of the performance, the applause thundered like summer rain on a rooftop. The encore also went down very well. Carried away by the music, the audience clapped in rhythmic unison. The musicians' faces flushed with pleasure.

Before the applause ended, Qiming and his colleagues slipped into the wings and gestured repeatedly in the direction of the stage manager. Then they left and soon were out of earshot of the applause in the hall. "You two go home," said Deng Wei. "I'll come later, after I pick up some deli food at Xidan."

He strode forward, his viola case swinging and his heels ringing loudly on the icy asphalt road. "Xiao Zhen," he added. "Go back to our place and bring that bottle of Maotai."

"Forget it!" Qiming caught Deng Wei by the arm. "This isn't the first time we get together."

"Of course not," replied Deng Wei. "But it's the last time!" At that, the four came to a halt in the cold, wind-blown street and stared at each other, suddenly gripped by a uncomfortable feeling. Definitely uncomfortable.

The first to recover her wits was Xiao Zhen. "Deng Wei can never talk like a decent human being," she said. "The last time? Does that mean 'The Last Supper'?"

"It doesn't really matter." Qiming smiled thinly. "After all, it is the last time."

"Last time or not," Yan broke in, "the important thing is to eat well!"

"Quite right!" responded Deng Wei. "Get a move on, then," Qiming urged Deng Wei and Xiao Zhen. "Yan and I will go home and slap together a few dishes."

And thus the quartet finally broke up in the darkness in front of the Music Hall.

"The Last Supper" turned out to be quite a party. The small round dining table was loaded with food: sausages, fried peanuts, spiced tofu cubes and tossed cabbage hearts. The main courses were red-braised chicken, steamed fish and stir-fried shrimp. The bottle of Maotai supplied by Deng Wei and Xiao Zhen occupied the place of honor at the center of the table. "Aiya!" sighed Qiming. "Who knows if we'll ever get any tossed cabbage hearts in the United States."

"What a hayseed you are!" replied Deng Wei. "Americans eat beef and drink milk. Who's interested in tossed cabbage hearts?"

"One can get tired of beef and milk, " remonstrated Xiao Zhen. "It could be that one would want some tossed cabbage hearts for a change."

Deng opened the bottle of Maotai and poured some of the fiery liquor for each person.

"Qiming," he said, raising his glass. "I've always said you've got good karma. This day was bound to come!"

Xiao Zhen also raised her glass. "I wish you two a life of happiness and well-being in the United States!"

"That's a bunch of crap," said Deng Wei impatiently. "All those who go to the United States find happiness and well-being. I don't happen to have such karma. And it all boils down to my family's failure to perform a sufficient number of good deeds, or to set up links in the United States. I've often wondered why my mom didn't get hitched to a Yank."

"All right, all right, all right!" broke in Xiao Zhen "You're always saying something offbeat. Would there be any you, if your mother had married an American?"

"Don't be so pessimistic, Deng Wei!" said Qiming expansively, draining his glass of Maotai. "Do you know what kind of a family I had? None of my ancestors ever made it any further than Beijing's city limits. I don't even have a relative in Tianjin, let alone the United States."

"What if I hadn't condescended to marry into your family," put in Yan. "And what if I didn't have an aunt hanging around over there? Thinking of going to the United States, kiddo? Forget it!"

"Hey!" exclaimed Deng Wei. "I've got something straight now!"

"Got what straight?"

"D'you know what the Americans' policy for immigration is? In plain lingo, it's a big prick policy. If you've got one of those gizmos tucked away somewhere in the U S of A, you get your visa for sure."

There was a roar of laughter.

Xiao Zhen, poking at Deng Wei's forehead with her chopsticks, giggled: "You make an ass of yourself every time you take a couple of drinks!"

"As they say: 'Don't expect to get ivory out of a dog's mouth,'" observed Yan laughingly. "Nothing good ever comes out of yours!"

"Hey, Sister!" said Deng Wei very seriously. "Don't act so holier-than-thou! Just remember that Qiming's ticket to the United States is that beautiful body of yours."

Qiming exploded with mirth and slammed his fist on the table. Yan, her face scarlet with embarrassment, vouchsafed only a thin-lipped smile. She was at a loss as to what to say to that irrepressible rascal.

"Don't blush, sister! You'll have plenty to blush about when you're in the United States. People there go around in the streets with bare asses and nobody stops them. Strip dancing is a legitimate profession. But what about us here? You look at a broad a couple of times in her big old cotton-padded trousers and you get called a hooligan. Why are people so uncivilized here?" He clucked his tongue disapprovingly.

"I bet you think screwing around is civilized, too," Yan threw back at him. "Where do you pick up such ideas? Xiao Zhen, I advise you to keep a close watch over him."

Xiao Zhen came to Yan's support. "What a picture you paint of the United States! Not everyone there is like you, you know."

"If you knew everything there was to know," countered Deng Wei, looking at Xiao Zhen, "there wouldn't be anything worth knowing. Seriously, though, the United States is so rich, so strong! They've got freedom, liberty. You do what you please there, whatever you feel like doing. You want to do such-and-such a thing? Go ahead and do it! You don't need to apply for permission. Nobody's there to stop you..."

"As for myself," observed Qiming, reflectively, "I don't even know yet what I'm going to do there."

"Don't worry about that," said Xiao Zhen. "I hear one can earn hundreds of dollars a month abroad simply by washing dishes."

"But I've never done such work," replied Qiming earnestly.

"Why, there's nothing to it," said Deng Wei, trying to pump up Qiming's courage. "In any case, they've got everything mechanized over there."

"Frankly, I'm not worried about going hungry," confided Yan. "I'm more..."

"Don't tell me!" interrupted Deng Wei. "You're worried about Ningning, right?"

"Now you just go along and don't worry about her," said Xiao Zhen reassuringly. "You've got us here. I promise we'll go every week to her grandmother's place. We'll take charge of everything. They'll be well looked after."

"Ningning is eleven years old, just at an age when she most needs a mother." Yan's eyes were reddening. "But I, her mother, pick this time to go to the United States. What kind of a mother am I?"

She broke down, and her tears fell like pearls from a broken necklace.

Qiming put an arm around her; her tears wet his shoulder. He tried to comfort her. "Don't have any worries on that score." His own voice was husky with suppressed emotion. "Ningning's a good kid, the best in the world..."

Late that night, Deng Wei and Xiao Zhen said their goodbyes. The little room, so filled with warmth and conviviality a few minutes earlier, suddenly seemed cold and forlorn. As Yan spread out the quilts on the bed, she smiled sweetly at her husband.

"This is our last night in China, so don't go right to sleep after taking a few drinks."

Taking his wife's hint, Qiming went up behind her and put his arms around her waist. He kissed the back of her neck and said, "I'm not letting any opportunities slip by!"

Yan twisted around. Eyeing him sternly, she said, "I won't have you watching bare-assed dancing in the United States."

"I won't watch such things. Not even for free!" Qiming unbuttoned Yan's blouse and stroked her shapely white breasts. "Besides, nobody has an ass as pretty as my wife's."

"Maybe you'll change and become a different person some day," murmured Yan, falling back on the bed with her arms hooked around Qiming's neck.

"I'll always be the same, no matter where we are..."

His last words were muffled by ardent kisses. It was as though they had never before experienced such joy and satisfaction. Heaven came down to them that night. Afterwards, they slept in one another's arms. And they dreamed a dream.

They dreamed about an America they had never seen, and about themselves. They dreamed about an undefinable but realistic happiness and security.

They dreamed this dream together. And in this dream they talked, and they clung to each other tightly, fearing that happiness would slip out from between their arms...

Not all of it was a dream.

The next morning, a Boeing 747 passenger flight took off from Beijing's Capital Airport. A young couple sat side by side in the plane with hands interlocked. Not for a single moment during the long journey did they leave one another. On several occasions they asked the flight hostess: "Are we heading for the United States?"

"Yes, for New York," replied the hostess once and again. She was understandably mystified: Why should the same question be repeated so many times?

Actually, Qiming and Yan were only trying to assure themselves that all this was not just a dream.

- 2 -

Wang Qiming and Guo Yan walked through the lounge of New York's Kennedy Airport, dragging heavy bags and suitcases and gazing around the labyrinth.

People of all races and colors congregated there. It seemed as though the whole world was represented. A beautiful woman in a huge perfume advertisement stared down at the couple who had made the long journey from their ancient Oriental land. Qiming was beginning to feel he needed more than one pair of eyes.

"Let's hurry!" Yan tugged at his sleeve to bring him back on course. "Why isn't Auntie here to meet us?"

"Now don't get excited. Your aunt is an American, and Americans keep their word. If she said she'd come, she'll definitely come."

A soft female voice came over the public address system. "What's she saying?" inquired Yan. "You watched *Follow Me*, that TV English class in Beijing, didn't you? So get your ears up and listen!"

Qiming stood still and listened with great concentration. After a while he shook his head. "She's talking too fast."

"You wouldn't understand her even if she spoke slowly," remarked Yan penetratingly.

"Let me hear a bit more," replied Qiming, flapping a hand in Yan's direction and listening with his head cocked to one side.

A few moments later Yan inquired: "Did you get anything?"

"She said..." Qiming paused a moment before continuing. "She said: 'Ladies and gentlemen...'"

"Is that all? Didn't she say anything else?"

"Of course she did. But I'll have to listen a little longer."

. "May I help you?" A young woman, obviously an airport attendant, walked up to them. This sudden onslaught in the English language caught Qiming entirely by surprise. He gaped at the young woman. "May I help you?" the attendant asked again, batting long eyelashes.

"Er, help, help, I..." stammered Qiming. "I go home."

"Where is your home?"

"I... I... go home."

"Yes, I understand." The airport attendant smiled and, very patiently, added: "You'd better tell me where your home is. Give me your home address and maybe I can help you."

Confused by the rush of English words and finding no better way to deal with the situation, Qiming kept on repeating the same sentence: "I go home."

"No problem!" The attendant was losing her patience. "The exit is over there. Go out and find a taxi, and tell the driver where you want to go." Qiming and Yan, together with their bags and suitcases, were finally deposited at the airport exit. Before they got their bearings a black man came toward them in a loose-limbed walk.

"Hey, what's up, man?" he inquired. "Oh, yeah. I know, man. You just got here. You need help. Let me tell you something, man. J.F.K. Airport is a very dangerous place. Come with me, man. See there? That's my car. I'll take you home, man."

The man from the streets of New York spoke with such a different accent than Qiming ever heard that he didn't understand a word. He stared at the man, his eyes glazed as though he were in a trance.

"Auntie!"

Yan's sudden shriek was like that of a shipwrecked mariner who sights a rescue ship after floating three days and nights on the ocean. Shouting and yelling, the two bounded to where Auntie was standing.

Yan's aunt, with her husband in tow, took a few steps forward and said: "I'm sorry, really sorry! I'm late because I got caught in a traffic jam. My apologies!"

Yan and Qiming made haste to bow and greet these American relatives, addressing them as "Auntie" and "Uncle" and making a big display of the civilities from an ancient Oriental culture.

Uncle was older than Auntie by at least twenty years. "Welcome to New York!" he enunciated with heavy Cantonese overtones. "You must be exhausted after your trip."

"Not at all! Not at all!" replied Qiming.

"Thank you, Auntie and Uncle, for coming to meet us!" added Yan, laying on more courtesies.

"Well, let's be going," proposed Auntie with a smile.

"Aiya!" wailed Yan. "Where's our luggage?"

Only then was it discovered that all their suitcases had vanished, leaving the new arrivals with only the bags slung across their shoulders.

The posh Cadillac was appointed with tasteful modern fixtures and wide, comfortable seats. Auntie was driving, and the car sped smoothly and silently on the freeway.

Qiming looked out of the window, drinking in the scenery, stimulated by the novelty of everything. Overpasses rose in several tiers one above the other at highway crossings. Dazzling car lights, spaced out in orderly files, stretched to infinity. Soon their car entered an undersea tunnel. Street lamps at the various exits flashed by. As the car emerged from the tunnel, exclamations of astonishment broke from Qiming's and Yan's lips. Like a mirage, twinkling with countless lights and appearing almost translucent, New York lay spread out before them. "This is New York," said Auntie.

Qiming and Yan were dumbfounded by the beauty of the scene. After crossing a toll bridge, the car rolled into busy downtown Manhattan. This gaudy and grotesque city, the world's biggest metropolis, filled the newcomers with boundless wonder and amazement.

The car lost speed. Here, all motor vehicles became snails that inched forward at the proverbial pace. Yellow taxicabs took up more than half of the roadway, negotiating the traffic with consummate skill, squeezing through interstices, exploiting every little opening, ceding not the least advantage.

The skyscrapers were rows of giants looking impassively down at the mass of people and vehicles below, at the cars swarming in the cracks between their toes. Colorful neon signs lit up the night sky, vying for attention in their variegated, garish profusion. A blue police car nudged right and left in the packed traffic, howling at the top of its metallic voice.

"Something's happened," exclaimed Qiming.

"Not necessarily," replied Auntie with a nonchalant smile. "Police cars are a major feature of New York. They rush around twenty-four hours a day."

Qiming stared at her in surprise. Several red fire trucks, immobilized in the stream of motor vehicles, wailed forlornly and helplessly.

"Most newcomers to New York panic easily," explained Uncle with ponderous thoroughness. "The least bit of excitement, and they start asking if anything's happened, if it's serious, and so on and so forth. Actually, nothing has happened. See for yourselves! Everybody's going about their own business as usual, aren't they?" Qiming looked out and, indeed, the indifferent pedestrians didn't spare even a brief glance at the clamoring vehicles. They hurried along busily, intensely, absorbed in their personal affairs.

"What a joint," exclaimed Qiming. "It's weird!"

Yan turned and white-eyed him.

Eventually they drove out of the downtown area and before long the noise and bustle disappeared. The scenes now were of a different kind. Groups of homeless people crouched in the dark recesses of dilapidated buildings, huddling for warmth over small fires. Unwashed vagrants sprawled on the sidewalks, pouring alcohol down their throats.

Two skimpily dressed girls winked and waved at Qiming through the car window, leaving him embarrassed and confused. "Is this America? New York?" Qiming asked Auntie, unable to repress the doubts that had begun to assail him.

"Yes, this is New York." Auntie was absolutely positive on that score.

The Cadillac stopped in front of an old house. Without getting out of her seat, Auntie turned to address Qiming and Yan.

"I've taken account of your financial situation as newcomers in the United States. The rent here is fairly cheap." She extracted an envelope from a brand name purse and held it out. "You'll find five hundred dollars and my telephone number here. Take it and don't stand on ceremony."

Qiming and Yan accepted the envelope. Getting out of the car, they advanced toward the house. The walls were scrawled over with graffiti.

"Are we going to live here?" faltered Qiming. It wasn't clear whether the question was directed at Yan or at himself.

"No," said Auntie, leaning out of the car window. "The apartments above ground are all too expensive. I've reserved a basement flat for you. Rent and deposit come to four hundred dollars. That, and the five hundred I lent you just now, make a total of nine hundred dollars. My husband and I will both be busy tomorrow morning. Call at eight-thirty tomorrow evening if you have any problems."

Having detailed the accounts, Auntie started the car and drove away. Qiming and Yan stared at one another in blank dismay, not knowing what to do next.

"Let's go in," proposed Qiming after a while.

"You go in first!" Yan gazed fearfully at the black cave of the entrance.

The inside of the building was very dark. A single light bulb only accentuated the spookiness of the surroundings.

Qiming pushed the door to the basement flat. It opened with a groan. An indescribable odor hit them in the face.

Yan gagged and coughed.

Qiming turned on the small yellow lamp.

An empty fruit crate from some supermarket, two backless chairs and a grimy mattress for a double bed—that was all the furniture in the room. Yan walked to the crate and slowly lowered herself onto it, cupping her face in her hands.

Qiming inspected their "home."

A smaller room opening off the main room contained a sizable kitchen. He turned on the gas stove; the vigorous flames were a pleasant surprise. A fridge, taller than a person, was in good working order. The bathroom next to the kitchen pleased him even more. He turned on one of the taps. Hot water!

He went back to Yan and stroked her hair.

"I'm scared," she murmured.

"Don't be afraid. I'm here. If this place frightens you we'll move somewhere else."

"Where to? Besides, you heard what she said. We already owe her nine hundred dollars."

"We'll earn some money and give it back to her! I'd heard before now that people here lack human feelings. Now I know it for a fact!"

"We're strangers in a strange land," said Yan apprehensively. "We could starve and nobody would give a hoot!"

"We won't starve. I still have some instant noodles in my bag. I'll fix them up for you. Meanwhile, go and take a bath."

"Take a bath?"

Qiming pulled his wife to her feet, took her clothes off and propelled her toward the bathroom.

"You go in first," he said. "I'll join you in a second."

"Don't tell me you're still in the mood for that!"

"You bet I am! Always for that, even if for nothing else. Come on, hurry up!"

That was their first night in New York. Two naked bodies held to each other tightly in the steamy bathroom. They had little else besides their naked bodies. They could do little more than hold to each other tightly.

. . .

Hurrying pedestrians surged out of the subway exit, reminding one of gouts of muddy subterranean water. Peoples of all races and colors—white, black, yellow, brown, red, mixed—and in all parts of the world had sent their offspring to the narrow island in New York called Manhattan. There was very little living space for them; and with practically all twenty-four hours of the day booked solid they lived at a frenetic pace. Like worker bees they followed their own fixed paths: from underground to the surface, from the streets into the buildings, and in express elevators to the mist-shrouded summits of skyscrapers. Ceaselessly they scurried about; but they created no sense of confusion. Their trajectories were quite unique, sometimes crossing but never interfering with one another, as well-ordered as the orbits of planets.

Qiming, too, was in such an orbit today. He climbed out of the subway, tugged at his suit which had been jostled out of alignment, then approached a street sign to orient himself. Clutching the slip of paper on which were written his notes from Auntie's phone call early this morning, he compared the writing on it with the lettering on the street sign.

Being reasonably intelligent, he wasn't baffled by the intricacies of getting around in New York and soon found the Chinese restaurant called the Hunan Garden. After hesitating at the entrance, he pushed open the door and went in.

Business hadn't begun yet. Several waiters were busy getting things ready for the lunch period. No one seemed to notice Qiming's arrival; the waiters went on with their various chores. One of the youngest, perhaps because he happened to be nearest to Qiming, finally noticed him.

"We aren't open yet," he said as he laid out paper napkins and cutlery. Qiming was quite particular about the kind of reception he got.

"My name's Wang. I've come to work here on Mr. Sun's recommendation."

The young waiter eyed him up and down. "Hey, boss!" he yelled. "There's someone for you at the door!" High heels clicked crisply on the parquet; a Chinese woman appeared. She was nearing middle age, fashionably attired and heavily made up.

"Good morning, sir. What can I do for you?"

"My name's Wang. I'm looking for work. Mr. Sun recommended me."

"Uh-huh! I remember now." Her demeanor became visibly cooler. "You're welcome here. The first three days of work are probationary and unpaid. Your work will consist mainly of washing dishes in the kitchen and cleaning up the stoves, lavatories and floors. Your pay will be eight hundred per month."

Qiming nodded and smiled. He liked the woman's straightforward manner.

"All right, that will be all." The proprietor expelled her breath as if to dismiss the subject. She then raised her voice. "Xiao Li! There's a Mr. Wang out here. He'll wash dishes with you." More clicking of high heels and she was gone.

Xiao Li, wrapped in a soiled apron, came out of the kitchen. "Ye gods! A dishwasher at last!" He wiped his hands on his apron. "I'll crack up soon if I have to double any longer as dishwasher and general handyman." Judging from his accent, he was from the Jiangsu-Zhejiang region in East China.

Qiming stepped forward. "My name's Wang and I'll be washing dishes," he said with stiff formality. "I welcome your instructions and advice."

"Nuts! You don't need instructions or advice to wash dishes. You just wash the damn things!"

"Okay, okay. Where do I wash them?"

"What's the hurry? There'll be plenty for you to wash after a while. Meantime, don't just sit on your ass. Come and chop onions."

Chopping onions isn't work fit for human beings.

Xiao Li's brief and explicit instructions made it sound easy. "Here's the chopper, and here are the onions. Slice two basketfuls and dice four!"

Ever tasted American onions? They're several times stronger than Chinese onions. After Qiming had made a few passes with the chopper, tears began to slosh down his face. And that's straight fact! He stood there with eyes streaming and nose running as if somebody had exploded a tear-gas grenade.

Slice? Dice? Qiming was in no shape to attend to such niceties. Hacking the things apart was as much as he could manage.

Xiao Li came over to "instruct" him. "If the boss sees you cutting them like that, she'll throw your ass out! Turn your head! Keep your face to one side. Get it?"

Qiming followed Xiao Li's advice, with fairly good results. Just as he was congratulating himself he heard the proprietor commenting behind him. "Say! Did you do this with the chopper or with your teeth?"

Qiming turned around. She was picking through the onions he'd just chopped. Admittedly, he deserved what she'd just said. His work was decidedly unattractive. Instead of uniform slices or cubes there were chunks of all shapes and sizes.

"Is that what I'm paying eight hundred dollars a month for?" The proprietor was quite annoyed. "You newcomers are all so dense, especially if you're from mainland China!"

Qiming felt very unhappy; he'd never been told off like that in all his life. He was about to object when she grabbed the chopper from him. Her delicate hands with their scarlet fingernails danced over the chopping board. The onions under her fingers turned obediently into neat, becoming slices and cubes. Qiming looked at the onions, then his eyes were drawn to the hands working on them. He became so entranced that he was still looking at them after the proprietress ended her demonstration.

"All right," she said. "It's ten-forty now, Mr. Wang. By eleven-thirty all the onions must be done, or else..."

She left the sentence hanging, but it was perfectly clear what she meant. Then she walked off, swaying gracefully on her high heels. Qiming watched her go, then picked up the chopper. Things went better this time, much better.

During the lunch period, the restaurant became a frantic battlefield. The waiters flew back and forth between the kitchen and the dining hall, calling out orders:

"One mu hsu pork with plain rice!"

"Two orders of egg fu yong without MSG!" "Two plates of Yangchow fried rice, and go easy on the eggs!"

"Mr. Wang," called the proprietor, taking off a moment to look into the kitchen. "Hurry up! You've got to move faster! We have a lot of customers!" Then she was back in the dining hall seeing to her guests.

"Long time no see, Mr. John! How are you doing?"

"Oh! You look different today, Jenny. Come this way!"

"Hi, Tommy! Is everything okay? Sure, I've missed you very much!"

Listening to the expert manner in which she handled the clientele, Qiming thought that here was an interesting woman. He had little time for other such reflections, however. He washed the dishes conscientiously, more so than at home. The green-colored detergent made the skin on his hands itch, and the white bleaching powder seared his eyes so that he could hardly see. But he had no time to think of such things, none at all. His only concern was to get the dishes clean, so as to bring a smile onto the proprietor's face.

But the more dishes Qiming washed, the faster they came. He fell behind and a mountain of dirty tableware rose on both sides of his work station.

The waiters began to complain. They were running out of drinking glasses, out of plates, out of bowls! The proprietress left the cash register and with a few swift steps flew into the kitchen. Bumping Qiming aside with her hip and throwing a glare at him, she rolled up her sleeves and without further ado started to wash dishes herself.

Qiming stood beside her, confused and thinking that he wasn't too far now from being fired.

"Why are you standing there!" yelled the proprietor, drying her hands. "Start washing!"

Qiming almost jumped. I must go on working here, he thought to himself. And I can do it. With a surge of energy he threw himself into his work. Beads of perspiration rolled down his face, and his fresh white shirt soon became soaked. Keep on washing! Go to it! Whatever it cost him, he had to have those eight hundred dollars a month. He wasn't going to let her can him. It was do or die!

– 3 –

Qiming had gone to the restaurant very early in the morning, and Yan was left to herself in their basement apartment. She would have liked to go out and walk around but she was really scared of losing her way, of not being able to find her back home again. She paced the room like a dog behind a fence. Now and then she stopped in front of the one little window and raised herself on the tips of her toes to peer out. Then she would resume her pacing. That morning she breakfasted on a few cookies left over from the trip to New York; in the afternoon, driven by boredom, she slipped out into the street.

Women are braver than men, and that's a fact.

Seeing a Chinese-owned general goods store, she walked in. The elderly proprietor came forward to serve her and they struck up a conversation. His name was Liu, and Yan was mildly surprised to learn that he was a retired Kuomintang general. Nothing in his bearing suggested a former general; all one saw was a shrewd little businessman. When Yan had told him something about her circumstances he proceeded to give her some advice.

"Mrs. Wang," he said. Yan felt somewhat uncomfortable at being addressed so formally. "Mrs. Wang, you're new in the United States, so you don't know the way things go here. The first thing to do is to make money. Without money you can't move a single step, you're one dead duck. This country isn't a charity institution."

As Yan listened, her neck slowly shrank into her shoulders.

"But you don't need to be afraid. The thing to do is to find a job, any kind of job, and never mind if it's good or bad. As long as you have work to do, you won't have any problems getting food and shelter."

"Could you help me? I'm a stranger here."

"I'll have to make a phone call first. Wait just a moment." With that, Mr. Liu went into the back room. Yan stood stiffly outside, pondering what she had been told.

After a while Mr. Liu came out again and handed Yan a slip of paper. "This is the address. Go there and say that Mr. Yao sent you."

Yan thanked him effusively. Seeing her out of the store, Mr. Liu continued to give her advice. "Take any work you get, and don't turn your nose up at it. In this country, sitting around and not making any money is about the same as committing suicide."

Yan thanked him again and stepped into the street.

New York. So this was New York.

Mr. Liu had recommended Yan to a garment factory. That very afternoon Yan took home a large bundle of semi-finished wool sweaters. Sitting in her basement apartment she concentrated on crocheting the pieces together. She worked several hours without stopping, hardly ever getting up. The work was tiring, but at least the fear and anxiety were gone.

It was two thirty in the afternoon by the time the lunch-hour battle at the Hunan Garden Restaurant came to a halt. The employees sat down at a large round table to eat. Too weary to have an appetite, Qiming spooned some soup into his mouth.

"Eat something! You have to eat if you're going to work like that!" The proprietor placed a piece of eel in Qiming's bowl with her chopsticks. Business had been good and she was rewarding her employees with an extra course, a dish of braised eels. Qiming thanked her and went on eating without looking up.

"You're new here, Mr. Wang, but you've managed to stick it out today. Not bad at all! I need people here, and you're young and strong. So work well!"

The employees listened to the proprietress speaking but kept their heads down in their bowls and didn't interrupt. As soon as the proprietor had left the table, however, the younger workers started to comment loudly on her words. The first to do so was Xiao Li. Aping her tones, he lauded Qiming. Everybody laughed.

Qiming was beginning to feel embarrassed when Xiao Li added for his benefit: "If anyone else had worked like you did today, he'd be out on his ass now."

Blowing out cigarette smoke, the master chef spoke with an air of great experience. "If you ask me, that broad's got her eye on Mr. Wang."

The Wok was even more blunt. "You're telling me, man! I've known that all along. She talks with her ass and gives the old come-on with her tits. You're in luck, Mr. Wang. You'll get a screw for free. Wow!"

"I'm a married man," began Qiming. "And my daughter is eleven years old already."

"So what?" said The Wok. "If you don't mind, neither will she."

"Maybe she's only playing around," observed Xiao Li, "and doesn't mean it for real."

"Who cares whether or not she means it for real," said the master chef. "Screw her first—that's for real! Get a load of that pair of hooters and..." The master chef stopped in the middle of his sentence. The proprietress was standing right behind him.

"Don't you guys have anything better to do than to tear down your boss behind her back? If you're that horny, go somewhere and pay somebody to get it out of your systems. But don't try to work it off blabbing about your boss! I've got my eye on him!? Fat chance! I wasn't born yesterday!"

Qiming held onto his temper and remained silent. He glanced at the fiery woman. Judging from her intelligent forehead and expression, she was a most capable woman;

but by the looks of her semi-exposed breasts and sensuous buttocks she could also be an uninhibited libertine.

"You work well for me, the lot of you, and if business is good I won't let you down."

"Does that mean we're to keep it up?" The master chef's quick jab brought a roar of laughter.

"You shameless ball of shit!" The words were sharp, but she kept on smiling. A mysterious woman, thought Qiming.

Qiming was kept busy the rest of the afternoon scrubbing stove surfaces, washing dishes, cleaning washrooms, sweeping carpets, cutting onions and shelling frozen shrimp. The newly-laundered white shirt he'd put on in the morning had taken on a yellow-brown hue by the end of the day. Qiming was utterly played out. At nine o'clock in the evening, all the employees said their good-byes to the proprietor and left the restaurant. Only Qiming remained to do some last-minute tidying up. The proprietor finished doing the accounts and walked languidly over to Qiming.

"Do you know how to get home?" she asked.

"Yes."

"I could drop you off somewhere."

"I think I can find my way." He was about to leave when the she called to him. "Wait a minute!"

He stopped in his tracks.

"Help me lock the front door."

"All right." Qiming submissively obeyed her every order.

Qiming dragged himself toward his "home". His legs were heavy, his fingers were stiff, and his head weighed a ton.

It was chiefly his head; it felt as though it were filled with paste. He tried unsuccessfully to make himself think lucidly. His brain was as numb as a block of wood, a lump of iron.

"Is this the way I'm going to live?" he asked himself. "Did I come to the United States to be a dishwasher?"

As he walked along he raised his hands and inspected them by the light of the street lamps. These hands, which had played the cello since he was eight years old and received such special care, had in one day been mauled into insensitivity by bleaching powder, detergents, and dirty bowls and platters. "What am I going to do about my cello? My playing? My career? What to do? No, I must look for opportunities to go back to it. I can't just leave it like that!"

Somewhere along the way he walked into a subway tunnel. Suddenly he stopped and pricked up his ears. The sound of a violin. Ah, that was a Beethoven violin concerto. The tone color was pure and beautiful, and the technique good. In fact, quite outstand- ing. Qiming thought at first that it was a recording played over the loudspeakers. But was it a recording? Listening closely, Qiming didn't hear any accompanying orchestra. He hurried forward and turned a corner.

A young man with blond hair was playing. He played very earnestly and with great dedication, his rumpled hair covering his forehead although not his eyes. Those eyes burned with flames lit by Beethoven himself. Qiming was drawn forward by the skillful performance and the stirring melody. He stopped in front of the violinist. Hurrying passers-by paid no attention to the musician or his music, but this didn't in the least affect the musician's ardor or Qiming's rapt enjoyment. As the performer launched into the concerto's cadenza, he cast a knowing smile at Qiming. Qiming returned the smile. A concert was being held in that subway tunnel, a concert by one musician for a single listener.

At the performer's feet, several coins glinted bleakly in an open violin case. It was unbelievable that such a gifted musician should be reduced to playing on street corners. Qiming, conscious of the fact that he couldn't hold a candle to this man in either talent or technique, sank into a painful frame of mind. Taking a ten-dollar bill from his jacket pocket, he laid it in the violin case and walked hastily away.

Behind him, the music went on uninterruptedly. Qiming hurried out of the subway without looking back.

A feeling of disillusionment, of desperation, welled up within him. In the blond musician he had seen the end of his music career. He broke into a run, not knowing himself what he was running away from. He ran and ran, without stopping.

Yan was still working on her sweaters when Qiming came home. He didn't tell her about his work; instead, he lit a cigarette with shaking hands. Yan rushed into the bathroom to run him a tub of hot water, loudly recounting to Qiming her experiences of the day.

"I've got work, too, Qiming! I'm crocheting sweaters at a dollar seventy cents apiece. This afternoon I finished four sweaters, which makes six dollars and eighty cents. Figure it out yourself, that's almost half a month's salary at the ensemble!"

As she emerged from the bathroom, bursting with enthusiasm, she found Qiming fast asleep and snoring on the bed. Gently she took off his clothes and pulled a quilt over him. Then she sat down beside him to crochet a sweater. Outside, cold wind from the Atlantic Ocean whistled ceaselessly among the withered branches of trees. Motor vehicles rumbled past on the street, shaking the basement apartment and almost seeming to drive through their room. Yan sat crocheting sweaters next to the little yellow lamp, working deep into the night.

Qiming had completed his three days of probationary work. On the afternoon of the third day he was doing the floors with a vacuum cleaner. He was also waiting with anticipation and fear for the proprietor to appear. Her coming would decide his fate. He was afraid of this moment, but was also hoping for it. He was dimly aware that he'd experienced such a feeling only once before, when he'd taken entrance exams for the Central Conservatory of Music. Then, he'd waited impatiently to be accepted but quivered at the thought of receiving a notice of non-acceptance.

Qiming allowed a wry grin to flicker across his lips at the realization that he had the same trepidation waiting to be a dishwasher as he'd had waiting to be accepted by the Conservatory.

The vacuum cleaner whined, the sound blanking out his thought. This mental blank was an escape hatch from reality and from his worries and misgivings. Someone tapped him on the shoulder. The action was so light Qiming failed to notice it.

The vacuum cleaner continued to whine with hypnotic intensity. The tap was repeated, only more sharply this time. Startled, Qiming turned around. The proprietor's face was so close to his own that he felt her warm breath waft sweetly across his cheek.

"What did you say?" Qiming shouted, trying to make himself heard over the racket created by the vacuum cleaner. The proprietor raised her foot and stepped on the vacuum cleaner's on-off switch.

"Couldn't you have turned off that damned contraption first?" she snapped.

"Yes...I, I didn't hear you."

"You're really stupid!"

"No! Ma'am..."

"Don't call me ma'am!"

"I think..."

"Think? Do you think too? You're a dumb cluck and you don't know how to think! You can't figure out even the most obvious things."

"But, I..."

Faced with this razor-tongued woman, Qiming had a temporary speech block. He gaped and his face turned scarlet. The proprietor observed the foolish look on Qiming's face with growing amusement. Finally she burst out laughing. "If I say you're a cluck, you *are* a cluck!" Then, lowering her voice she continued: "Come to work tomorrow. I want to see if working in this restaurant will sharpen your wits a bit! Also, I'll be a sucker for once and raise you a hundred dollars."

Qiming's eyes brightened. He gazed with disbelief at this pungent, forceful woman.

"Don't stare at me like that! You give me the jitters!" she said with a smile, as though scolding a child. "But maybe it's me who's stupid. I can't figure out why I like a guy like you!" She plucked a thread of lint from Qiming's hair and flicked it into the air with delicate fingertips. Then with an eloquent glance at Qiming she spun around and walked away.

A month, thirty days, can be a long, long time. The days seemed to drag by especially slowly for Qiming who worked like a coolie and was "washed" with perspiration as he washed the dirty dishes. On the other hand, he felt a certain satisfaction as he reflected that he had at least some sort of a job, which was not necessarily the case with many of his compatriots from mainland China.

To kill time—and perhaps not only to kill time—Qiming half-seriously took stock of his boss. This attractive, self-assured, capable woman ruled the restaurant and retained in her service a sizable contingent of men, providing them each with a passable job and a foothold in the United States as well as bending them to her will and making them forget completely their male pride.

The very first time Qiming learned her name—Ah Chun—he deemed it quite apt. Ah Chun, Spring, brought warmth and a few chill gusts as well.

"Here's your salary," said Ah Chun to Qiming as he entered her office. "Nine hundred dollars. Be careful with it. Don't get mugged on your way home."

Qiming took from Ah Chun the envelope containing the nine hundred dollars. The twenty-dollar bills made a hefty stack. He adored these twenty-dollar bills. They created an impression of weight, of plenitude and prosperity. And even though this impression was spurious and the thickness of the wad did not augment the nine hundred dollars by a single cent, it nevertheless gave Qiming a feeling of substantiality and self-confidence. It gave him a momentary sensation of uplift; it enabled him to forget for the time being his bone-grinding weariness and to pull back his shoulders.

It hadn't been easy, earning those nine hundred dollars. And they made such a thick stack! He secreted the money in the safest place he could think of—an inside pocket next to his heart, then stepped out into the streets of Manhattan. In the subway he kept his arms protectively crossed over his chest.

The contents of that inside pocket were more important to him than anything else. He felt as though something were searing his chest, and he couldn't tell whether it was the money warmed by his body temperature or simply the awareness of having those honest-to-goodness greenbacks. In any case, his chest burned, his head felt dizzy, and his throat was dry.

On this day he understood how vitally important money was to people, to a person who was trying to survive in this country. He knew this stack of bills represented his first real foothold in the United States.

Then he was assailed by a sudden fear that someone was going to grab his nine hundred dollars. He instinctively covered his chest with his hands and alertly eyed the people around him. To a bystander he must have looked like a well-trained police dog.

Qiming finally walked out of the warm subway tunnel into New York's cold and clammy March air. He was still wearing the down-filled windbreaker and faded blue jeans he'd brought from Beijing. These were covered with large spots of grease. And, yes, his walking shoes, once white, were now a dark gray.

He walked with rapid steps along the streets of New York. No one paid any attention to him. Nor could they know his past, or imagine the agitation that filled him. If anyone had, by some outside chance, glanced at him more than a second they would have seen a typical New York wage earner with nothing special to distinguish him from any other. And that was the whole truth of it. Money brought some rare laughter to their cold and damp basement apartment.

As Qiming handed the stack of bills to his wife she suddenly waved a check in front of his nose.

"What's that?" Qiming had guessed what it was, but he asked the question anyway and put surprise and elation in his voice.

"A check! For four hundred and eighty-five U.S. dollars! I earned it!" She couldn't have felt prouder of herself. Flourishing the check, she waltzed around the room, jumped onto the fruit crate, rolled on the bed and skipped about until Qiming threw his arms around her waist.

They hugged one another tightly, their breaths caressing their faces.

"Listen to me," said Yan, brushing aside Qiming's kisses. "Nine hundred goes to pay back Auntie. Three hundred goes for rent. And we'll send a hundred to Ningning!"

"Good!" Qiming was in complete agreement.

"All right," said Yan, getting up from the bed and seating herself on the crate. "I've got to get back to work." Happily humming a tune from Ode to Beijing, she picked up a sweater.

"Work? Are you going to work late again?"

"Yes, of course."

"Let that boss of yours do some late shifts! We're human beings, not machines!" Furious, he banged his fist on the crate. "Isn't his name Ma? Horse? Well, tell Mr. Horse that you're a human being, not a beast of burden. Make him understand that!"

"Why are you so het up? Mr. Ma isn't forcing me to do this. I want to work late, to earn a few extra dollars!"

"Human beings will accept any hardships and swallow any insults simply to survive!"

"We're not the only ones to suffer hardships. Most newcomers here go through the same thing, don't they? One year of such hardship and we'll save some money, send you to university, and the hard days will be practically over!"

"Forget it! With my half-baked English it'll be several years before I manage to pass the TOEFL test. Then I'll be in my mid-thirties before I get into college and in my forties when I graduate. Who will want me then? And besides, what's the use of getting a good education? Xiao Li at the restaurant busted his ass five years to get his M.A. in marine biology and he's still washing dishes. And take my boss Ah Chun. D'you know she's a graduate of Columbia University? She switched to the restaurant business because she's got a strong personality and wouldn't take crap from any Westerner. As for me, I don't feel like doing the roundabout through college. The best thing is to go straight into business and make money!"

Yan went on crocheting her sweater and made no comment.

"Mrs. Wang, don't wear yourself to a frazzle. Tomorrow's Sunday, so let's go out to look around."

"Look at what?"

"At the sun in the United States!"

"The sun in the United States?"

"I dive into the subway early in the morning and wash dishes all day, and when I get back home it's dark already. We've been here a month and I still don't know whether the sun here is round or four-cornered! Whatever you say, I'm going to find out tomorrow what the sun looks like in the United States!"

- 4 -

Manhattan in midsummer is one big furnace. Thousands of air conditioners, running twenty-four hours a day, suck a fetid miasma out of the bowels of one-hundred-story leviathans and spew it into the streets, so that cramped little Manhattan is basted with a moist, turbid stench as it roasts in the heat.

Qiming's basement apartment had become unlivable. Every day he put ice cubes on himself, trying to keep cool the way body temperatures are lowered for heart surgery and corpses are refrigerated. But even that didn't help. Enough was enough. It was time to move.

As far as moving was concerned, both Qiming and Yan belonged to the get-up-and-go type. Besides, they had no furniture and their "friend" at the airport had relieved them of the little luggage they'd brought. That made moving easier, if nothing else.

They bought a newspaper and after much finger pointing found a bed-and-living-room apartment for rent at four hundred and eighty dollars. Newspaper in hand they went to look for it.

Not bad. Not bad at all. A large kitchen, quite clean; the dining space big enough to seat six or even eight people; the tiles in the bathroom still white and fresh-looking; the bedroom and living room quite stylish, the latter large enough even for a party.

Why dawdle? Shell out!

The apartment paid for, the two began to move furniture in. But you just said they didn't have any furniture and that all their luggage had been stolen, didn't you? Quite right. But their not having any furniture didn't mean that none was to be found in the streets.

The heat was stifling. Never mind clothes; even a birthday suit was too warm for that kind of weather. They somehow managed to wrestle a used king-size double bed into their bedroom, Qiming with his shirt sticking to his back and Yan looking like her hair was glued to her forehead. As Yan leaned against a wall to catch her breath Qiming went out again, throwing back: "Take a rest!"

And so Qiming, looking like a drenched chicken, made several more trips and lugged back a sofa set with two armchairs, and then a wardrobe and a desk. On his last trip with a 27-inch TV braced against his belly, he staggered up the stairs on wobbly knees and with the half-squatting gait used by comic characters in Peking Opera.

"You don't even know if it works or not, or if you can see anything in it," Yan said. "Why didn't you check it out before bringing it home?"

"Huh! I call that real smart!" Qiming shook his head with a wry grin. "Where d'you expect me to check out an idiot box I pick up on the street? Where do I plug it in?"

Yan helped him set up the TV and then plugged it into the wall socket. Loud and clear sounds came out of it, but the screen remained blank. "I told you so! All that wasted effort!"

"I'll bring those bastards out of the box!" Qiming slapped the TV set, punched it a few times, then fiddled a while with the knobs, and finally figures appeared on the screen: several girls doing a dance.

"Hey! How's that! It works now!" Qiming said proudly. "It's okay now! Now you know why they say the Chinese are intelligent!"

The kitchen at the Hunan Garden Restaurant was as unbearably hot as the inside of a steam cooker. It wasn't even equipped with a ventilator, not to mention air conditioners, and the two little fans spinning pathetically next to the open window were no match for the four big cooking stoves.

Everyone's pores were wide open, and exposed skin glistened greasily like that on the roast suckling pigs sold out front. Faces were stiff and expressionless, indicating a general unhappiness. People went around like mines with their fuses sticking out. They were okay if left alone, but one careless word was enough to set off an explosion. Even Ah Chun, who usually spoke long and loud, had pitched her voice down a few decibels.

Qiming was close to suffocation. Drops of perspiration fell from his head into the dishwashing sink as he bent over it. The waiters kept on dumping dirty dishes beside him, sometimes splashing gobs of oily sauce onto his face.

Sing! He felt an urge to sing at the top of his voice to clear out the heat-compounded morass of frustration that clogged his chest.

Sing! Why not! A couple of verses from *Taking Tiger Mountain by Stratagem*!

> Through the forests
> Over the snowy plains,
> Spirits higher than the sky...

The ear-splitting blast of Peking Opera ripped through the hubbub and rooted Qiming's colleagues to the spot. They gaped at him wordlessly, then broke out in a ragged ovation that was three parts cheering and seven parts jeering.

After the first verses, Qiming went on to sing the orchestral accompaniment. This, combined with the clatter of woks and the thumping of choppers, resulted in a fairly respectable musical composition.

"All right!" shouted Xiao Li. "You're a genuine artist! Just get a load of that voice!"

"I liked that bit from *Silang Visits His Mother*," commented The Wok, also shouting.

"Who told you that was from *Silang Visits His Mother*?" Xiao Li yelled at The Wok. "I bet you never even heard that opera!"

"Then what was it?"

"That was from *Luo Cheng's Challenge at the Pass*."

Qiming shook his head, undecided whether to laugh at or deplore his friends' ignorance. All at once, he noticed a tingling sensation in one of his hands submerged in the dishwashing sink. He lifted it out of the water. A shard from a broken wine glass stuck knife-like in his palm, in the angle between thumb and index finger. He grasped the piece of glass with the fingers of his left hand and gave it a jerk. Blood welled out, dripping bright red into the sink.

Sweating from the pain, he pressed a finger on the wound and looked around for a roll of adhesive tape. He found one and, silently clenching his teeth, laid a strip over the gash, then a second strip. He then plunged his hands back into the sink. His blood slowly dissolved in Picasso-like patterns on the surface of the water.

During the lunch break, he stayed alone in the kitchen to wash out the wound with cold water. It hurt and he drew in his breath with sharp hisses. But he didn't exclaim out loud. He must not do that; he still had to work. Stick it out! he told himself. It'll get better in a while! He suffered the pain in silence, gritting his teeth, all the parts of his face twisted out of their normal positions.

When Ah Chun failed to find Qiming among the employees at the dinner table she came into the kitchen, arriving just in time to see his grimaces as he sluiced his wound.

"This won't do," she said decisively. "You'll have to go to the hospital."

"It'll be all right after I wash it out," Qiming protested. "I've still got work to do in the afternoon."

"Afraid of spending your money?" Ah Chun asked with brutal directness. "If you don't go soon to the hospital and it gets infected, you might not be able to save that hand with the little money you make! Go on, off to the hospital!"

Qiming walked out of the restaurant into one of Manhattan's hottest afternoons. Sunshine, penetrating the interstices between tall buildings, scorched his face. He screwed up his eyes like a convict newly released from prison and still unaccustomed to bright sunlight.

Commuting to and from work by moonlight and starlight, as it were, Qiming hardly ever saw such sunshine, or New York in such sunshine. He stopped at the subway entrance, reluctant to go in. He wanted to walk a few blocks and use this rare opportunity to enjoy the sunlight and see something of New York.

New Yorkers dashed across his field of vision. Women, in a bid to keep cool, had stripped down to the barest minimum of clothing. But they failed to interest Qiming. He suddenly had the feeling that these people had nothing at all to do with him. For the most part well-fed, fashionably dressed, and bustling about each on his or her own business, they passed by him without giving him a glance, not even noticing his lonely presence. Here, in one of the world's busiest and most crowded spots, he felt completely forgotten.

1

. . .

2

At the factory where Yan was employed Boss Ma paced back and forth in his office in a towering rage. He was waiting for Yan to come in so as to vent his spleen on her. The instant she appeared in the doorway, he started to yell at her.

"See what you've done! This is all your doing! Two boxes of sweaters have been sent back! Two whole boxes! The client returned them because the collars on all of them are too small! I put you in charge of quality control, so why did you pass them?! The client refuses to pay for them. What am I to do now!"

Yan was too tense to speak. Tears sprang up in her eyes.

"I'll make you pay for them!" Boss Ma was still shouting. "What you earn in a whole month won't even pay for one box of sweaters!"

Yan was becoming frightened. She started to cry. Apparently gratified by the sight of Yan's tears, Boss Ma calmed down a bit.

"I'll...fix them," ventured Yan tremulously. "Your deliveries won't be held up."

Boss Ma suddenly came up behind Yan and wrapped his arms around her. "Okay, okay! I was only teasing you. I'm not going to make you pay for them..."

Yan struggled to get free, pushing at him with all her might and dodging his lewdly grinning face.

"Don't be like that!" Boss Ma was panting now. "I'm not going to hurt you. I'll protect you. Protect you."

Yan finally wrenched herself out of his arms. With a gesture of disgust she walked to the door of the office and stopped there.

"Your deliveries won't be held up," she repeated, then walked out.

At home she carried the two boxes into the living room and set herself to repairing the sweaters. She thought of quitting her job to get away from that lecherous old goat. But all their expenses had risen overnight after they'd taken this new apartment, and new jobs weren't to be had simply for the asking. And besides, she couldn't let Qiming know what had happened today. With his temperament he'd pick a fight with Boss Ma, and that would be a disaster. No matter how you looked at it, there was only one thing to do. Put up with it.

She picked up a snapshot of Ningning. It showed a lively and lovable Ningning standing beside a bowl of goldfish in Beijing's Zhongshan Park. Yan didn't miss her daughter so long as she wasn't reminded of her. But at the sight of Ningning in the picture, she couldn't hold back her tears. Throwing herself face down on the pile of sweaters, she began to sob.

...

Qiming was at home on sick leave. The difference between going on sick leave in New York and in Beijing was that you got paid as usual in Beijing, whereas in New York you didn't get a red cent. Yan took good care of him, and said things to distract and reassure him when he began to moan and groan. "Don't fret," she said to him. "I know you won't be earning anything the next few days, but I can bring some extra work home from the factory and make up for what you're losing. We won't be out by too much. Making money is easy in the United States."

Qiming sighed. "It doesn't feel good to be supported by one's wife!"

"It isn't me who's supporting you, or you who are supporting me. We support each other."

"If this were Beijing, a little cut like this wouldn't faze me."

"Yes, it would. You'd be afraid of not being able to play your cello."

"Play the cello?" Qiming had a short, bitter laugh.

"Oh! I nearly forgot!" Yan quickly opened a drawer.

"What have you got there?"

"A letter."

"From whom?"

"Deng Wei. It came yesterday afternoon."

"Quick! I want to read it! That rascal!"

"Read it out loud, so that I can hear you."

"All right, you listen and I'll read. Hey! This guy's handwriting hasn't improved one bit!"

"It isn't that long since we left Beijing. How much improvement do you expect?" said Yan, laughing. "Go on, read!"

Qiming began: "Dear Qiming and Yan, How are you doing..."

"Get a load of that! He says 'Dear'! Gives me goose bumps!" Qiming flicked the letter with his index finger and laughed. "Not yet in the States and he goes Western already!"

"Go on reading!" urged an amused Yan, without looking up from her work.

Qiming went on reading:

> "First of all, let me congratulate you on your success in the United States. You're riding

> high now, but you have not forgotten friendship even though you've made it good. That really impresses me. Our positions are different now. You're prosperous, happy and free. As for Xiao Zhen and myself, how shall I put it? Things haven't changed. At the Ensemble it's three-meals and hit-the-sack. We rehearse a bit in the morning, shoot the breeze in the afternoon, go to bed early at night. It gets boring. Don't laugh when I tell you Xiao Zhen had another abortion last week. She's at home now, watching TV..."

Qiming interrupted his reading. "That Deng Wei! The only thing he's good at is getting his wife pregnant."

"Don't talk about people that way. Go on, read!"

Qiming returned to the letter.

> "Ningning is a really sweet kid. We go to see her every week..."

At the mention of Ningning, Yan put down the sweater she was working on. Her eyes glistened.

> "She often tells people her Mom and Dad are in the United States and are going to get her over there soon. She's a real little princess. All the kids in the neighborhood and at school envy her. That kid is real generous. She's always sharing her goodies and toys with the other kids. In this she reminds me of the two of you: unselfish, loyal to friends. Don't forget us. When you're out for a drive or accumulating riches, think of your old buddies. Here's wishing you greater prosperity and advancement! Yours enviously, Deng Wei"

Qiming laid down the letter and laughed bitterly. "Enviously?" he said. It wasn't clear whether he was speaking to Deng Wei or to himself. "You poor sap!"

Yan remained silent. She was thinking of Ningning.

. . .

Working day and night for several days, Yan made up the lost income. But when she went to work one day, her legs seemed to have turned into rubber. Gimlet-eyed Boss Ma noticed at once that something wasn't quite right.

"Miss Guo!" he said with a great show of concern. "You look pale. Come into my office for a cup of coffee. It'll buck you up!"

Yan shook her head without speaking.

"You work very hard, Miss Guo. But today we're sending out a delivery and you'll have to have your eyes wide open. My business depends entirely on you!" He patted Yan's shoulder.

Avoiding him, Yan replied: "I'll do my best, Mr. Ma."

"Of course, of course."

Yan walked into the workshop with the sensation of treading on air. Her eyes were red from lack of sleep and she had a splitting headache, but she kept on going. She had to; if she lost this job, both of them would be out of work.

By three o'clock in the afternoon, the sweaters still hadn't been counted and boxed. She asked another worker, a woman by the name of Bai Xiumei, to tell the others to hurry up. She herself continued to inspect the goods, opening her eyes as wide as she could. But her vision became more and more blurred; she seemed to be looking at the sweaters through a fog. Suddenly, as though by magic, they began to whirl in front of her eyes. Everything whirled; things went topsy-turvy, turned upside down. Yan blacked out and fell to the floor. Vague shadows floated before her eyes. She wondered where she was. She couldn't speak, but clearly heard her fellow-workers talking.

"What's happened?"

"Maybe she's fainted from hunger."

"It's exhaustion. She's been driving herself too hard."

"I'll bet she's pregnant."

"Call an ambulance."

"Quick, call 911!"

Summoning up some strength from Heaven knows where, Yan managed to force out the words: "No! Not... to...the...hospital. I don't have any insurance!"

Whatever was said after that went unheard. Yan was out cold.

. . .

Qiming wasn't there when Xiumei and some other women workers brought Yan back home. He had gone to an employment agency. He'd never felt quite right about letting his wife support him. He wanted to stand on his own feet and get a better job than dishwashing at the Hunan Garden Restaurant.

The employment agency was in New York's Chinatown. An agency they called it; actually it was merely a small room thirty feet square with a young woman named Chen in charge of the business. Miss Chen appeared to be quite busy. Piles of forms covered her desk and three telephones rang incessantly. The room was crowded with people, all of them Chinese. Coming chiefly from Hong Kong, Taiwan, Singapore, Malaysia and mainland China, they yackety-yacked in a variety of dialects. The place sounded like a frog pond.

Qiming squeezed through to the desk. "I want a job," he said to Miss Chen.

"Leave your phone number and address," replied Miss Chen in her official voice. "We'll send you a notification."

"I want it today!" said Qiming unequivocally.

"What do you want today?"

"A job."

"All right, let's see what we have." Miss Chen flipped through a stack of forms. "There's a dishwashing job at Long Island. Want it?"

"No. Do you have anything else?"

"There's one here. Also dishwashing, in Albany. Want that?"

"No."

Miss Chen closed the file and looked at Qiming. "Do you have any special skills? And how's your English?"

If my English were good, thought Qiming, what would I need you for?

"Do you have any special requirements?" continued Miss Chen.

"Yes. I want a job that doesn't require hands."

Surprised, Miss Chen shrugged in a very American manner. Several other applicants laughed.

Qiming strode out of the employment agency in a huff. He couldn't stand being laughed at. As he walked along the streets he suddenly realized how precious that grueling job at the Hunan Garden was to him. He stopped at a street-corner phone booth and dialed the restaurant's number. By chance it was Ah Chun who answered.

"Is that you, Mr. Wang? You can stay home and rest for a while longer. Don't be in a hurry to come back to work. I have a new dishwasher."

"What?" Qiming became excited. "I never said I was quitting!"

"I know. But I'm running a business. And you know each person has his work cut out for him here!"

"You should have...let me know earlier!"

"I didn't have time. I was too busy."

"But I still have some money coming to me."

"Come and pick it up whenever you want to. Good-bye." Ah Chun had hung up.

Qiming slammed the receiver down on its cradle. "The bitch!" He cursed out loud. Nobody on the street took any notice of him; their indifference only made Qiming more furious. Raising his voice, he worked off steam with a string of Beijing expletives.

Still no one looked at Qiming. They were too engrossed in their own affairs to pay any attention to him. At last, completely deflated, Qiming turned toward the setting sun and made his way home.

The moment he stepped through the door he saw Bai Xiumei seated on the edge of the bed and Yan lying sound asleep, a damp towel folded over her pale forehead. With his heart in his mouth, he asked: "What's the matter with Yan?"

Xiumei motioned to him to be quiet. "She fainted. From exhaustion."

Qiming tiptoed over to the bed and laid a hand gently on his wife's forehead. Only now, apparently, did he have the opportunity to take a good look at her. She was thinner, her face pale, dark shadows around her eyes. Qiming stared at her for a moment. Abruptly he turned around and walked toward the door.

Xiumei called after him, wanting to know where he was going. He didn't reply, but he knew exactly what he was about to do. He was going to the Hunan Garden Restaurant. He would hold on to that job even if it cost him his hand.

- 5 -

On the way to the Hunan Garden Restaurant, Qiming formulated a number of plans to give Ah Chun a piece of his mind. He could tell her off for being heartless and unjust, or he could simply stalk out after the accounts were settled and slam the door. All the plans looked good, at least in theory. All were quite dramatic, and would allow him to let off some superheated steam.

Thinking such thoughts, he unconsciously quickened his pace; he could hardly wait to see Ah Chun's expression when his accusations awoke pangs of conscience in her. He walked faster, almost running toward the Hunan Garden Restaurant. It was getting late. Lights had come on in residential buildings and businesses were closing up for the night.

Qiming could see the restaurant in the distance now. The doors hadn't been locked yet and lights were burning inside. He stopped outside the restaurant and stood on the sidewalk for a few moments, rehearsing what he would say to the woman. Then he approached the doorway and was about to go in when he saw a chilling spectacle.

Through the window he saw a shaky Ah Chun taking money out of the cash register and stuffing it into a bag. Beside her loomed a burly man. He was holding a handgun against her head.

Qiming realized at once what was happening. He quickly stepped to one side to get under cover. He'd seen such scenes on television, but this was the first time he found himself in a real-life situation and he was both excited and a little frightened. Maybe he should charge in. But the gun was pointed at Ah Chun's head; besides, he himself was unarmed, and going in would invite a bullet into his guts. Or maybe he should simply clear out. But the sight of Ah Chun's fear-contorted face kept him rooted to the spot. He couldn't leave her just like that. He looked again through the window. The man was ordering Ah Chun to hurry and she was complying. She had no other choice.

Now all the money had been stashed away in the bag. With his free hand the man grabbed Ah Chun's arm. Qiming ran to a nearby phone booth, intending to call the police. He had just punched the first two numbers when he saw a blue police car driving down the street. Dropping the receiver, he raced towards the car.

"Police! Robber! Robber! He there!" He still spoke half-assed English, but the police officers quickly caught the drift of what he was trying to tell them. Hopping nimbly out of their car, they moved in on the restaurant. This was the first time Qiming witnessed New York policemen engaging in this aspect of their public functions. They were obviously well-trained and highly experienced—veterans of many similar operations. Holding their revolvers muzzle up, they sprinted almost soundlessly to the restaurant door and kicked it open with a loud crash.

"Freeze!" they yelled, aiming their weapons with both hands at the man. "Police!"

The startled robber stood still.

"Put up your hands!"

The man seemed to be about to obey, then suddenly reached for his gun. The policemen's revolvers barked. The officers had pulled the trigger simultaneously and the blast was deafening. The man slumped to the floor.

Qiming rushed over to Ah Chun. She screamed, her legs crumpled under her, and she collapsed into Qiming's arms.

Police cars drove up one after the other, their headlights penciling bright scrawls in the darkness of the street.

Qiming tried unsuccessfully to draw apart Ah Chun's arms which were clamped around his neck. She clutched him tightly, shivering against his chest.

The police cars began to leave, and the restaurant gradually reverted to its usual night-time tranquillity. Qiming cleaned up the dining hall of the restaurant, then returned to Ah Chun's office.

"I want to draw my salary."

"Why? We aren't at the end of the month yet."

Qiming looked at Ah Chun. She had recovered her sangfroid and was bent over her accounts. Women are the world's most unfathomable enigmas, he thought. Just a while ago she was trembling with fear in his arms and now she was as cool as a cucumber.

"Because," he said, "you have a new dishwasher."

"That doesn't cause any problems. He's leaving tomorrow."

"What for?"

"For you." Ah Chun raised her eyes from her accounts and looked earnestly at Qiming.

Qiming's heart leaped. He felt he was on the verge of solving this woman's enigma.

"But you said you wanted to fire me."

"Yes, I did," replied Ah Chun, weighing her words. "I hoped that would make you come back sooner. And you came."

Qiming nodded.

"It's a good thing you did." That said, Ah Chun retreated into the cool aloofness of a female employer. "Take another day's rest and come to work the day after tomorrow. Oh, that's right! How is your hand?"

"It's all right now! Perfectly all right!" Qiming assured her, exaggerating somewhat.

Ah Chun nodded, then went back to her accounts as though nothing at all had occurred this night.

Qiming walked out of the restaurant and slowly expelled his breath at the stars twinkling in New York's night sky. It goes without saying that he hadn't noticed Ah Chun following him with her eyes.

. . .

Christmas was just around the corner. It was snowing heavily in New York. How heavily? With flakes as big as goose feathers, as we say in Chinese? Not quite. But you could say the snow was coming down like layers of cotton fluff.

New York was in a festive mood and the general enthusiasm was in no way dampened by the fall of snow. Santa Clauses in red suits swarmed in the streets, ringing golden bells and doling out gifts to passers-by. People were buying presents in the department stores and stuffing big and small parcels into their cars. The heart-warming strains of Christmas carols floated in the air. Radio City's special Christmas programs had been brought out into the streets and pretty girls were kicking their lovely legs with neat precision. Millions and millions of colored lights outlined the marvels of New York City, their glow filling half the sky.

Yan sat alone under her lamp, working on a rush order. She had no time for the extraordinary scenes of festivity outside. Boss Ma had told her this batch of goods had to go out before Christmas Eve, or else he'd be stuck with them.

Contrary to what one would expect, New York's Chinese restaurants did little business during the holidays. Shrewd proprietors used this opportunity to redecorate their shops. Qiming had been asked by Ah Chun to stay and repaper the walls—which he'd been doing all day.

"You won't be able to go home now," said Ah Chun. "There's no more public transportation."

"And why's that?"

"Because of Christmas. But don't get excited. I'll drive you home in my car. But I'd like to take you out for a drink first."

"Do you drink, too?"

"Only coffee."

They went in Ah Chun's car to a cafe. The interior was tastefully decorated and well insulated from the pre-Christmas noise and excitement outside. Ah Chun and Qiming sat facing one another beside a flickering candle. She told him her life story.

Rotating a coffee cup in his hands, Qiming inserted a question: "So what did he do afterwards?"

"He spent all his time in nightclubs and fooling around with women."

"How did he make a living? By betting at the races?" asked Qiming. "How could a talented person like that fall to such depths?"

"He was a weakling, a pathetic little worm."

Ah Chun took out a cigarette and Qiming lit it for her with her lighter. He inspected her face. She was very beautiful, not in an exaggerated, garish way, nor with the subdued poise of young girls with aristocratic backgrounds. Hers was an enchanting, mature beauty.

"People change when they have money," said Ah Chun.

"Is that true?"

"Yes. Especially with you men."

"Not necessarily. I wouldn't change if I had money."

"You? It's a law of nature. No one can escape it. Neither can you."

"You don't know me very well."

"I don't have to. All men are like that."

"Tell me, Ah Chun, why did you start your restaurant?"

"My name isn't for everyone to use!"

"I'm sorry, Boss."

Ah Chun flashed him a charming smile and said softly: "You're very obedient. Why did I start that restaurant? I wasn't going to let him squander and gamble everything away. After the divorce I started the restaurant with money from my personal savings and from selling my jewelry."

"They say you used to work in a large American firm."

"Yes, I did. That experience was even more frustrating. I worked like a slave, but it didn't do any good."

"Why not?"

"Why not? Because I'm an Asian, and Asians get very few opportunities for advancement, no matter how hard they try."

Qiming nodded.

"Nor is it a picnic running a restaurant," Ah Chun went on. "I've been thinking. If things don't work out I'll shut down the Hunan Garden and go into some other business."

Seeing her worried expression, Qiming changed the subject. "Do you have any children?"

"No. I decided I wasn't going to pass my woes on to the next generation." Ah Chen raised her glass to hide her eyes which were swimming in tears.

Qiming was astonished. He had never imagined that this intelligent and capable woman would have such a barren and tragic spiritual existence, or that a forceful female like Ah Chun could at the same time be so emotionally fragile. He stared at her, bemused.

"Let's go!" Ah Chun forced back her tears. "I'll take you home." She stood up, keeping her eyes averted.

It was a red BMW luxury sedan, and she'd added her own embellishments to it: a pair of typically Chinese good-luck symbols hung from the rear-view mirror and the steering wheel was wrapped with pink velvet. On the windows were a number of stickers with whimsical legends: "NO RADIO," "I LOVE NEW YORK," and "BEWARE OF THE DOG."

Taking the driver's seat, Ah Chun stretched herself lazily. She took off her high-heeled pumps and tossed them over her shoulder onto the back seat, then thrust her feet into a pair of embroidered Chinese slippers that lay on the car floor. The practiced dexterity of her movements made Qiming smile.

"What are you grinning about?" asked Ah Chun. She turned to look at him.

"Nothing," replied Qiming, removing the smile from his face.

"Well, don't laugh at me." She started the engine and drove the car into the street. "You know, I envy you. At home you have someone who cares for you and loves you.

Not like me. I could work myself to death and nobody would give a damn."

Snow continued to fall in white, fluffy layers. Several yellow-painted snow plows ambled back and forth, pushing aside the snow and piling it on both sides of the highway. The car seemed to be rolling between high walls of snow. Ah Chun drove very slowly.

"White Christmas!" said Ah Chun, breaking the silence. "Beautiful, isn't it!"

Qiming looked at her from the corner of his eyes. She was very beautiful tonight, whiter and more beautiful than the snow-mantled scenery outside the car. The car's engine purred monotonously.

"Do you like it?" she asked suddenly.

"Yes, I do. I mean, no. What are you talking about?"

"My BMW, naturally!"

"Oh, I like it. Of course I do. I'll never drive an expensive car like this."

"Yes, you will."

"What's that?"

"I said you'll have a car like this one."

"Don't make fun of me."

"I'm serious."

The car crept forward, Ah Chun gripping the steering wheel with both hands. Her half-bared bosom rose and fell. She seemed to be a bit tense. Reaching forward, she turned down the heater and switched on the radio. The strains of country music came over the car's hi-fi audio system. Ah Chun hummed along with the music.

"Do you understand the words?"

"Hardly."

"I'll interpret for you."

As each verse came over the speakers, Ah Chun translated it into Chinese. Her voice was pitched sufficiently low so as not to interfere with the singing. In fact, it blended in quite harmoniously with the plaintive melody and lyrics.

If you love him
Send him to New York,
`Cause that's where Heaven is.
If you hate him
Send him to New York,
`Cause that's where Hell is...

"Lovely," said Qiming softly.

Ah Chun glanced at him but didn't say anything. She knew that the comment was meant for herself as much as for the music. The BMW drove off the highway into a narrow street. The snow hadn't been cleared from the roadway and its surface was very slippery. At a turning Ah Chun braked to slow down, but the car skidded without warning and swerved across the roadway. Both Ah Chun and Qiming were flung about on their seats.

"Watch out," said Qiming. He grasped Ah Chun's arm.

Ah Chun was an experienced driver. Shoving in the clutch, and with a few deft turns of the steering wheel, she spun the car straight again. Ah Chun slowly let out her breath. Then she laughed. "Mr. Wang, I'll thank you to give me back my arm!"

Only now did Qiming realize he was still grasping her arm. He quickly let go.

"Did I hurt you?"

"It was like being squeezed by a pair of pincers. That's the last thing I need. How do you expect me to steer the car when you grab my arm like that! You dumb jerk!"

Qiming laughed and began to massage her arm. Ah Chun didn't object; she smiled sweetly at Qiming. The BMW came to a stop not far from Qiming's home but he didn't get out.

Outside was a world of white. Festoons of colored Christmas lights winked, lighting up the interior of the car and Ah Chun's face. On it, Qiming read both agitation and indecision. Ah Chun turned her face up and moved closer to Qiming. Her brimming eyes looked searchingly at him.

Then she closed her eyes, and her lips, lovely, sensuous and quivering, approached his own. Qiming bent his head to meet her moist, burning, rosebud-colored mouth. Perhaps it had happened all too suddenly and unexpectedly.

Before he could melt into their kiss he began to struggle away from her. Tearing his lips from hers, he held her by the arms. "I'm sorry, Ah Chun. It's my fault."

Ah Chun didn't insist. Two tears trickled down her cheeks. Qiming couldn't resist taking her in his arms again. But this time Ah Chun pushed him away.

"That's all. You'd better get out now."

He tried to intercept her lips but she turned her head aside. Qiming reflected for a moment, then opened the door. He got out without even saying goodnight. Ah Chun didn't start the car at once.

As Qiming approached his house he saw Yan with a coat thrown over her shoulders, standing in the doorway and looking out.

When she caught sight of him she ran forward and flung her arms around his neck. "I was beginning to think you wouldn't come back tonight," she said, almost like a child.

Qiming looked back and saw Ah Chun's car in the distance. It was still there. He felt his heart pounding.

"My boss was afraid you'd worry," he explained. "So she gave me a lift."

"How nice of her!" said Yan, opening the door.

Just before he stepped into the house, Qiming glanced back and saw Ah Chun's car driving away in the snow. His feelings at that moment were impossible to define.

That night, as he lay in bed beside Yan, he didn't feel at all sleepy. Eyes wide open, he stared out of the window. Yan said softly: "I bought a suit of clothes for Ningning this morning."

"Uh-uh."

"And a Christmas card as well. I'll send them off tomorrow morning."

"Okay."

"I've also laid aside two hundred dollars for my parents. Those will also go tomorrow."

"Uh-uh."

"After paying the rent and deducting everyday expenses, I've been able to put seven hundred in the bank this month."

"Good."

"I bet you're tired out. You're getting skinnier and skinnier. The sales have started, so I'll get you a pair of smaller-size Levi's. Your waist measurement has gone from large down to medium. And now I'll have to buy small-size ones. You work too hard."

Qiming didn't answer.

"Are you asleep?"

Qiming wasn't asleep, of course. He was reenacting once more in his mind his kiss with Ah Chun. In twenty years of marriage this was his first amorous brush with another woman. As he listened to Yan talking to him he regretted very much what had happened. Yan was a good woman. The best. He really shouldn't have done it.

Sometime during the night he opened his eyes in the darkness and looked at the figure of his sleeping wife. Remorse overcame him. He put his arms around Yan.

Yan asked sleepily: "What do you want?"

"Yan!"

"Yes?"

"I love you."

"You wake me in the middle of the night just to tell me that?"

"Yes. I want to tell you: I love you!"

– 6 –

The atmosphere in the Hunan Garden Restaurant wasn't quite right, these days. The reason was that Ah Chun had announced to everyone that Wang Qiming had been promoted and would henceforth be the general manager of the restaurant.

A lot of nasty remarks flew around the kitchen.

"That broad, she's full of new angles and screwball schemes." said The Wok, banging down a cooking pot. "And she goes and does anything that comes into her noodle."

"What the hell does she think she's doing, making that jerk general manager!" The head chef was really peeved. "O.K.! I'm waiting to see how he pans out."

"What she wants is a pretty boy to play with. So she puts this guy on a leash. She works his ass off daytime, and he's got to shack up with her at night. She's a cool one, that dame!"

"Don't underestimate these mainland China guys either. They know a few tricks of their own."

Xiao Li silently went about his own business.

Qiming and Ah Chun could hear all that was being said. Qiming was on pins and needles. He wanted to go into the kitchen and argue things out. But Ah Chun held him back and wagged her hand.

All at once, silence fell over the restaurant. Something was about to happen. A moment later, the master chef and The Wok threw off their white jackets and untied their aprons. Striding over to the proprietress, the master chef announced: "You'd better start looking for someone else. I'm not working here anymore."

"I've got something else lined up," The Wok chimed in. "So I'd appreciate it if you'd settle my accounts."

Not liking how things were turning out, Xiao Li came to the rescue. "Okay, okay! Knock it off, fellas. It isn't as though you didn't know the boss's temperament. And we've worked together all these years. So let's sit down and talk things over. How about it?"

Neither the master chef nor The Wok paid any attention to Xiao Li. But neither did they move from where they stood.

Ah Chun knew exactly how to deal with such situations. She was sitting at the cash register. Cocking her head to one side but not looking at them, she lit a cigarette. "I heard you guys," she said. "So you want to quit? Well, I'd like to quit, too. Big, strapping men like you, with such narrow, petty minds? I can't believe it! And I can't believe you've never had tiffs or squabbles at home with your wives. So a few words stick in your craw and you want to quit? Shame on you!" Slyly, she was working herself off the hook. She took a drag at her cigarette. Then she changed tack.

"All right, maybe I was in too much of a hurry with my arrangements for Mr. Wang. That's my mistake. But put yourselves in my shoes. All day I'm running in and out doing this and that, and on top of that there are the accountants and the lawyers to deal with. There has to be someone to hold up the restaurant end. Besides, all these years I've never let you down or treated you badly, have I? But now when I'm in a pinch you drop me cold and stand around, waiting to laugh at my troubles. I'm a single woman. Who is there to sympathize with me?" Ah Chun began to sob. "People always talk with sugar on their lips. 'We care for you, we love you,' they say. Then you find out it's all bullshit. Why was I born so unlucky?" She threw away the cigarette and began to cry in earnest.

The master chef and The Wok were satisfied. They looked at one another and exchanged sly grins, then picked up their jackets and aprons and went back to the kitchen.

Seeing the situation was more or less under control, Ah Chun dried her tears, made a couple of phone calls, and went out on some business matters.

All afternoon Qiming felt ill at ease. Several times, hearing the gossip and barbed comments issuing from the kitchen, he wanted to go in, but restrained himself as he remembered Ah Chun's words. Absentmindedly he swept the floor. I've been here over a year now, he reflected. Do I have to work here? Am I going to work in restaurants for the rest of my life? No, I wasn't cut out for this kind of thing. He made up his mind to leave the Hunan Garden. When Ah Chun returned, he went up to the cash register and hesitated a moment. But Ah Chun pushed him along.

"So you want to quit."

"Uh-uh."

"What are your future plans?"

"I don't have any."

Ah Chun thought for a moment. "Fair enough. Try to break some new ground." She opened the cash register and took out two envelopes. "This one contains your salary." Then she pointed at the second, fatter one. "Jobs aren't always immediately available. This may help you along." Apparently she'd been expecting this.

"No, I can't take it." He pushed the envelope back toward Ah Chun. Ah Chun fell silent. Lowering her eyes, she extracted a visiting card from her purse and held it out to Qiming.

Qiming didn't look up. He took the card, picked up the slimmer envelope and turned to leave.

At the doorway he turned around and said softly: "Don't forget to lock the doors at night before doing the accounts."

Ah Chun nodded.

Qiming walked out of the Hunan Garden Restaurant.

Ah Chun followed him with her eyes, her fingers kneading the envelope Qiming had refused. She had a feeling that she'd never see him again. But again, something deep inside told her that he'd be back.

Qiming, sitting in the subway car, took the visiting card out of his pocket and inhaled its fragrance. On it were printed Ah Chun's telephone number and Long Island address.

Yan was dragging a large bundle of semi-finished sweaters into the room. As she looked around, she saw Qiming lying on the couch. "Hello! How come you're back so early today?" Setting down her things, she went into the kitchen and started to cook dinner.

"I've quit," announced Qiming, springing up from the couch.

"Haven't you just been promoted manager?"

"That's why I quit. I can't cope with it."

"Then go back to dishwashing."

"Go wash dishes yourself! I can't stand it any longer."

Seeing that Qiming was losing his temper, Yan tried to placate him. "Don't get excited. If you don't want to work there, we'll look for another restaurant."

"Restaurants, restaurants! Is that all you can think of? I've been there more than a year and I'm fed up—fed up with being miserable, fed up with being exhausted, fed up with being pushed around by those bastards. I'm fed up with restaurants. Those places aren't fit for human beings."

"It doesn't matter. Starting tomorrow I'll do more overtime and bring back more work to do at home. We'll still be able to put money aside."

"That's what I hate about you! All you know is to work like a drudge. You don't use your brains. How many people get rich through mere drudgery? Look at my boss. Now that's a capable woman! Chinese, English, Cantonese, Mandarin. She's got it all at her fingertips. She's good at anything she does, knows how to use opportunities and adapt to situations. But what about you? You don't learn, and you don't know anything. Married to a woman like you, I'll never get anywhere. Talk about being unlucky!"

Yan was furious. "I am what I am! So what do you want to do about it? I'm the one who is unlucky, married to a jerk like you and having to suffer such misery. Go ahead!

Marry any woman you like!" She began to cry and ran into the bedroom.

Qiming knew he'd gone too far. Guiltily, he went to the kitchen and took up the cooking where Yan had left off. Very soon a hot meal was laid on the table. "Mrs. Wang, dinner's ready!" he called toward the bedroom. Not receiving any reply, he went in and tried to get Yan out of the bed. "Come on, call it off! You're not a baby any more."

"Get out of my sight, you ungrateful sonovabitch!" Her sobs became louder.

"I was only joking."

Yan rolled around to face the wall. Her shoulders shook from crying. Knowing Yan as he did, Qiming realized that no amount of cajoling would be of any use now.

He went back to the living room and flopped on the couch. He wanted to think things over, to think about what he should do next. Qiming racked his brains into the middle of the night, but failed to turn up any good ideas.

The food on the table had been left untouched.

When Yan came home from work the next day, she took a small notebook out of her pocket and tossed it to Qiming who was lying on the couch, looking very gloomy.

"What's this?" asked Qiming.

"See for yourself!"

Qiming turned the pages of the notebook. It was full of names, addresses and phone numbers.

"An address book," said Qiming uncomprehendingly. "Do you want me to look up somebody's address?"

Yan couldn't help laughing. "How stupid can you get! Those are client's addresses I copied on the sly in Boss Ma's office." Qiming's face lit up with sudden understanding.

"Great going, Yan!"

"You big dope! The only thing you're good at is blowing up at me!"

"Oh, hell! It won't work."

"What's the matter?"

"Boss Ma will be fighting mad if he finds out."

"So what? If he can do business, why can't we!"

"You're right. A man's got to be ruthless to succeed."

"Don't be afraid. As I see it, you can do as well as he does if you take the plunge."

"Oh, hell!"

"What's wrong now?"

"My English. Englishmen and Americans don't understand it!"

"Hah! Even Boss Ma pops his words out one by one like popping popcorn. There's no reason your English shouldn't be better than his if you'd spend some time on it. Besides, when you yelled at me the other day you threw in a few words of English, didn't you? That shows your English is improving."

Qiming reddened. "Those were cuss words."

"I should have guessed that," laughed Yan. "They came off too glib. Anyway, learn from me."

"What? English?"

"No. How to make sweaters."

"I must learn designing. I'll design them and you'll make them. We'll show everybody in New York we people from Beijing are as smart as anybody else."

After that talk, Yan bought a secondhand electric iron and Qiming learned how to use it. He pressed all the sweaters Yan brought back from the factory, and that counted as increasing their income.

Come evenings, he went to one of the cheaper night schools to learn English. He studied conscientiously. Whenever there was a free moment he could be seen sitting under a lighted lamp, cradling a textbook or a thick dictionary like some old professor and mumbling to himself. He went at it so hard his head swam and he was definitely getting wacky.

One evening he lay sprawled on the bed with a dictionary, muttering to himself: "Y-e-s, y-e-s. Why the hell can't I find it!" Yan was working on a sweater in the same room. She giggled.

"What are you laughing about?"

"Do you need a dictionary for the word 'yes'?"

"Oh, shit! I must be going nuts."

Qiming learned English somewhat differently from most people. He paid little attention to grammar, to things like subjects, predicates, objects, tenses and active and passive voices. He concentrated on conversation. Most people learn writing, reading, aural comprehension and conversation in more or less that order. But Qiming had a different objective in mind and he started at the other end by first learning to speak. Maybe because he had taken music lessons since he was a child, he had a very good ear and a highly developed sense for different sounds. So after a few months he was able to speak tolerably well; without much of a vocabulary yet, to be sure, but he wasn't afraid to open his mouth. Words he learned the evening before he'd use the next day. Use them while they're fresh, he would say, and nothing gets wasted. And because he had such a sharp ear, every sentence he constructed and every word he pronounced sounded very American, very New Yorkese.

As a result of his lopsided approach to learning the language, he ended up with a typical New York accent and a remarkable collection of swear words, but he didn't know how to read or write; he became a bona fide American illiterate. But all that's for later.

. . .

For a hundred and fifty dollars, Yan bought a knitting machine from one of her colleagues.

Qiming was ecstatic. "I've always loved to take machines apart, ever since I was a kid," he remarked.

"What's that?" said Yan. "I buy something for a hundred and fifty bucks only for you to take it apart?"

"That's not what I meant. I was saying that I'm good at fiddling around with machinery. In this machine I see the goose that'll lay golden eggs for us."

That knitting machine became Qiming's constant companion. Every day he sat with it, knitting and knitting, never bored or tired, until he became quite skilled at operating the thing and at creating new designs with it.

He didn't find such work tedious. Practicing on the cello used to be a good deal more monotonous, what with doing scales and arpeggios and chords day in and day out. Five years, ten years, fifteen years, he'd spent on that kind of thing.

Industry and hard work, combined with intelligence and creativity, produces results. Within a few weeks Qiming learned a great deal about making sweaters.

In the United States, success comes from doing things others have never done and not being afraid to fantasize. No one pays attention if you only follow the beaten path.

Qiming had come to this realization.

One day he made two sweaters, using some of Yan's leftover wool. He inspected them carefully and decided they weren't bad. The colors on them were well matched and they looked quite respectable. That evening when Yan came through the door Qiming jumped up and, before she'd had time to collect herself, thrust one of the sweaters at her. "Try it on! Quick! I have a feeling I'm nearly there."

Happily, Yan took the sweater.

Qiming watched her. He was tense and excited. After she'd tried it on, Qiming made her put on the other one. The two sweaters set off Yan's well-developed yet slender figure to full advantage. They looked beautiful with her willowy waist, up-thrusting breasts and long, slim neck.

"You're fantastic!" exclaimed Qiming.

"You mean the sweaters are fantastic."

"I mean both you and the sweaters are fantastic!"

Then the two sat down.

Suppressing their agitation, they tried to calculate calmly what trumps they held in their hand, how to go about marketing and cornering clients, and how to come out on top in this game. Together, they drew up several marketing strategies. In each of them the first step was for Qiming to go the next day to Fashion Avenue.

The next morning, Qiming, dressed in a natty suit, strode briskly up New York's Seventh Street, which is also known to the world as Fashion Avenue. Buildings of up to a hundred stories stand one next to the other, their lower levels dominated by fashion stores.

Mannequins were deployed in various poses in the display windows. In some of the windows there even were live models. Wearing garments of many styles and colors, they dazzled Qiming with the variety and profusion of the goods they advertised.

"Can I do it?"

Intimidated by all the fashionable, eye-catching displays, Qiming was beginning to feel somewhat nervous. He stopped to look around, then touched the samples in his bag, uncertain whether to continue. Rows of container trucks clogged the streets and alleys. Latino stevedores shuttled between the trucks, pushing carts piled high with ready-made garments.

"Buck up!" said Qiming to himself. "Since you're already here, pull your shoulders back and get on with it. No one's going to laugh at you. And even if someone does, so what? A guy has to start somewhere."

Men and women of all colors and races hurried past him on the sidewalk. A tall model in a sexy yet stylish getup wove by on her long legs, gracefully swinging her hips. Several men, who Qiming knew were in the big boss class, swaggered past arrogantly with cigars clamped between their lips and talking loudly.

Street vendors selling hot dogs, ice cream, fruit or peanuts lined the pavements, their cries rising above the general hubbub. Qiming took his courage in his hands and advanced toward one of the buildings. A uniformed doorman politely opened the door for him. He stepped into a gleaming elevator, placed a finger on the number 56 and pushed. The elevator zoomed upward. The motion of the high-speed elevator made him feel dizzy and he opened his mouth wide to relieve the pressure on his eardrums.

When the elevator door opened again, he saw the show room he was looking for. A pretty girl slid open a window and greeted him with a "Hi!" Qiming returned the greeting.

"I have some samples I want to show you," he said.

"Okay. Come with me, please."

He followed her into an office. Sitting behind a round desk was a woman with a haughty expression. The young girl explained why this Oriental was calling.

"Let's start," said the woman behind the desk, raising her eyes.

Qiming quickly took out of his bag three sweaters he'd designed and knitted and held them out to her with both hands.

"Too simple and too Eastern," said the woman. "I'm not interested." With that, she lowered her head and went back to her work.

Qiming found his way to another room. With both hands he held up his sweaters to show them to people sitting behind a window. They shook their heads without even bothering to open the window. When he came to a third show room, a hefty man, apparently the owner, showed him in.

He carefully inspected the sweaters and kneaded them with his hands to feel their texture. "All right," he said. "Tell me the price."

"Seventy five," replied Qiming, quoting the price Yan and he had calculated.

The hefty man dropped the sweaters. "Are you crazy? Seventy five for cheap, poorly designed things like that? That's really funny. Go back home!"

Qiming wasn't discouraged. If he'd felt nervous and uncertain before going into those show rooms, he had no more apprehensions left now. He calmly assessed the reasons for the failure of his first sortie.

"Too simple and too Eastern." He kept turning these words over in his head. He examined one by one the displays on Fashion Avenue, absorbing and mulling over what he saw. A flood of new ideas and designs rose up in his mind.

Back in his apartment, he sat at the desk and recapitulated the new concepts he had formed on Fashion Avenue. He had started to learn music in primary school but had never been involved in fine arts, yet he had some ideas of his own on the subject. Paintings shouldn't be too realistic, too detailed or too true to life. Nor should they be too abstract or too far into modernistic trends. Fashion designing, he reflected, was not so far different from fine arts. He lowered the neckline by another inch and a half, and widened the sleeves by a full five inches. The result looked like the costumes worn by fairies and goddesses in a recent Chinese dance drama. Colorwise, he boldly selected a deep purple.

The design completed, he sat down at the knitting machine and began to make his new creation. Now and then he would stop knitting to pick up a pocket calculator and punch in a few figures. His original drawing was gradually covered with a scrawl of solid and dotted lines, numbers, Chinese characters and English letters.

Qiming didn't eat anything the whole day, and even failed to see Yan when she came back to the apartment after work.

"That's really great!" Yan's sudden comment, coming from behind his shoulder, made him jump. The next day he returned to the same building on Fashion Avenue.

This time he chose a small display and sales room tucked in a corner of the complex. An elderly man with a strong Italian accent came forward to meet him. He nodded repeatedly as he looked at Qiming's work.

"Good! Good! I like it very much. How much do you want for it?"

"Seventy five dollars."

"O.K. I'll take it."

Qiming was overjoyed. But he tried not to let too much happiness show.

"Can you make these?" asked the elderly man, picking up seven or eight sketches and showing them to Qiming.

"Yes, I can," replied Qiming, without a moment's reflection.

"Good. I want them completed by next week," said the elderly man, very firmly.

"They'll be done."

Qiming hurried along Fashion Avenue, elated, walking on air, winking and waving at the mannequins in the display windows. This was the first time he'd received any kind of recognition since he'd come here. He knew now what he was to do in the United States.

– 7 –

The living room in the apartment became Qiming's workshop. For a full week, he hardly moved a step from his workshop. The only time he did so was when he went to the toilet. And even there he would be punching keys on his pocket calculator. Seven drawings, to be completed in seven days. That meant he had one day to complete each sample, one day to produce a sweater of a style no one had ever seen before.

Demanding? Yes, very. Never mind a complete novice, even a person with years of experience in the business would think twice before accepting such an order. But Qiming had to do it. He had no other choice.

He knew these seven drawings represented more than seven sample sweaters; they traced the outlines of his future in the United States. In Beijing one would say that these seven days were his "hurdle." If he got over this hurdle, broad vistas would lie before him. If he didn't, he'd have to go back to washing dishes. Or worse, if things went badly.

There was no retreating, he could only go forward. Grit your teeth and go to it! Such was Qiming's decision.

By Beijing standards a week's work consists of eight hours a day with Sundays off. Qiming couldn't afford such a luxury, let alone American working hours.

Qiming figured on working sixteen hours a day. The other eight hours would have to do for eating and sleeping and trips to the toilet. Working this way, chockablock, without weekends off, seven days would mean a good, solid seven days. They'd give Qiming one hundred and twelve hours to work in. So by changing the method of calculation, seven days had been turned into fourteen days.

Terrific calculating! That was the way to do it!

Excellent as these calculations seemed, however, they didn't work when Qiming really got down to the job. In the first sixteen hours, or the first day, he didn't succeed in finishing the first sample! Qiming broke out in a cold sweat. It suddenly became clear to him that his calculation was useless. That was merely a plan, a project, wishful thinking!

He should look at it as seven sweaters in seven days. The simplest way of reckoning was: one sweater per day. Can't get it done? Then don't sleep! No more thinking in terms of days and nights and mornings and evenings. No more considerations about sleep. Just get your head down and go at those sweaters twenty-four hours a day! Whether at night or in the daytime he could hardly keep his eyes open from lack of sleep. His arms and shoulders ached. The moment his hands stopped doing something they would start to shake.

The swishing of the knitting machine went on without interruption. The lights in the room were never switched off, night or day. His meter count would be way up. So what! There was plenty of electricity in the United States. If people kept the lights on when watching TV or dancing, why should he save power when he was working?

When Yan came home from work in the evenings, her heart ached at the sight of Qiming with his hair uncut and his face unshaven, looking like a convict doing a stint of hard labor. As soon as she came in, she would pick up the completed strips of sweater, and without a word or a moment's rest would crochet them together. Her work was very fine, very meticulous.

"You put much more heart into this than when you work for Boss Ma," Qiming remarked with a grin.

"Naturally!" Yan pressed her lips together in a tight smile. "We'd be morons if we marked time doing our own work!"

In seven days Qiming slept maybe about twenty hours in all, and took one bath. Lying in the bathtub, he fell asleep and nearly drowned. Yan helped her dazed husband get out of the tub and then toweled him.

"You're getting very thin," she said feelingly.

"Yeah."

She helped him into his small-size jeans, and was shocked to see that his waist had slimmed down by another finger's breadth.

"What else can I do!" she exclaimed. "Even these small-size jeans won't hang on around your hips."

"That's easy. Buy me another pair at a children's store."

And in this way, the seven sample sweaters were completed by the end of the seventh day.

As she admired them, Yan's feelings were a mixture of joy and sadness. She didn't know what to say, or how to say it. She turned to call her husband who was getting ready to deliver the goods, only to find him asleep on the couch, already in a clean shirt but with his tie half-knotted. At a loss as to what to do, she knelt down beside him and gazed at his face. After a while she shook him. He got to his feet groggily and let his wife finish knotting his tie and help him into his suit jacket. He squeezed his eyes shut and then opened them again.

"Are you quite awake now?" she asked.

"Yes, I am," he answered.

"Then go to Fashion Avenue and knock them dead!" She radiated encouragement and hope.

Qiming nodded confidently. "Yan! You just wait and see!"

The garment display and sales room was operated by an Italian designer called Antonio. To Qiming's mind the name Antonio brought pictures of a robust and dashing young man.

This Antonio, however, was a gentle and refined old man of rather short stature, the one who had met Qiming once before. Of course, this little oldster had once been a dashing young man; and if a dashing young man were here now, he would quite probably end up as a little oldster. This irrelevant reflection popped up in Qiming's mind as he watched Antonio examine the samples. For some reason

Qiming found this thought quite amusing. Antonio scrutinized the sweaters one by one. His examination was critical and stringent, albeit highly professional. Qiming felt some apprehension as regards the workmanship.

Whatever his fears, however, he couldn't let the least sign of them show on his face. In the United States, revealing lack of confidence is not much different from jumping in a river or hanging oneself.

Antonio at last straightened up again.

"Good," he said in his not-too-fluent English. "I'm satisfied."

A big weight dropped from Qiming shoulders. Antonio took a few rolls of paper from a cabinet and spread them out on his desk.

"Here are twelve sketches," he said. "Take them, fill them out and make samples from them."

Qiming bent over and looked at the rough drawings one by one. "Young man," Antonio continued. "You must complete the samples by the twentieth of August. I know this is a tough deadline. But neither you nor I can help that, because there's to be a world-ranking fashion show in New York at the end of September. I don't want to miss this opportunity. Nor do you."

Qiming nodded. One thing he had learned since coming to the United States was the significance of the term "opportunity."

Antonio took a checkbook out of a drawer. Qiming stared at the checkbook. Antonio quickly wrote a few figures in it and signed his name. "Take this, young man," he said, holding out the check.

Qiming glanced at it out of the corners of his eyes. Two thousand and four hundred dollars. His pulse rate increased several fold.

"Thank you, thank you!" He took the check and shook Antonio's hand.

Antonio gave him a pat on the shoulder saying: "Drop in, young man. You're always welcome here!"

Qiming walked out of the show room. The check exhilarated him. Twenty-four hundred dollars in a week. That meant nine thousand six hundred dollars a month! A-OK! Who'd have believed it! He forgot his weariness, his Oriental reserve, and ran and skipped down Seventh Avenue. New Yorkers are a blasé lot, however, and no one vouchsafed more than a glance at Qiming's joyous antics.

Qiming began to spend some time walking around in the streets to gather data on current American fashions. Notebook in hand, he looked into one clothing store after another, standing for a long time before each display. Previously, one of his biggest headaches had been to go shopping with Yan and look at clothes. He had thought it a pure waste of time and energy.

"A guy could do a lot of things in that time," he'd often say. But now he looked at show windows and visited fashion stores with the greatest enthusiasm. To survive, he had to become a different person.

Actually, it was quite easy. Without thinking, he turned a couple of corners and was suddenly aware that the display windows were different from those he'd seen earlier. Pictures of male and female sexual organs and love-making in various positions, enormously enlarged, were openly exhibited in the windows. Photos of naked women, blown up larger than life, hung on the exterior walls of stores. Apart from these stores there were a few movie houses lined up close together, all showing X-rated films. Sex clubs, also standing a row, vied for customers. What was this place?

Qiming remembered that when he was at the Hunan Garden, the master chef and The Wok had talked with great gusto about some place near Times Square, on New York's 42nd Street. They'd called it the "hottest spot in town."

Qiming found a street sign and went up to it. Sure enough, the lettering on it said clearly: 42ND STREET.

Driven by curiosity, Qiming decided to take a look inside one of the movie houses. It was a small, dirty movie house, and smelled of urine. Qiming at first couldn't see a thing in the darkened theater, but when he made out the pictures on the screen he gave a start of surprise.

A pornographic film, too revolting to describe, was being shown. He seated himself. Before he knew what was happening, a near-naked Occidental woman reeking of cheap perfume plumped down on his lap.

"Feel like going into a one-on-one?" she asked without any preliminaries.

Qiming was taken aback. When he'd collected his wits, he hurriedly shook his head.

"I'll give you a wonderful time. I'll bring you happiness."

This was obviously the professional spiel of the girls in this establishment. Although spoken with cloying sweetness, it gave Qiming a scary feeling. The experienced woman, without waiting for Qiming to say yes, pulled him to his feet and into a small dark room. Was this some kind of theater box? wondered Qiming.

From here one could see quite clearly what was being shown on the screen. The cubicle was only large enough for two people. No sooner had Qiming seated himself than the woman's long hair began to bob and sway above his groin. The woman soothed him with obscene endearments, pulling down his pants, and trying to make him relax. But Qiming was too tense, and nothing came of her efforts.

"Are you chicken!" said the woman, slapping his buttocks. "Get up. It's finished."

Qiming nervously pulled up his pants and began to leave. The woman stretched out her arm, barring his way. He quickly handed her twenty dollars. The woman put out her hand once more. Qiming shook his head.

"Cheapskate!" hissed the woman. She pushed him out of the cubicle.

Buckling his belt, Qiming ran out of the movie house into the street. Without looking either right or left, he dove into the subway and headed straight for home like a good little boy. That was the last time he dared to gad about in the streets of New York.

All new immigrants dream one dream. That dream is to buy a car. And every new immigrant finds out on arriving in the United States that this dream is one of the easiest to turn into reality.

There are so many cars in the United States that they've become a plague and a scourge. Buying a car here is the easiest thing in the world. But making one's other dreams in the United States come true, such as living well and eating well and sleeping well—dreams that don't even count as dreams before one comes to the United States—is harder than jumping straight into Heaven. One has really got to be on the ball.

Qiming passed his test for a driver's license without a hitch. He then spent four hundred dollars on a 1976 Buick. One of the pleasures in life for Americans is driving around in their cars. Since he was in the United States and had his own car, Qiming decided to have a good time the American way. Why not?

Over a long weekend, Qiming invited a few people to go with him to Jones Beach on Long Island. All of them were people he knew quite well. One of them was Xiao Li from the restaurant. Another was a painter named Chen Fen from the Central Academy of Fine Arts in Beijing. Then there was Chen Fen's wife, Yang Lan, who had come to the United States with Chen Fen as an accompanying spouse and was now working as a baby-sitter for an American household.

Since all of them were ordinarily up to their ears in work and had no time for outings, they began to chatter and shriek with laughter as soon as they got into the car. It was as if they'd never had such a good time.

The car rolled along, wheezing and grunting, its tires flattened by the weight of the passengers and its chassis almost scraping the ground. They had lowered the windows and a pleasant breeze caressed their faces. A carload of hard-up buddies; a carload of good cheer. All of them laughed and shouted and carried on like birds let out of their cages.

"Ah!" Chen Fen's exclamation made all others look at him, wondering what had happened.

"Ah! The sun, the sun of America!" Only now did his companions realize he was composing poetry. Trying hard not to smile, they listened to him as he declaimed his poem.

I thank you, I love you.
For only you do not belong to someone.
Only you are fair and impartial.
Even the great,
And the stinking rich,
Are entitled to just one share
Of your light and warmth.
Even I,
Who am flat broke,
Am entitled to my own share
Of your light and warmth.
No one can stop you,
No one can curb you.
Ah! The sun! The impartial sun!

No one, and that included Chen Fen as well, could honestly say that the poem was first-rate or that Chen Fen was any great shakes as a poet. However, there was a line or two in the poem that struck a chord in the breasts of these hard-up buddies.

"Ah, sun!" shouted Qiming after Chen Fen had finished. "You're a real square guy!"

"Ah, sun!" yelled Xiao Li. "How I wish I could see you every day!"

"What's come over you guys today," remarked Yang Lan. "You've all gone gah-gah over the sun!"

"I hardly ever see it," said Qiming.

"Me either," said Xiao Li.

"But I get to see it every day," added Chen Fen. "There in Central Park on Fifth Avenue I sit under the sun all day long, painting those unpaintable fat women, painting until my tongue is on fire and my head spins."

Yan, sitting in a corner of the car, started to sing softly the first stanzas of *Ode to Beijing.*

> Brilliant morning clouds,
> Gild the city of Beijing.
> Solemn melodies,
> Announce our country's dawn...

The others stopped talking and joined her in a ragged chorus.

> Ah! Beijing,
> Beijing...

The car had arrived at Jones Beach. Jumping out, they walked hand in hand to the edge of the water and gazed over the ocean. The horizon stretched endlessly in the distance.

"What's over there?" asked Xiao Li softly, looking out over the waves.

Every one of them knew that if they could walk on the ocean and keep on walking and walking, they would come to a city. That was the city all of them had come from. They knew the people in that city, people who spoke with the terminal "r" of the Beijing dialect and who rode to work on bicycles. Qiming even thought he heard the sound of the orchestra tuning up in the rehearsal hall and Ningning practicing on her instrument.

They stood there a long time. The tide came in and sea water soaked the hems of their slacks..

- 8 -

When Qiming came back from night school he found a manila envelope in the mailbox downstairs. The name "Antonio" was written on the upper left hand corner.

Without waiting to get to his apartment, he tore open the flap and looked inside, then gagged with sheer joy. He raced up to the fourth story and, without pausing to catch his breath, barged into the apartment, shouting:

"Yan! An order! An order has come!"

Wiping her hands, Yan hurried out of the kitchen.

"An order? Let me see it!"

"Look! It's from Antonio!"

The two huddled together. With gasps of emotion they haltingly read the writing on the order, now and then exchanging excited glances.

"All put together that's a hundred and eighty thousand bucks' worth of business! A hundred and eighty thousand!" Qiming could hardly contain his elation. "And with three monthly deliveries and payments, that comes every month to...to..."

"How come you can't even figure that one out?" The agitated Yan stared at her even more agitated husband.

"I can't, I just can't." Qiming laughed. "That comes to sixty thousand per month! Sixty thousand!"

"Qiming!"

"Yes?"

"We've made it."

"You bet, Yan! We've made it!" Qiming picked Yan up and raised her above his head like a ballet dancer does with his partner.

"Hey! Stop it! Put me down! You're like a kid!"

Yan took the order slip and looked at it carefully. Qiming paced back and forth in the room, unable to calm himself. "One hundred and eighty thousand, one hundred and eighty thousand. Dammit! One hundred and eighty thousand!"

Suddenly, Yan said, "What do we do about that?"

"About what?" Qiming looked uncomprehendingly at his wife. He was still dazed with euphoria.

"Sixty thousand dollars' worth of output per month is no laughing matter," she said, reflectively. "That's close to an entire factory's output."

"What's wrong with that?"

"Capital."

"Capital? What capital are you talking about?"

"To fulfill this order we'll need seventy thousand, no, eighty thousand dollars for wool alone. Where will we find such money?"

"Eighty thousand!"

"Wool apart, there's also the labor. For such a big job we'll need at least twelve people to do the knitting, sewing and ironing. These people will have to be paid, and that means more money. Where do we get it?"

Qiming stopped pacing. He sat down. Yan also sat down and, facing each other, they racked their brains for ideas.

At long last Qiming ground out between clenched teeth, "We'll borrow it!"

All morning the next day Yan and Qiming took turns making phone calls. The phone came close to falling apart from all the work it was doing. None of the banks they contacted, whether operated by Americans, by Japanese, by Germans, or by Chinese, were willing to extend them a loan. The reason was very simple. Neither of the two had established any credit record.

"What the hell is this, anyway?!" said Qiming, slamming down the receiver. "People who've never borrowed from a bank go down as having no credit record, no loan history. But those with their asses chock-full of

IOUs, and who go around with the palms of their hands turned upwards, are said to have good credit records. I can't see the logic of it!"

Yan went on making calls.

"You might as well save your breath!" Qiming flared up. "Those bastards don't use normal logic in their thinking. Somebody ought to clean them out with bum loans!"

"Quiet!" Yan interrupted him. "I'm calling my aunt!"

Qiming flopped down on the couch and raked a hand through his hair.

"Hello, is that Auntie? This is Yan."

"No soap! I'm telling you!" said Qiming.

Yan gestured to him to shut up.

"How are you doing, Auntie? Yes, both of us are fine. We're here to trouble you again. It's like this. Qiming and I are doing business and we're short of funds. If your finances are up to it, there's a great future for the business we're in."

"I'm sorry," said Auntie. Her voice coming over the phone still sounded quite cordial. "Your uncle has been having some cash flow problems lately. Nor do I have anything to spare. I'm afraid it will be difficult."

"Then could you manage just a small..."

"Yan, both your uncle and I are strapped for cash at the moment. I'll call you as soon as our finances improve."

"Thank you, Auntie."

"And how is Qiming?"

Yan made signs to Qiming that he should say a few words to Auntie. He hastily made negative motions with his hands.

"He's fine. He went to work today. He said to say hello to you."

"Well, give him my regards. Goodbye."

"Goodbye." The phone clicked.

In utter despair Yan stared blankly at the wall in front of her.

For a while they sat in silence, plunged in pure, unrelieved disappointment. Was this business, this bird in the hand, to escape from them just like that?

"These Americans," observed Qiming, as though summing up, "don't like to lend out their money. I wonder how they got to be like that."

"What's the use of talking about such things? Think of what to do! We can't go to Americans, they won't lend. Nor can we go to any Chinese, they don't have any money."

Qiming sprang to his feet. "There's someone who might lend us the money!"

"Who's that?"

"Ah Chun!"

"Who's Ah Chun?"

"The owner of the Hunan Garden."

"Why go to her?"

"She's Chinese, and she has money."

"She might not be willing."

"We can always try."

He snatched up the phone which was still warm from being handled all morning. "Hello! My name's Wang. Is the proprietress in?"

"What proprietress?"

"Ah Chun."

"Ah Chun? She isn't here any more."

"Then what..."

"She's sold the restaurant."

The other party hung up.

"Well?" asked Yan.

Qiming thought for a moment, then ran upstairs to the bedroom and rummaged around until he found the card Ah Chun had given him. Rushing downstairs again, he dialed Ah Chun's number. The beeping of the phone's tonality synchronized with his heartbeat. A languorous female voice came on the line: "Hello!"

No question about it. It was Ah Chun. He recognized her voice, and his face flushed red.

"Is Ah Chun at home?"

"Oh? So you've finally remembered me!" Ah Chun's tone of voice was, as usual, hard to define. It disconcerted, inspired respect, and held just a touch of warmth.

"How are things?"

"Not so good."

"I hear you've sold the restaurant."

"That's right."

"What are you doing now?"

"Nothing."

Qiming paused and glanced at Yan. Yan was busy doing something. Her head was lowered, but Qiming knew she was listening.

"I want to see you." Forming the words cost Qiming an effort.

"So do I."

"When?"

"Now."

"Where?"

"At my house."

"Good. See you in a while."

Qiming hung up.

"Is that necessary?" asked Yan huffily. "Just tell her you need money. If she has it, you borrow some. If she doesn't, forget it."

"There's hope. Enough to make it worth going there." Qiming threw on a jacket and hurried out.

Qiming started the old jalopy and, burning with impatience, drove onto the highway. Anticipation, eager anticipation, made him step hard on the accelerator.

His mood was rather peculiar. Was it joy over the possibility of getting a loan? Or was it agitation at the prospect of seeing Ah Chun soon? Qiming couldn't say.

The jalopy's carburetor wasn't able to handle the excessive amounts of gas it was receiving, and the car drove toward Long Island trailing dark smoke. Qiming stopped the car in front of a white house close to the sea. Swiftly alighting, he walked up the path and pressed the doorbell.

A moment later the door opened. Ah Chun appeared in the doorway, holding a wine glass.

Clad in a semi-transparent black negligee, she looked very sexy. The curves of her small, exquisite body were completely revealed. Qiming noticed at once that she wasn't wearing anything under the negligee. It was half a year since he'd last seen her and she looked more gorgeous than ever. Qiming stepped through the door. Seeing the pink carpet, he bent down to take off his shoes. His eyes strayed to Ah Chun's white-skinned, carefully pedicured feet.

Ten scarlet dots flickered before his eyes. The door clicked. Ah Chun had locked it. As he straightened up he became aware of the heavy fragrance of cognac.

"How are you, Ah Chun?" he asked.

"Fine." They were very close to each other. Their eyes met.

"I..."

Before Qiming could continue, Ah Chun threw herself against him and with an ardent kiss cut off the rest of his sentence. The aroma of cognac enveloped him. He felt Ah Chun's arms clamp around his neck. There was a tinkle as Ah Chun's wine glass dropped to the floor.

Embracing one another, they tumbled onto the soft pink carpet. They held each tightly, locked in a deep kiss. Ah Chun was now like a ball of fire, a white-hot cluster of flames that melted away all reserve or reticence.

These flames instantaneously reached every nerve in Qiming's being, igniting a fierce conflagration within him. Every cell of his body was on fire. Kissing, they undressed each other. She pulled off his shirt and jeans, and he cast aside the filmy negligee, her last line of defense. It floated down to the pink carpet like a soft, dark cloud. Tremulously, the man and the woman became one.

Two raging fires combined and burned all reason to ashes. Time and again, tender rhythms climaxed in cries, each time more passionate. In the end, happiness and contentment suffused Ah Chun's face, now wet with perspiration and tears.

Qiming lay beside her, spent and breathing deeply. They stared at the ceiling. Neither of them said anything. After a while Ah Chun lit two cigarettes and handed one to Qiming, then placed an ashtray on his midriff. Two plumes of smoke rose slowly to the ceiling.

"Let's talk," said Ah Chun flatly, blowing smoke from her lungs.

Qiming felt he couldn't broach the subject in such a setting. "Talk? There's nothing to talk about."

"You said over the phone you wanted to see me about something. So let's talk."

"No. Some other time." Qiming felt that discussing money matters now would be too much out of keeping with what they'd just been doing. I just didn't seem right.

Ah Chun looked expressionlessly at the ceiling. "I know very well you wouldn't have come here without a reason," she said quietly.

"Listen, Ah Chun..."

"I don't want to hear anything false or hypocritical. I know you've come for a reason. You haven't been longing for me, or pining away for me, or..."

"Ah Chun!"

"Don't interrupt. I won't like what you have to say, but I'm very glad you thought of me when you had a problem. That's exactly what I want. So let's talk!"

"But...but I can't bring myself to say it."

"Then I know what it is. In the United States, people say anything. There's only one thing they find difficult to say."

"What's that?"

"That they need to borrow money."

Qiming had no reply to that. He respected her for her competence and admired her beauty. But the one thing that really fascinated him was the uncanny accuracy of her judgments. That and her determination, which was stronger than most men's and not to be moved by honeyed words.

"Am I right?"

Qiming turned to look at her. "Yes."

Qiming could only admit it. There was no point in playing games with this woman; she knew what was on your mind. Maybe she knows better than I do, reflected Qiming.

Ah Chun suddenly stood up.

"Where are you going?" asked Qiming, catching her hand.

"I can't talk money like this. Money is something naked, and I can't stand talking about naked things when I'm naked myself. You'd better get up too. Go take a shower." She walked to the staircase, then stopped and looked back. "Never mix money and love," she said. "Never!"

She went upstairs.

When she came downstairs again after washing up, Qiming was sitting fully dressed on the couch and looking at a newspaper.

"All right," said Ah Chun, sitting down beside him. "Are you borrowing the money to do business?"

"Yes. To go into business."

"What kind—if I may ask?"

"A sweater factory."

"Good. A sweater factory is a good idea."

"Why?"

"Other businesses are too risky. The competition's too great. A sweater factory's your best bet."

"Thanks."

"For what?"

"For your encouragement."

"I never encourage people. I'm only helping you analyze things and choose your path."

He stroked her ear with his hand.

She allowed his fingers to caress her.

"Monthly output?"

"Sixty thousand dollars' worth."

"Let me do some calculating." She closed her eyes and snuggled into his arms. After mumbling to herself for a few seconds, she opened her eyes again. "You'll need between sixty and seventy thousand dollars' capital."

"Seventy thousand."

"At the very least, otherwise it wouldn't be a factory."

"You're so intelligent."

"Don't flatter me."

"That's not flattery. It's the truth."

"You shouldn't flatter your creditor so blatantly when asking for a loan."

"I've already separated love and money."

"You learn fast."

Ah Chun got up from the couch and went behind her desk. Opening a drawer, she took out a sheet of paper. She wrote something on it with an incisive, experienced hand. Qiming watched her, finding it hard to believe that only half a minute earlier this woman had been lying in his arms. Ah Chun finished writing and laid down her pen.

"Come and sign this, if you agree to it."

Qiming went to the desk and picked up the sheet of paper. On it was written that Ah Chen was making a loan of seventy thousand dollars to Qiming at fourteen percent interest and to be paid back within ten months. The terms of the IOU were clear, concise, and airtight.

"You're in luck," remarked Ah Chun. "I've only just sold the restaurant and some money happens to be lying around."

"Thank you, very much."

"I plan to invest in a larger restaurant and I'm looking at a few places now. I'll be needing money myself soon, so please pay me back on time."

Qiming greatly admired her level-headed forthrightness as well as her business acumen. He looked at her face, trying to read it, trying to read her mind.

"Sign it, please!" Ah Chun smiled briefly. Pointing at the IOU, she added, "Before I change my mind."

Qiming cheerfully signed his name.

Ah Chun produced her checkbook and wrote out a check for seventy thousand dollars.

Looking into her eyes, Qiming asked, "I'm to send you some money on the first of every month to pay this off in ten months, is that right?"

"That's correct."

"How shall I send you the money?"

"Mail it."

"Why? I can bring it to you. That way I could see you on the first of every month."

"Don't wax lyrical."

"I'm not waxing lyrical. This is a very real matter. I'll be able to see you, and that's very important."

"No. You won't have the time, especially in the first year after your business gets started."

"You have no faith in my feelings."

"It isn't that." Ah Chun smiled understandingly. Coming around the desk, she stopped in front of Qiming and drew a finger over his jaw and cheeks. "Why are you people from mainland China all like this? Romantic, full of good sentiments, but so impractical. Look to your business and forget everything else. Don't let anything distract you."

Qiming nodded automatically. Then, afraid of hurting Ah Chun, quickly shook his head.

"Don't pretend. Just do what I say," said Ah Chun, advising him as an older sister would.

She saw him to the door.

"Ah Chun," said Qiming suddenly, "I'm grateful to you. I...I care for you!"

Ah Chun smiled again. She fully understood. "I know. But don't tell me everything. Keep some of it in here." She pointed at his heart.

Qiming nodded gratefully. "But I'd like to know how you see me, what you think of me."

"You already know."

He tried to kiss her once more. Turning her head, she evaded him.

"Now go. Your wife will be worried."

– 9 –

Thousands of pounds of wool filled the living room and bedroom in Qiming's apartment. The only places not piled high with wool were the double bed he and Yan slept on and the table used for ironing.

The square table, small sideboard and couch which they'd picked up for free on the streets but nonetheless had spent much effort bringing home, were carried down the stairs again with a great deal of effort and left on the sidewalk for newer immigrants to take away. The smell of wool pervaded the entire apartment, tickling their nostrils and making them sneeze constantly.

Yan took on an assistant; not a stranger, but Xiumei who had worked with her at Ma's sweater factory. Xiumei had come to the United States from Taiwan. She and Yan had gotten along very well at the factory. Besides, she was industrious, not much of a talker, and absolutely loyal and honest, which gained her Yan's high regard. She was also a most reliable and competent assistant.

The new business went into operation. The workers Qiming and Yan had hired walked into the half-apartment, half-workshop rooms with great curiosity.

Naturally they were curious. They wondered what kind of business was being run by a penniless punk who'd been in the United States little more than a year. When Qiming and Yan weren't around their comments and guesses flew thick and fast.

"I've got to give it a good think before I decide to stay on here," one said. "Who knows whether or not that guy can pay us our wages!"

"You've got to hand it to these mainland people," said another. "I've been here close to twenty years and I'm still dreaming of becoming a boss. I want to see what makes this guy tick."

One man with a political bent remarked: "If you ask me, this guy's got connections. I bet the Chinese communists are giving him money to mark off some territory in New York and do united front work!"

All these people had heads to think with, and all were entitled to conjecture and theorize according to his or her logic or train of thought. But getting to the truth was an altogether different matter.

None of the workers came anywhere near to guessing what Qiming and Yan really had in their minds.

Why? Because Qiming and Yan didn't react in any way to what their workers were saying. The only thoughts in their heads were about knitting sweaters and making money. These were already enough to make them run around in circles, and they couldn't care less what other people were thinking or saying about them. The important thing was to get this little factory off the ground at once.

Yan showed unexpected managerial talents. In the first days the factory went into operation, it was she who told her new employees what to do:

"Oh, Mrs. Zhang! This batch will be the first to go out, so please rush them along a bit. Everybody knows you've got quick fingers.

"Mr. Lu, you're a really fast worker, and there's no doubt about it. But I'd be just a bit more careful if I were you. If you make a mistake, you're the one who'll have to do the job over again. Isn't that so?

"Sister Ailian, I can assure you there'll always be work to do. So long as we stick to schedules and get the goods out on time, there's no reason why we shouldn't get more and more orders. So don't be afraid."

"Auntie Yang, you'll get every cent of your salary, and I'm not talking big. Don't you worry!"

Dealing with these workers was no picnic. Most of them had been "stolen" from other factories by Yan and Xiumei through personal connections. One couldn't let them go unsupervised, neither could one afford to offend them. The Chinese make a big thing of the Golden Mean, the median path. Actually, one of the most difficult things is being a middle-of-the-roader.

When the workers had each taken some work and gone home, Xiumei said to Yan, "You shouldn't be too polite when you're running a business, Yan. You're only just starting up and this is your first order. It'll be bad enough if quality problems show up and you can't get your money back. What's worse is you'll lose credibility. That'll be a total disaster."

"I realize that. But if I offend people and we can't complete the order by the delivery date, that too will be a total disaster."

"But what happens if defectives turn up?"

"Don't worry. I'll fix them." Xiumei smiled. "If all bosses were like you, businesses..."

"...would all be on the rocks. Right?" Yan chuckled.

Xiumei laughed in reply. "I hope that doesn't happen to you. Good bosses are hard to come by."

Shaking her head, Xiumei walked out of the room.

Yan lowered her eyes, thinking about Xiumei's words. Xiumei was right, absolutely right. Yan made up her mind to learn to be a bit more tough.

Having made this decision, Yan felt easier. She looked around the room for Qiming but didn't find him.

"Qiming! Qiming!" she called.

"I'm here!" Qiming was sitting not far from Yan but was surrounded by mountains of wool.

"What do you want?" asked Qiming.

"Nothing." Yan laughed. "I couldn't see you and I wondered if you'd been buried alive under the wool."

"It hasn't come to that yet. At most I'll faint from the heat."

Yan approached Qiming, making her way through stacks of wool. An exclamation of surprise broke from her. "I say, Qiming! You're not wearing anything. And with all those people around just now!"

Qiming, bare from the waist upward, was wearing only a pair of shorts. Sweat ran down his neck and close-packed beads of moisture glistened on his back. "I'm wearing shorts, aren't I?" said Qiming defensively.

"I'll turn on the air conditioner."

"I've tried that. There isn't enough power. It's either the air conditioner or the electric iron. You can't use both at the same time."

"Talk about the tortures of the damned!" sighed Yan. She went off to iron sweaters.

"Huh! They say great hardship produces great men," muttered Qiming to himself; whether in self-encouragement or in self-ridicule, it was hard to tell. Qiming was getting all he could take. To cut down on expenses he was doing several jobs at the same time: designing, calculating drawings, ironing sweaters and negotiating with suppliers; and to make their factory more competitive he took it upon himself to deliver wool to the homes of women workers who had children to look after. Call him a boss? You could just as soon say he was a coolie. But never mind what he was; what did that matter so long as he made money! Placing the telephone next to the ironing board, he clamped the receiver with his shoulder and spoke to his client:

"Yes, tomorrow afternoon...The whole batch, naturally...Right, I have all the labor I need here. Your business won't be held up, Antonio. I've looked at your drawings, and I've added some of my own ideas. How do you feel about that...? Thank you, it's nice of you to say that. Then I'll start working according to this drawing...Very well, I promise to deliver the goods on time. Ciao!"

He put down the receiver and turned to Yan.

"Yan! The products made to drawings 334, 335, 226 and 215, one hundred and ten pieces in all, must be ready by tomorrow morning."

"No problem!" replied Yan. She turned to Xiumei, who had just come through the door. "What do you think?"

Xiumei did some calculating. "There aren't many factories that start delivering right after they go into business," she said. "We could do it by tomorrow morning, but we'd have put in extra time tonight."

"Why not?," said Qiming. "Do or die! This first batch is the one that'll get us credibility."

"But you'll have to watch out. The client doesn't always insist on such quick deliveries. You can't put in extra time every night!"

"Don't worry about that. Antonio knows the sweater business. He also does designing and sales exhibitions, and he ought to know how much work goes into a sweater."

The day sped by in frantic activity. The three of them didn't even have dinner. What "dinner" they had consisted of slices of bread and some canned food Yan bought at a supermarket.

They worked as they ate, their hands busy with the jobs they were doing. And so no time was wasted; the work got done and the three had their meal—and enjoyed it, too.

The electric iron in Qiming's hand never stopped working. Even when a wool manufacturer called up to ask for payment, Qiming kept on ironing and dealt with the man with the receiver tucked in his shoulder.

Xiumei was sewing shoulder pads and trade labels onto the sweaters. Her nimble fingers moved so fast it made a person dizzy just to watch them. The Chinese have a name for it: Thread chasing after a flying needle.

Yan had the most irksome job. She had to revamp all the substandards. She first took them apart then made them over. No matter how many defects a sweater had, it came out of her hands looking terrific.

The night melted through their fingers. Morning was approaching.

Yan propelled Xiumei into the bedroom, telling her to lie down for a while. When she had put Xiumei to bed and came back to the living room, Qiming was crouched over a paper carton and already snoring. His head was pillowed on the sweaters they had worked so hard to complete.

Qiming woke up the next morning at eight o'clock. He looked at his watch and remembered he'd promised Antonio to deliver the sweaters by nine. Scrambling to his feet, he routed Yan and Xiumei out of bed and together with them loaded the sweaters onto his old Buick.

They crammed the cartons into the trunk, back seat and front seat, leaving only enough space for Qiming to drive. "Has your head cleared yet?" Yan apprehensively asked her bleary-eyed husband.

"Yes," he replied, screwing up his tired eyes so as to see better.

"Are you able to drive?"

"Yes."

"Take care!"

"Uh-uh! I'll take care."

Qiming's answers still hadn't put her mind at ease.

"Drive slowly, don't overturn the car!"

"I won't," said Qiming, getting into the driver's seat. "If only because the fruits of our labor are in it!"

He pulled the door shut and started the engine.

"Both of you wait here for my good news!"

Yawning, he drove the lopsided jalopy down the street.

Qiming had left the house, and Yan's thoughts had flown after him. She knew she should start on the next batch of sweaters, but for some reason she wasn't able to calm her fears. "He must be there by now," she said to Xiumei. "What do you think?"

Looking up at the wall clock, Xiumei replied very objectively, "He'll be a while yet."

She went back to her work.

"I wonder if Antonio will like this batch of sweaters."

Xiumei smiled. "Ours are among the best in all of New York. If Antonio knows his sweaters, he'll like ours for sure."

"That's what I say too."

The two were quiet for a while. It was Yan again who broke the silence.

"Tell me, Xiumei. The samples Qiming designed, will they suit Antonio's tastes?"

"Why shouldn't they? After all, the drawings are his."

"Qiming's got a lot of nerve. He takes one look at Antonio's sketches and then starts to make changes on them and to add his own ideas. Some of the designs he makes from the sketches show quite big changes. Antonio's an old designer and that might hurt his ego."

"Americans aren't like that," replied Xiumei after a moment's reflection. "If a thing is good, it's good. If a design is attractive, it's attractive. Antonio and your husband work together on the designing and they seem to be getting along quite well. I hardly see such side issues cropping up."

"That's good."

"Don't be concerned."

"O.K."

Xiumei couldn't help smiling. "I started making sweaters in the United States a year earlier than you, and I know ours are..."

"What?"

"Really tops!"

And so the two chatted as they worked. Yan waited nervously. She was as restless as a cat on a hot roof, now dropping her work to go and look out of the window, now fishing for some soothing remarks from Xiumei.

Near midday, Yan heard three beeps from a car on the street. "He's back!" she cried, rushing to the window.

Sure enough, it was Qiming driving back in the old jalopy. "Why is he driving so slowly?" she muttered anxiously. "Why does he look so pooped?"

She hadn't the courage to go and meet Qiming. The door opened. Qiming leaned wearily against the door frame, looking at Yan. Xiumei greeted him. "So you're back? Did you deliver the goods?"

Qiming nodded. Unable to stand the suspense any longer, Yan asked her husband: "How did it go? Was Antonio satisfied?"

Without replying, Qiming slowly extracted a slip of paper from his jacket pocket and waved it at Yan. Yan and Xiumei could see it was a check. "Take it," Qiming said with an effort. Then, pointing at the figures on the check, he added, "It's for sixty thousand dollars."

Yan was silent. She wanted to run into his arms. She wanted to kiss him, hold his thin face in her hands, wash away his exhaustion with her tears. But she did none of these. She stood where she was, not moving a single step. Covering her face with her hands, she began to cry like a little girl.

Neither she nor Qiming noticed Xiumei leave the apartment. Swaying on his feet, Qiming walked over to Yan and put an arm around her heaving shoulders.

"Don't cry, don't cry!" he said gently. "Yan, we've made it in the United States!"

Yan sobbed: "I shouldn't...cry. But I...just can't help it."

"I know."

"Let's... No, is there anything you want to do?"

Qiming whispered something. Yan didn't catch what he'd said. "What's that?" she asked.

"Go...to...bed."

Yan nodded and let her husband put his arm around her waist. Holding onto each other, they went into their bedroom.

After a deep, satisfying sleep, they woke up to find it was almost evening. The setting sun was splashing a streak of orange across the window screen. Neither of them was in a hurry to get up. They lay in bed, looking out the window and languidly enjoying a rare moment of sweet happiness after their recent ordeal. Lying face toward the ceiling and stroking Yan's bare arm and bosom, Qiming recalled his encounter with Antonio when he delivered the sweaters. She listened to him, resting her head on his broad chest, as lazy as a kitten.

"He was busy consulting with some other clients when I came in the show room. But he saw me. D'you understand? He came over to me. He left his clients and came over to me. Get it? That shows how much he thinks of me. He said, 'Hi, my Chinese boy.' He called me his Chinese boy."

Yan snuggled into his armpit and giggled.

"Don't laugh," he said. "This old Italian guy looked at our sweaters. He was thorough, very thorough. His eyes are really sharp, like hawk's eyes. Nobody can fool them. They don't let pass a single defect, not even the tiniest fault. I can swear to that."

"Did he find any?"

"There aren't any defects in our sweaters, that's the most important thing! He can look as hard as he wants but he won't find bones inside an egg. I'll admit, though, I could hear my heart thumping. I thought it would jump out through my throat. He really had me guessing. Finally he looked up at me and said: 'Very good, my Chinese boy!' Then he made out the check."

"He's a nice man."

"True. But what counts most is, the stuff we gave him is first-rate." Qiming went on confidently: "All our workers are top-notchers. Their handiwork is almost faultless."

"Another very important thing is that our relations with them are good."

"How do you explain that?"

"They say we don't put on airs, that it's a pleasure to work with us."

"That's what's called 'cadres merging with the masses.' Only when cadres live and work together with the masses can they mobilize the masses' initiative."

"That sounds very familiar."

"That's what we've been taught since we were kids, and now we're benefiting from that education."

Yan and Qiming laughed gaily.

"I'm hungry." said Qiming, gently reminding his wife.

"Let me boil some noodles for you."

Qiming held down Yan who was about to get up. "I've got an idea."

"What idea?"

"Let's go out to eat. It's time we had dinner at a restaurant."

Yan almost gaped with astonishment. Then she joyfully threw her arms around Qiming's neck. "No kidding?" she exclaimed. "Let's go! Right now!"

Qiming tried to extricate himself from her arms. "Sure, right now," he laughed. "But we'll be thrown out of any restaurant if we go there naked as we are now!"

. . .

It was a Chinese restaurant specializing in Chuanyang cuisine. Not the best restaurant in the United States, of course, but it left a deep impression on them as it was the first restaurant they'd visited as clients since coming to the United States.

They ordered roast duck and a couple of stir-fries. They ate ravenously and quickly. Too much so; the table looked as if it had been swept by a hurricane.

Qiming still hadn't had enough. He asked the proprietor to make a soup with the duck's bones and put in some Chinese cabbage and tofu. "Nothing's as satisfying as cabbage and tofu," he said.

The proprietor told them this restaurant had a tradition of serving "one duck two ways." Soon the duck soup was brought in, made the way Qiming wanted it.

Thereafter, whenever Qiming and Yan had sent out a delivery they would come to this restaurant to enjoy "one duck two ways" as well as to discuss their business and how much they were going to pay each worker. One could say the restaurant served them as a part-time managerial office.

If the proprietor was an observant person, or if he had the habit of talking about his customers, he would probably say to his friends and relatives a year later that the couple from Beijing who always ordered "one duck two ways" had changed a great deal in the past year, at least on the surface.

The first time Qiming came to the restaurant he was wearing blue jeans. These were soon replaced by a suit with the jacket always well pressed. The ties he wore became more and more expensive and elegant.

Yan's clothes, too, began to change, naturally in the direction of better styling and quality. Not only that. Gold and silver ornaments appeared on her neck, wrists and fingers. Most noticeable was the makeup she began to wear—red nail polish and lipstick which did make her look younger and more attractive.

Of course, the changes were not limited to the young couple from Beijing but affected the proprietor as well. The first change was a subtle difference in the way he addressed them. At first he called them Mr. and Mrs. Wang; now he was saying *Wang Laoban* and *Wang Taitai*—which in English mean Proprietor Wang and Madam Wang. He also said flattering things about Yan's new clothes, which of course cost Qiming quite a few extra dollars in tips.

Qiming became more and more accustomed to such service. The fact of it is, it doesn't take any effort to get used to such things.

Once, when Qiming and Yan were in the restaurant, flushed and stimulated with good eating, a thought suddenly struck Qiming. Pulling Yan out of her chair, he marched with her to the back of the restaurant.

"Where are we going?" asked Yan. Without answering, Qiming made straight for the work area. The air in the room was thick with steam and vapor.

Qiming immediately found the dishwashing sink. A young Chinese was bent over it, washing dishes. Sweat poured down his face and neck and piles of bowls and plates rose on either side of him. Watching the frenzied efforts of the young man, Qiming went into a brief trance.

Yan realized what was on his mind and stood beside him without uttering a word. The proprietor had followed them into the work area.

"Aiya, Wang Laoban!" he exclaimed. "You're a man of many interests. Would you like to see how our ducks are roasted? I'll show you."

"No," replied Qiming. His eyes hadn't left the young man. "I just want to watch this."

"Very well, very well," said the proprietor, a puzzled expression on his face.

"Dishwashing is hard work," Qiming said to him. "Very hard work."

"Yes, yes."

"One earns less than a waiter, and one doesn't get any tips."

"Yes, of course."

"This young fellow is a good worker," Qiming told the proprietor.

"That's right. He's a good worker." Not knowing what Qiming was driving at, the proprietor simply agreed with whatever he said. As Qiming watched the young man his hands went to his pockets, feeling first one and then the other.

Yan knew what he was looking for. She drew a five-dollar bill from her chamois purse and handed it to Qiming.

Taking the money, Qiming went up to the young man and stuffed it in the pocket of his apron. The young man stopped working to stare uncomprehendingly at Qiming.

"Say thank you!" the proprietor hastened to admonish the young man. "Say thank you to Wang Laoban!"

"Thank you, Wang Laoban," repeated the young man, wiping perspiration from his forehead.

"Are you from Beijing?" inquired Qiming.

The young man nodded.

"Work hard, buddy," he said. "And some day you'll make good."

The young man nodded dumbly. Qiming slapped his shoulder and walked out.

- 10 -

Qiming and Yan's business had been growing over the past year. Their output had almost doubled. Their bank savings and operating capital together reached a seven-digit figure. They'd already finished paying back Ah Chun's loan some time ago. And they had rented a factory workshop on Roosevelt Road.

The newly-rented workshop was quite large—large enough for five or six ironing tables. In sum, what they had now wasn't merely a tiny garment workshop. They were running a regular factory, a full-blown, honest-to-goodness factory. In Qiming's bright and spacious office the telephone rang incessantly.

Sitting across a corner of his large desk, he took one call after another. To be honest, doing business isn't difficult, nor is designing clothes. What really gives a person headaches is answering the phone.

The calls came from clients, from wool manufacturers, from lawyers, workers, banks and accountants, one call following the other with hardly a break. And Qiming took them one by one, switching voices and expressions for each call like a comedian in a one-man stage act, a different countenance for each call, a different attitude for each interlocutor. Qiming was beginning to feel quite exhausted.

"Oh, Antonio. How are you doing? On this matter you can rest one hundred percent assured. There's absolutely no problem. All deliveries will be completed before next Sunday."

"Mr. Zhang? I have to tell you I'm very unhappy about your request. Don't you realize what time this is? And you want to go on leave of absence? This work doesn't wait for anyone, so you'd better think it over...Salary? We can talk about that..."

"Oh, hello. Of course your wool is all of the best quality. I don't doubt that...Payment? Of course I'll pay...Are you crazy or what? I can't pay today! The first of next month, and that's a promise. I'm running a business and you've got to put yourself in my shoes...O.K., the first of next month! See you."

Putting down the receiver, he said to Yan. "That was the last call I'm taking today. If any more come in, say I've gone out."

With that, he left for his work table. But less than five minutes later Yan called him back to the office. This time the call was from their accountant. The man's anxious and resolute tone of voice had made it impossible for Yan to lie to him and say that Qiming was out.

"Ask him to come to the phone quickly." The accountant's voice made one think of dark, heavy clouds before a rainstorm. "Or else he may incur heavy losses."

Qiming was hurriedly summoned. When he picked up the receiver he was still in a mood to crack jokes.

"Hello," he said, smiling. "Are you about to run off to Mexico with my money?"

Very soon, however, the smile disappeared from his face. He moved his bottom, one side of which had been propped against the corner of his desk, to a chair and sat down heavily. He listened with utter concentration, and the look on his face became somber.

"What's the matter?" asked Yan impulsively.

Qiming waggled a hand, indicating that he didn't want her to interfere with his listening.

"You mean to say..."

That was all he said; after that he remained silent. He listened darkly to what the accountant had to say, knitting his brows and biting the cap of his pen. He listened like this for a full five minutes. Finally, he said: "All right, I understand it now. Goodbye." He put down the receiver. Head lowered, he stared silently at the phone.

"What's going on?"

"Something serious."

"What about?"

"Money."

"What's the matter?"

"We must..."

"Must what?"

"Spend some money."

"Spend some money?"

The more Yan heard, the less she understood. She anxiously shook Qiming's arm. "Tell me, what money? Why do we have to spend it?"

Qiming stood up. "The accountant has checked our accounts. He did it very carefully. You know, we have a lot of money. A lot of it!"

"And so?"

"According to the tax ratios, we've got to spend at least sixty thousand dollars, otherwise they'll have to be handed in to the IRS."

"What? Sixty thousand dollars!" Yan was shocked. "Spend all that? But there are only a few days left before the end of the year!"

"I know that," said Qiming impatiently.

"But why?"

Qiming looked at his wife. "This is the United States. If you own a lot of money and it goes above a certain limit, you've got to pay a large proportion of it in taxes. That is, unless you invest it as capital, or spend it!"

"That's ridiculous! You work your fingers to the bone making some money, and then you're not allowed to save it. What kind of a system is that!"

"What kind of a system? It's the American system."

"Time is so short! How are we going to spend that much money?"

"So now you're worried, too!" said Qiming resentfully. "You're always holding on to the money, never spending anything. All I hear from you is 'I hate to spend it, I hate to spend it'. Look at the coat you're wearing. It's still the one you brought from Beijing! Save. Save. Now your saving has landed us in trouble!"

"Don't blame it all on me," said Yan. "What about yourself? That old buggy of yours is about to fall to pieces, but you still can't bring yourself to get a new one!"

"O.K., O.K.! Let's not get at each other! We're both Chinese, and one word we'll never forget is 'save.' You can do that in Beijing, but you can't do it here. Here they make you spit it out again."

Qiming suddenly saw the light. "It's O.K. I've got it figured out now! I'll get a new car. That'll get rid of twenty thousand."

"What about the other forty thousand?" asked Yan.

"I'll talk to our accountant. He knows people in real estate. I'll ask him to look at a house for us and help us spend the rest of the money." Even as he said the last words he felt they went against all human logic. "Damn it! This is crazy! Here I go begging others to help me spend my own money! What the hell is this, anyway?"

Five days later, Qiming and Yan drove their new sedan to Long Island and stopped in front of a handsome three-story house.

"You can get out now," Qiming said to his wife. "We're home." They got out the car. After taking only a few steps, however, Yan stopped in her tracks.

"What's the matter? Aren't you feeling well?"

"It isn't that." Yan looked up and Qiming saw that her eyes were brimming with tears. "I can't believe it. Is this a dream?"

"No, it isn't a dream."

"Is it true, then?"

"It's true," said Qiming, very positively. "Come on!"

He swept Yan up in his arms and, like a pair of newly-weds, they went into the house.

The elegant living room was fitted out with a beautiful chandelier, expensive carpets and a full set of imported Italian furniture. The fireplace had been trimmed with chrome-plated steel. A Steinway stood in the living room.

There was also a palatial bedroom and a kitchen remodeled in the latest fashion at a cost of twenty thousand dollars.

Qiming felt Yan's breath quicken. Her arms were wrapped tightly around his shoulders. He put her down on the sumptuous bed and removed her clothing and underwear piece by piece.

"In broad daylight? Don't! Please!" She was as flurried and tense as a virgin.

Ignoring her half-hearted resistance, Qiming infused in her the flames of passion already burning within himself.

On the third day after they had moved into their new house, Qiming received a call from Ah Chun. He at once invited her to their house and Ah Chun readily agreed to come.

"Who was it?" asked Yan.

"Ah Chun."

"We should ask her to come here. After all, we owe everything to her help."

"I've already invited her."

"For when?"

"This evening."

"What does she like to eat?"

"She likes...I don't know."

The realization that Ah Chun would be coming to see them filled Qiming with conflicting emotions. He liked her, but he was also afraid that his new home might depress her. For some reason he couldn't get rid of a feeling that the more luxuriously his house was appointed and the better he and Yan lived, the more unfair he was being to Ah Chun. It was an odd feeling, but it was there.

Yan wasn't thinking of anything, of course. She bought some pricey seafood and went to the kitchen to cook a home-style banquet in honor of Ah Chun. Qiming went out to buy a bottle of XO brandy. Yan was quite surprised when she saw it.

"Does she drink?"

"Yes...Well, I don't really know, but it doesn't hurt to be prepared." He, of course, remembered the odor of cognac on Ah Chun the day he'd held her in his arms at her house.

"I don't...think it's very nice for women to drink and smoke," said Yan.

Qiming made no comment.

Dusk had fallen when Ah Chun rang the doorbell. Her behavior was quite easy and unaffected. Before Qiming could present her to Yan she was already introducing herself.

"My name is Ah Chun. Susan in English. You must be Yan!"

"Yes."

"Oh, what a beautiful house! I'm not boasting about my judgment, but I predicted a long time ago that you and Mr. Wang would have a good future. What I didn't expect was that you'd succeed so soon. Good for you! Your progress is the fastest I've ever seen among new immigrants. I admire you from the bottom of my heart!"

"It's very nice of you to say that," said Qiming.

"You should know," said Ah Chun gravely, "I never praise anyone without good reason."

Yan showed her around the house.

"I can see the artist in you both," said Ah Chun. "Such marvelous decor, and such charming color tones!" She added in English: "You have very good taste, Mrs. Wang. I love it."

Ah Chun had the habit of inserting here and there a few words of English when she was speaking in Chinese. She seemed to believe that was the only way she could express herself clearly. In the dining room, she exclaimed again at the sight of the bountiful dinner. "Oh, seafood! Lobsters! They're my favorite! And XO, I like this brand!"

Without waiting to be invited, she sat down at the table. Seating herself, Yan said to Ah Chun: "Qiming and I should both thank you. You've given us so much help!"

"You're being too polite, Mrs. Wang. You should put it to Qiming's good luck, and to the fact that I had some money at the time. If you tried to borrow some now, I could only say: Sorry, I don't have any."

"But the fact remains that you lent me those seventy thousand dollars," said Qiming earnestly. "It was that which gave me my start."

Ah Chun didn't reply. She stared at him for a moment, then lowered her eyes and began to shell a lobster. They first had a round of drinks, then began unhurriedly to attack the seafood entrees.

"What are your plans now?" Qiming asked Ah Chun.

"I've been looking around for half a year," replied Ah Chun. "And just last week I found a very suitable restaurant. It's in New Jersey."

"Don't forget to let us know when it opens," said Yan warmly.

"When it opens? It will be a long time before that happens. I've only just applied for a loan."

"Are you short of money?" asked Qiming.

Ah Chun smiled.

"Yes! The shoe is on the other foot now. Now it's my turn to borrow money from you."

"How much do you need?" asked Qiming earnestly.

"Yes," said Yan. "Tell us how much you need."

Ah Chun chuckled.

"I see both of you are simple souls really," she said. "I was only joking. I've already asked my bank for a loan. I don't think I'll have any problems."

Qiming face showed his disappointment that he wouldn't be able to help her.

"But I'll come to you if the loan is less than I need," Ah Chun added.

"Is that a promise?"

"It's a promise!"

Qiming nodded, again earnestly. Ah Chun was the kind of woman who never had enough time. When she got up to leave, she'd only had two drinks and had eaten only part of her lobster.

"Stay a bit longer!" Yan pleaded.

"Next time," replied Ah Chun. "Today isn't a weekend day, and I'm sure you have to get up early tomorrow."

Yan was touched by Ah Chun's considerateness.

Qiming rose to get Ah Chun's coat. She let him help her into the coat. "Come to see me," she said.

"I will," replied Qiming softly.

At the door, Ah Chun kissed Yan on the cheek. The two women had become quite friendly, almost bosom friends. "It's cold out," said Qiming to Yan, stopping her at the door. "I'll see Ah Chun off."

He went out with Ah Chun. The night was calm. A misty moon shed its light over the landscape. As Qiming looked at Ah Chun, so soft and beautiful in the moonlight, a wave of tenderness swept through him.

"Ah Chun!"

"Yes?"

"I...Tell me how much money you're short of."

"This is a risky venture and it needs a large investment. I...Well, we'll see."

"If you're not too sure about the whole thing, it won't hurt to wait a bit longer."

"I know."

"Ah Chun!"

"What is it?"

"I want to do something for you."

"I thank you."

Ah Chun opened the door of her car and was about to get in, but Qiming held her back.

"You must give me an opportunity."

"I will."

"Ah Chun!"

"Listen to me," said Ah Chun. "Your wife...is a good woman."

"I know that."

"And so am I."

"Of course I know that. You're the best woman in the world. The very best!"

She looked at him with eyes that reflected both sadness and joy. He, too, looked at her, fearing she would vanish before his eyes.

"I'll be seeing you!" Ah Chun held out her hand.

Qiming took it, grasping it tightly. Although he was hurting her, she didn't withdraw her hand.

"So long!" Qiming suppressed an impulse to kiss her. "Ah Chun..."

"Go home now!"

"Ah Chun..."

"Go home now. We've said our farewells."

Ah Chun jerked back her hand and got in the car. She could see the squeeze marks left on her skin by Qiming's fingers.

Qiming was still looking at her. She waved at him and started the engine. Lowering the window, she said: "Take good care of yourself!"

Then she stepped hard on the accelerator. The car rolled into the street and was soon lost to sight.

-11-

Another two years passed. Qiming's business was flourishing. He used his earnings to buy two houses that he rented out. This was a very lucrative venture. The monthly rentals were more than sufficient to make timely payments on Qiming's bank loans; he was turning a profit.

"I've got it figured out," Qiming said with deep conviction. "Buying a house is better than raising children. Even the best kid in the States won't be able to provide his parents with eighty thousand dollars a year."

In early 1986, they moved into another house. The red brick building standing amid a lawn and flowers blooming all year round was one of the classiest in New York's Queens district.

No matter how busy or tired Qiming was, he had only to look at his home to feel relaxed and at peace. Home? What was home? It was this little red brick house he could come to after the rough and tumble of society and the business world, after the exhaustion of constant play-acting and juggling and finagling; a place where all his anxieties and fatigue melted away once he was within its walls. Yes, that was home.

As a successful young businessman. he was self-assured, energetic, and adept at dealing with all the clients, lawyers, workers, accountants, tenants, revenue officers, bank employees, community leaders, members of Chinese chambers of commerce, and diverse types of rich people. In a crowd of important and not-so-important people he handled himself—and others—quite well. A socializer with a clever tongue and a ready wit, yet he didn't tailor his attentions to the stature of the people he met, which made him quite popular. All this, of course, helped him in his business.

The more his business activities grew and expanded, the bigger his ambitions became. But in the United States no one condemned him for this or accused him of greed. On the contrary, everyone here respected and liked him for it. Such respect and affection was by no means hypocritical; they were sincere. He became a center of attention not only in New York's Chinese circles; even genuine Yankees among the achievers in the business community would point at him behind his back and say: That guy from mainland China is highly successful; he's only forty but he's got everything already. For him the American Dream has come true.

Americans worship three kinds of people: Sports stars, film stars, and successful businessmen. Of all kinds of people, why these three? The reason is simple. These three have something in common: Money. They all possess money in astronomical amounts. That's right, the Americans worship money, to put it quite bluntly. That's what is called American culture—an out-and-out mammonist culture.

Surveying their achievements one day, Yan asked Qiming, "Qiming, we've got everything now—houses, cars, property, and money. Are we missing anything?"

Qiming thought a moment. "Yes," he said. "We're missing one thing."

"What?"

"Our daughter."

...

Passengers were filing one by one through Customs Inspection at the JFK International Airport, and then walking towards the exit. Qiming and Yan ran through the doorway into the lounge, afraid they might be late.

They still had clear memories of their fear and alarm when no one was there to meet them on their own arrival in New York. They didn't want their precious daughter to feel cold-shouldered as they had once felt. They pushed to the front of the waiting welcomers and peered around, searching for a girl from China, their long-yearned-for flesh and blood, their Ningning.

"Do you see her?" asked Yan.

"No." Qiming looked ahead, craning his neck. "She should be here."

"Yes, she should."

Their hearts were pounding with anticipation.

Suddenly, Qiming shouted, "She's arrived. Look! Over there!"

It was their daughter, Ningning, all right. She was taller and looked quite different from the child they had left in Beijing. Her hair was drawn back in a ponytail, and she was wearing a red sweater and a pair of close-fitting jeans. She'd really changed; she had grown into a lovely, radiant young lady.

"Call her! Call her!" Yan urged her husband.

"Ningning! Ningning!" shouted Qiming.

"Ningning!" Yan was also shouting. "Mommy is here! Mommy and Daddy are here."

Both their voices quivered. Both were weeping. Both waved and waved, hoping that Ningning would notice them.

She had! Their daughter had seen them! Ningning smiled at her parents and waved.

"Ningning!" Qiming was still shouting. Yan leaned on her husband's shoulder and sobbed audibly.

When Ningning was a few steps away, Qiming stepped over the barrier and hugged his daughter. He kissed her on the forehead.

"Dad! Mom!"

This simple greeting from their daughter was enough to make both Qiming and Yan shed tears all over again. As they walked out of the airport lounge, Qiming and Yan asked one question after another.

"How are you?"

"Were you sick during the trip?"

"You recognized us at once, didn't you?"

"Did you have any lunch on the plane?"

"Have you been thinking of your dad and mom?"

As Ningning answered these questions she looked curiously around the airport, the largest in the world, and at all the different kinds of people that can be seen here. During a brief pause between questions her parents were firing at her, Ningning asked her only question:

"Is this the United States?"

"Yes, it is," replied Qiming without hesitation. "This is New York!"

It was a simple question. But after answering it Qiming stopped in his tracks. He remembered that he'd asked the very same question when he had arrived in New York.

Outside the airport, the three got into the car. Ningning insisted on taking the seat beside the driver's.

"Dad, is this your own car?" she inquired.

"Yes, it's ours."

"It's up to snazz!"

"It's what?" Qiming asked his daughter.

"Up to snazz. You know, snazzy, really smart," explained Ningning. "If you'd drive this car in Beijing, you'd really quake 'em down. Isn't that so, Dad?"

Qiming was amused by Ningning's use of the slang current among Beijing teenagers. "Yes, I suppose so!"

"Since you've got this quakey car, I won't have to dahdee here."

"Dahdee?" asked Yan from the back seat. "What's that?"

"Mom! Don't you know what dahdeeing is? I guess that's because you've been in New York too long. Dahdeeing means taking a taxi."

"Don't you ride a bicycle in Beijing?"

"Ride a bike?! You lose share if you do that!"

"She means lose face," said Qiming, grinning. "She talks like a real Beijinger, this kid!"

Qiming was grinning not so much because Ningning's use of slang was especially amusing as on account of the fact that anything she said on this particular day sounded good and fell like music on his ears.

Yan didn't say much. From where she sat in the back seat she stroked her daughter's soft ponytail as though she couldn't get enough of doing so. On her part, Ningning found everything she saw novel and interesting and great fun. She was working her eyes overtime. She burned with curiosity about the cars, the skyscrapers, and continually asked questions about this and that.

When they got home she went upstairs and downstairs and into the living room and bedrooms, touching things as though just looking at them wasn't enough. Yan took her upstairs to the bedroom she'd prepared for her. "This is your room, Ningning!"

To her surprise Ningning pouted her lips. "No, Mom," she said. "I don't want this little room. I want the big one downstairs."

"But that's the living room, silly girl! It's not for sleeping in."

"Why can't people sleep in the living room? Why so many rules here in the United States? I'm going to sleep in the big room. They say America's a free country, don't they? One ought to be able to sleep where and how one wants to!"

"All right, all right. In any case, this is your home. Sleep wherever you want to," said Qiming, trying to smooth things over. "Come! Let me take a good look at you!"

He made her stand in front of him and looked her carefully up and down. At sixteen she was nearly as tall as Yan, and slim and graceful. Her fair-complexioned face was fine and delicate and without the least blemish. The large, liquid eyes were even more beautiful than Yan's. And her high-jutting bosom added a touch of maturity to her appearance.

"You've grown!" said Qiming with feeling.

Ningning looked at her father with amusement.

"Let the child sleep for a while and get over her jet lag," said Yan. "Ningning, get some sleep!" But Ningning wasn't feeling any jet lag at all and had no intention of sleeping now. She went alone into the garden, onto the lawn and among the flowering bushes, and inspected her new home.

Qiming and Yan stood at the window and watched their daughter. "Ningning has grown up," said Qiming.

"Yes."

"Her temperament isn't quite like it was before."

"In what way?"

"I can't pin it down, but in any case she isn't as compliant as you are."

"Then she's like you, stubborn and mulish."

Qiming laughed. He liked to hear that. He felt that his daughter was much like himself, receptive, quick to react, and unsubmissive. This pleased him.

"But," he said. "She has no idea of what we went through here these years."

"Of course not."

"I'll have to tell her."

"Oh, go on! Forget that stuff about 'recalling past bitterness to appreciate the present happiness.' " said Yan. "Even in China people don't do that anymore! What I do feel is that we owe her a lot for all these years we haven't been with her."

"We'll make up for everything we owe her.!" Qiming meant it.

. . .

Qiming and Yan went to all lengths to make up for the love and attention Ningning had missed out on. They gave her everything she wanted. The things she ate were the most nutritious, the best-tasting, and the most expensive money could buy. The clothes she wore were the most fashionable, of the best quality, and of course the most expensive as well.

Now and then Qiming would say something to the effect that maybe they were spoiling Ningning. But each time Yan would reply: "The reason we went through all those hardships was to give her happiness, wasn't it?"

Qiming had nothing to say to that.

Actually, Qiming talked about not spoiling Ningning, but he pampered her much more than Yan did. Every weekend after Ningning's arrival he took her out to have some fun together. Father and daughter made the rounds of New York's entertainment spots, parks and restaurants.

More than at any time in the past he was generous with his money, even prodigal. But he felt this was only natural and as it should be. After all, it was for her sake that they had suffered all those hardships.

That's the way Qiming looked at it. Let alone giving up a bit of time and money, he would be doing only what was right and proper even if he spent his whole fortune on Ningning, wasn't that so?

Without debating the matter with himself he went out with her and paid out his dollars, asking for nothing more in return than a contented smile. As for Ningning herself, she didn't find anything unusual or untoward in this.

From the time the sixteen-year-old girl had set foot on American territory she was doted upon and spoiled, and she had only to say the word to satisfy any of her material desires. Such a situation would have been unthinkable in Beijing, but here in the United States she took it for granted. All this was only natural and didn't require her to waste any thought on whether it was right or not. Just stretch out your hand and take, close your eyes and enjoy.

She thought everyone in the United States lived like this or did the same thing, and that was really great! She never tried to find out how her parents had struggled and strained themselves to acquire what they had. And since she didn't think about such matters, she asked for things with an easy conscience, and asked continually.

One day as they were having breakfast she looked Qiming in the eye and asked loudly, "Dad, do you have any extra cash at the moment?"

"What do you want to buy?"

"I want a sports car."

Qiming was speechless for a moment, then he set down the glass of milk he had been holding.

"What did you say you wanted?"

"A sports car."

"What do you want a car for? You don't even have a driving license!"

"I can get one quite soon."

"But why would a kid your age want to have a car?"

"Is that question worth asking? A lot of kids at my school have their own cars."

"American high schools have a lot of problems. You should learn from their good aspects, not their bad things."

"What good things, and what bad things?" Ningning pouted sulkily. "You're always saying how good the United States is. But now when it comes to spending some money for me, suddenly there seem to be both good and bad things!"

"We're not discussing a country's merits. The question we're discussing has to do with a car, and whether or not a high school girl like you should have one."

"Right! I must have a car!"

"You're not old enough."

"Very soon I'll be eighteen. Get the car first, and I'll drive it when I'm old enough."

"You'll get it when you're eighteen."

"That's only a few days away, so get the car first!"

Qiming looked at his wife. She looked back at him, nonplused. "We'll discuss the matter," said Qiming finally.

Ningning knew of course what "discussing the matter" meant. Jumping up, she ran over to her father and kissed him.

"Dad! You're so nice!"

. . .

One Saturday, the three of them, all in high spirits, went into the city to look for a car. The highways were clogged with weekend traffic, so they took the subway.

The last time Qiming had been in these dank and dirty subway tunnels was four or five years ago. In fact, he had not been there since he had gone into business.

Just as he came to a turning in the tunnel he heard the strains of a Beethoven violin concerto. It sounded so familiar, so intimate!

Dragging Ningning and Yan to make them walk faster, he turned the corner. Once more he saw the long-haired young man he'd come upon five years ago. He was playing the violin with the same earnestness and conscientiousness. Qiming stopped in front of him, recalling the time he was working at the Hunan Garden.

"What's there to look at!" said Ningning, tugging at Qiming's arm. "I see him playing the violin here every day when I go to school. Nobody pays attention to him."

Only a few coins lay in the violin case. The performer smiled at them as he played, seeming to recognize Qiming. Or maybe he hadn't recognized Qiming at all and was smiling merely as a plea.

Deliberately, Qiming took a fifty-dollar bill from his wallet and laid it in the violin case. None of the others could guess what his motives were for doing this, and Yan watched his motions with wide-eyed mystification.

"You've got to be crazy!" commented Ningning, pouting.

Having put down the money, Qiming walked rapidly away with Yan and Ningning. Behind them the playing stopped and they heard an exclamation: "My God, today is my lucky day!"

. . .

They were at a Chevrolet dealer's store, and Ningning had chosen a black 1986 sports model.

"Why black?" asked Qiming, frowning.

"Black looks nice," replied Ningning defensively. "It's got snazz!"

"I just don't get this snazz business!" muttered Qiming as he went to the manager's office to pay for the car and go through procedures. They could come and get the car after twenty days.

As they walked out of the store Ningning said she was hungry. She took them into a well-known seafood restaurant. The interior of the restaurant was almost devoid of adornment. The lighting was very dim, which gave the customers and waiters coming and going in the aisles a stealthy, furtive appearance. All the tables and chairs consisted of logs spiked together and were extremely uncomfortable. The walls of red and gray bricks were without any covering except for a few raw wooden boards on which the grain was visible. Some fish, lobsters and the like were painted on the boards, as though by a child.

"Why come to such a place!" said Yan, in spite of herself. "It's so dark and gloomy!"

"Mom, don't you know? This place is tony. It's in. It's the vogue these days!" Ningning knew quite well what was in fashion and what wasn't.

"And why is it tony?" Qiming asked his daughter, seeking enlightenment.

"Because it's primitive, rugged, aboriginal!"

"Oh!" Not wanting to disappoint Ningning, Qiming pretended to understand.

"Hey! Dad! Being a fashion designer, you should know all about such things," remarked Ningning. "You'd be a big hit if you made your fashions primitive, rugged and aboriginal!"

"Primitives and aborigines don't wear any clothes, so what do you want me to design?"

"Dad! Now you're being sarcastic!"

Qiming patted her on the cheek. Ningning squirmed her shoulders petulantly.

"Where did you learn all these things, Ningning?" Yan couldn't help asking.

"Where? In the United States, of course!"

"Here, in the United States? Your Dad and I have been here all these years and we haven't picked up as much as you have."

"You're getting old and slow on the uptake."

Ningning probably didn't mean her words the way they sounded. Nevertheless, Qiming and Yan looked at each other to see if they were actually getting old.

Were they getting old? Qiming asked himself the question. Or perhaps it wasn't they that were old, but Ningning who was too young.

Qiming studied his daughter under the dim lights. Strangely enough, in spite of the weak illumination he could see his daughter more clearly, more lucidly, than when he looked at her in the light of the sun.

Ningning was too clever for her own good. Without proper guidance she might get into trouble. It wasn't so very long since she'd arrived in the United States, but she was adapting very quickly, especially language-wise. Within half a year her English had passed muster. And since she liked to watch TV her pronunciation was accurate and pleasing to the ear, and even took on a touch of New Yorkese. What gave Qiming a headache was the large store of invective and dirty words she had acquired without anyone teaching them to her.

A waiter came up and Ningning did the ordering with practiced ease. She asked for three lobsters, two portions of oysters, two dozen clams, and champagne as an aperitif.

"You've picked up these ways very quickly, Ningning," said Qiming. "But what counts in the United States is the skills you learn. You should be going to college next month, shouldn't you? How are you coming along with the S.A.T.?"

Ningning unceremoniously interrupted her father. "Let's not talk about it this evening," she said, taking a sip of champagne.

"And why not?" asked Yan.

"Because today's a weekend!"

"It seems to me every day is a weekend for you," said Qiming.

"Be quiet, Qiming!" said Yan. "Today is really a weekend."

The lobsters were served and Ningning began to shell hers like a professional.

"That isn't right, Mom! Do it this way!" As Ningning ate, she served as instructor to her mother.

Qiming drank some champagne. He hadn't intended to say anything more about the pre-college exams, but seeing how quickly Ningning was becoming Americanized he felt most uneasy.

"Ningning," he said at last. "You haven't been in the United States very long, so there's one thing I must tell you. We Chinese who come to the United States shouldn't imitate everything we see here. We should keep up our good Chinese traditions."

The words came out flat and insipid. Even Qiming felt that what he'd said sounded like something a communist party secretary would say.

Ningning, shelling her lobster, couldn't repress a giggle. "I never thought I'd be hearing a political pep talk here in the United States!"

"All right, all right, Qiming," said Yan. "Seeing as it's a weekend, don't start lecturing her now."

"Lecture or no lecture, there's one thing she's got to know," said Qiming. "We Chinese couldn't become true Americans even if we wanted to. And that's a fact!"

Ningning laid down her knife and fork, wiped her mouth with her napkin, then propped her elbows on the table. "Dad, I'm really confused now. When I first came to the United States you said I was a greenhorn and a bumpkin. You told me to get on the ball and adapt to the life here as quickly as possible. Watch TV, answer the phone, make friends with Americans, you said. Isn't that so?"

"Yes. I did say that."

"But now you're saying, don't imitate this, don't learn that, stay Chinese. If I'm to stay Chinese I might as well have stayed in Beijing like a good little girl. What did I come to New York for? I can't figure out what you want me to be. An American? A Chinese? An American with a Chinese flavor? A Chinese with an American flavor?"

Qiming had no answer to that. Frankly speaking, he hadn't figured out what kind of a person he himself should be. And his feelings with regard to Ningning were just as contradictory. Before she had arrived in the United States he had looked forward to her coming; and then, when she'd come, he feared she wouldn't adapt and urged her to fit herself into the American society as quickly as possible. But when she'd done just that, he became afraid again—this time that she'd get into bad ways—and tried to drag her back.

How should he put it to her?

"It's like this," he started, taking a gulp of champagne. "In my opinion our Chinese concepts of the family and morality are still the best. What I mean to say is, you should know your own mind and stick to what has to be stuck to."

"Of course I have my own ideas."

"I'm worried that you might...you might..."

"Might what?"

"Be taken advantage of."

"How?"

"As a girl is taken advantage of."

Ningning snickered. "You're worrying the Chinese way."

"So what's the American way?" pursued Qiming.

"You're an old fogy!"

"Ningning!" Yan broke in. "You mustn't talk to your father like that!" At this point, the strains of the "Birthday Song" came over from the other end of the restaurant.

It was some customer's birthday and the band was playing the tune in his or her honor. All the customers joined in the refrain. The three of them sang with the rest, clapping their hands. The singing cut short a discussion which had threatened to turn into a dispute. When the song ended, Ningning laid both her hands on the back of Yan's hand.

"Mom! My birthday is coming next week."

"I haven't forgotten."

"What are you giving me for a present?"

"What do you want?"

"I would like to have..."

"What?"

"A dog!"

"Nothing doing!" Yan was very firm in her refusal. "That's absolutely out of the question!"

"I must have a dog!"

"I can give you something else."

"No! I want a dog!" Ningning was loudly insistent. "Both of you go to work and leave me at home all by myself. I get bored!"

"Keeping a dog is too much of a hassle. Someone has to feed it, give it water, take it to the vet when it's sick. Who'll do all that?"

"I will! I will!"

As Qiming listened to Yan and Ningning arguing, a thought suddenly crossed his mind.

"Ningning!" he interjected. "I'll get you a dog."

"Qiming!" Yan glared at him.

"I'll buy Ningning a dog. She really needs one."

"Dad! You're a real sport!"

She kissed his cheek.

When they had returned to their house, Yan complained to Qiming that he was being too indulgent toward his daughter. Qiming explained, "With a dog at home, she'll come straight back from school. She'll be less likely to run wild."

"I guess you're right," said Yan.

- 12 -

It was Ningning's birthday. An extra-large-size birthday cake lay on the marble top of the dining table in the living room. On the cake was written: "Happy Birthday to Kathy!" Ningning's English name was Kathy. And yes, the cake also carried an eye-catching numeral—18.

Multicolored paper chains festooned the ceiling of the living room. Bright spotlights hung on both sides of the fireplace. The tables, the piano and the couch were piled high with birthday presents. A barbecue on the lawn behind the house gave off thick smoke and the fragrance of cooking meat.

Qiming and Yan would be coming home after work. The crowd gathered here consisted of seventeen or eighteen year-olds, some twenty or more of them. Boys and girls, whites, Asians, and blacks were dancing a samba, rotating at the waist and wiggling their bottoms to the sound of music. Ningning was all tangled up with a boy, face to face, chest to chest, and hip to hip. The Chinese called this kind of dancing "dogs in heat."

"Kathy!" said the boy who was dancing with Ningning. The music was too loud and he had to shout.

"Yes?"

"Are you feeling good today?"

"I'm feeling great!"

"Do you know that new song?"

"What song?"

"I Want Your Sex!"

"Uh-huh, I know it."

"May I have your sex?"

"What did you say?"

"I want your sex."

"Me too."

"Now? Here?"

"Get out of here!"

She had shouted the words to let the boy know that was not to be considered here. The boy grinned, not at all embarrassed.

To shouts of "Happy Birthday" a new group of young people came into the living room. They were dressed differently from the others. They were clad from head to foot in black: black T-shirts, black pants, and black gym shoes. Their leader was a husky Chinese boy with handsome, finely-drawn features.

"James!" squealed Ningning, running to him.

James swept her up in his arms and gave her a deep kiss. "Baby," he said. "I've brought you a present."

"What is it?" asked Ningning.

James started to take a paper packet out of his pants pocket. Ningning knew what it held. She quickly pressed down his arm. "No, not here!"

"What's the matter?"

"We can't do it here."

"Why not?"

"My dad's coming back very soon."

"So what?"

"No, no! It won't do!" Ningning shook her head vigorously.

"All right. Later, then." James put the paper packet away and began to dance with Ningning.

The music became wilder.

The young people went into a frenzy. The door to Ningning's bedroom stood ajar. Pungent wisps of smoke floated out of the room. Inside, a number of young people were sprawled here and there, taking turns at smoking a reefer. Young as they were, they exhibited all the mannerisms of a group of *lao yanqiang*, or veteran dope smokers.

When their turn came each took a long drag, pulling the smoke deeply into his or her lungs. Then with eyes shut and lips pursed they slowly expelled a plume of pale, white smoke. These young people, all with dull, staring eyes and untidy clothing, took on an expression of utter bliss after a puff of the marijuana.

Ningning, in the living room, smelled the smoke and ran up the stairs. "Hey, fellas! You can't do this in here!"

Loudly scolding her companions, she threw open the window and fanned the air with her hands.

"Want to give it a try?"

The boy smoking the reefer held up the butt and waved it at Ningning.

"Get out, all of you!"

"You shouldn't chase us out," said the boy. "Come on, take a drag!"

At this point, James came in the room.

"Get out! Beat it!" His authority was supreme. At his command, the marijuana smokers scrambled to their feet and went out of Ningning's bedroom.

Only James and Ningning were left in the room. He kicked the door shut with his heel. Ningning had just finished opening the windows. She turned around and saw something not quite right in his expression.

"James?"

James stepped up to her and grabbed her like a hawk pouncing on a chicken. His movements were forceful and determined, leaving Ningning no room for resistance. He pressed his lips heavily against Ningning's mouth and sucked hard. Ningning frowned. Muted sounds came through her nose.

She tried to push his arms apart, but he seized her hands and twisted them behind her back. Then he forced her down onto the bed, under himself. With his heavy body pressing on her she could hardly breathe. His hands groped at Ningning's breasts and groin and his mouth clamped onto hers like that of a huge leech.

"Come on, baby! Don't play games with me!"

He unbuckled his belt.

. . .

The party had broken up.

Ningning and Wendy—daughter of a worker named Ah You at Qiming's factory—were cleaning up the mess. Ningning was pale and she looked very tired.

"Why haven't your Dad and Mom come back yet?" asked Wendy.

"It's better they didn't."

"Why?"

"When they get back it'll be the same old story."

"What story? What'll they do?"

"Start lecturing me."

"About what?"

"About being a Chinese or an American."

"How do you see it?"

"Me?" asked Ningning, pointing at herself. She shook her head. "I don't know."

Wendy looked quizzically at Ningning.

"Do you feel it's tougher being a Chinese or tougher being an American?"

Ningning was somewhat nonplused by Wendy's last question. She gave it some thought, then replied, "I feel it's tough being a woman."

There was no end to Wendy's questions.

"Do you love your Dad?" she asked.

"No, I don't."

"Why not?"

"I don't know. Anyway, I hate him."

"Is it because he lectures you?"

"Maybe."

"Maybe! He loves you. Our parents always care for us, are always good to us."

"Is that so?" countered Ningning, not without irony.

"Yes, it is. That's why we should listen to them and try to make them happy."

"I know that."

"Do you?"

"In theory I do. But I still hate my dad. There's nothing I can do about it!"

"You shouldn't talk like that."

"He never asks about me. He doesn't know when I do something good, nor does he know when I do something bad."

"Does he know about your smoking?"

"No."

"About James?"

"Not either."

"You sure can keep secrets!"

"Well, keep mine for me, too!"

"I know," said Wendy. "Don't worry.""

- 13 -

Dusk was falling as Qiming's car sped down the highway. He drove impatiently. Yan sat beside him, holding a small white dog on her lap. It was their birthday present to Ningning.

They had left the factory quite early and had bought the dog at a place far away in New Jersey. It was a Maltese, a world-famous breed which the Chinese call "Aristocratic Lady." The frightened dog was trembling all over and had hidden its head under Yan's arm. Maybe it was wondering where its new owners were taking it.

"I hope Ningning won't be angry because we're late," murmured Yan.

"She won't." Qiming was very confident about that. "She'll jump with joy when she sees the dog."

"I hope so."

The speedometer needle crept past the 70 mark. Yan reminded her husband, "Watch out for the police."

As their car passed through the Holland Tunnel they came on a traffic jam. Qiming thumped the steering wheel. "What the hell?" He looked at his watch. Ten-thirty.

"We're too late," he said. "I'm afraid we'll miss the party."

"I figure it's about over now. She called me and said her friends had started arriving at one in the afternoon." Yan stroked the little dog's head. "Let's give him a name."

"I've got one for him. We'll call him Jerry." Qiming remembered the name from a television cartoon which was almost a household word.

"Jerry, Jerry. Your elder sister will be most happy to see you!" Yan raised the dog to her face, intending to kiss it. But it licked her face.

"That tickles, you naughty boy." Yan laughed. "Now that Ningning has this dog, I think she'll stop gadding about after school. I'm afraid she might fall into bad company." Yan sighed, "It's really got me worried."

"The Americans say 'teenage is animal age.'"

"What does that mean?"

"It means kids of seventeen or eighteen behave like animals."

"There's some truth to that, even though the wording is nasty." Yan continued, "That boy of Mrs. Zhang's—the lady who knits sweaters—got mixed up with one of the Chinese gangs."

"Really?"

"Yes. Last year the boy was hit by three bullets, and since the family couldn't pay the medical fees here, they sent him back to Nanjing for treatment. That was a year ago, and he still doesn't dare come back."

"Poor kid."

"Xiumei has a cousin, a girl about the same age as the boy. Soon after she came here from Taipei she picked up a drug habit. Her father gave her a terrible beating and the next day she left home. To this day she hasn't been found. I'm really afraid."

"For whom?"

"Ningning."

"She won't get into anything like that," said Qiming positively. "We both know what kind of kid she is, don't we? She's always been intelligent and obedient, and she never gets involved in things that don't concern her. Am I right?"

"Yes. Of course I have faith in her."

It was to drive out a feeling of uncertainty that Qiming and Yan were praising Ningning so determinedly. Both were worried, Qiming especially. His heart pounded every time he heard his daughter speaking her pure New Yorkese.

At last they reached home. Holding the dog, Yan got out of the car first and made straight for the living room.

"Happy birthday!" she called, raising the dog above her head. The little dog, who perhaps had a phobia of heights, scrabbled about with its legs, looking very cute.

"Mom! My dog!" Ningning ran across the room and took the dog, hugging it tightly in her arms. "Steady, honey!" she cried. "Oh, you're lovely!"

Qiming frowned when he saw the mess in the living room and smelled the foul air. Without a word he went upstairs. He wanted to take off his suit and relax in his gym outfit. The moment he reached the landing a strong, unfamiliar odor hit him. He walked up to Ningning's bedroom. With the door left slightly open and the odor coming from the room, Qiming knew what had happened. Without changing his clothes he went downstairs again and whispered something in Yan's ear. She turned pale. Ningning was still teasing the dog and hadn't noticed. But Wendy saw, and then stood up.

"Auntie! Uncle! I'm leaving now. See you again!"

"Thank you, Wendy!" said Qiming. He didn't look at her but kept his eyes on the floor. "You've been a big help, Wendy." Yan spoke warmly. "Thank you. When you get home, tell your mother to come to work a little earlier tomorrow. There's a batch of sweaters to rush out."

"I'll tell her." Wendy went out the door.

When the last guest had left, the room became very still. The air was muggy, like before a summer downpour. Qiming sat on the couch, glaring. He lit a cigarette and frowned. Yan sat down beside him. She knew a storm was about to break. So she sat beside her husband and signaled him that he shouldn't lose his temper or be too hard on his daughter. She poked him in the side as a reminder. But Qiming ignored Yan and brushed her hand aside. She knew now that a clash was inevitable, and waited nervously.

Ningning was still playing with the dog. She sensed the tension in the air. But she hummed a tune, seeming not to care.

"Ningning!" Qiming began his interrogation, trying hard to inject some calm into his voice and straining to keep his voice steady. "Have you learned to smoke?"

Ningning quivered, then quickly composed herself. "Sometimes," she replied with easy unconcern. It was her indifference rather than the reply itself that nettled Qiming. He raised his voice.

"My question was, have you learned to smoke!"

"Yes." She decided she might as well admit it.

"Is it marijuana?" he pursued.

"I...don't know."

"Who taught you?"

"Someone."

"Who?"

"Must you know?" Ningning countered coolly.

"It isn't vital," acknowledged Qiming. "What is vital is why you did it."

"For fun." She said the words quite casually. Then she got to her feet and with a flip of her ponytail started to go upstairs to her bedroom.

"Stop!" Ningning kept on walking.

"Stop!"

"I want to go to bed!" she said.

"No way."

"I want to sleep. You've got no right to stop me." Ningning turned her head and looked at her father, her eyes filled with hatred.

"I have the right. I'm your father."

"Even a father has no right to do that. This is a free country." Ningning was shouting now. Her voice, usually so pleasant was brittle and angry.

Father and daughter had reached a stalemate. Ash from Qiming's cigarette dropped to the floor unnoticed.

Yan went across to her daughter and said patiently, "Ningning, talk to your father properly. Don't be like this. Everything your father and I are doing is for you. You should know that."

Ningning didn't answer.

Yan's eyes were turning red. "For whose sake do you think your father and I have worked so hard to make some money, if not for you? Why do you think we brought you here from Beijing, if not to provide you with a good life, good opportunities and a good future? Don't let yourself be led astray. I'd gladly work myself to death, if only it would bring you happiness!" Yan wept.

"For my sake, for my sake!" said Ningning fiercely. "You keep on saying it's for my sake! But what have you really done for me? For me?"

Qiming had never felt so wronged. Slamming his hand on the table, he rose to his feet and shouted, "You ungrateful brat! Who do you think we're doing everything for, if not for you? Tell me!"

Ningning cocked her head and, again quite casually, said in English, "Who knows."

Qiming couldn't stand her casual way of speaking. He couldn't stand her attitude, her New York English. "I'll thank you to be more respectful," he roared. "And from now on you're not to speak any English at home! I can't stand it, and I won't tolerate it!"

"You used to insist that I talk in English, and now you hate it when I speak English. How do you want me to talk?" Ningning had switched to Chinese, which only made her sound harder and more adamant.

"I want you to talk like a decent human being!" Again Qiming banged the table.

"Qiming!" Yan wanted to stop him talking, stop her daughter talking, stop this explosive confrontation. But how could she? There was nothing to do but helplessly watch her husband give way to his anger, and watch her daughter's hatred.

"You ought to speak truthfully, like a decent human being! At least to your parents." His voice quivered.

"Okay. I'll talk!" Ningning dropped the dog on the floor and began to speak. Her pent-up feelings poured out. "What did you do for me in those five long years from the time I was eleven to the time I was sixteen? Do you know how many times I cried, and how I cried? And do you know what I was thinking about every day? You don't know. You don't know anything. Honest, I longed for you. When New Year or the Spring Festival came around, I missed you very, very much. I know you sent me lots of money, but I didn't need money. What I needed was love. What I needed was my father's broad chest and my mother's warm bosom. Did you give these to me? Dad, Mom, I'm not a good girl. I'm not what you think I am. So don't place too many hopes in me. I...I...you don't know me!"

"Tell us what it is, Ningning. At least it will help us understand you." Yan was almost pleading with her daughter. She had a premonition that her daughter would be telling her things she didn't want to hear, telling her about some tragedy.

"Go ahead! Tell us!" said Qiming, suppressing his anger.

"All right. I'll tell you, if that's what you want."

Ningning was lost in thought for a while. She sat in silence, looking much older than she actually was. She seemed all at once to have aged.

"Without your love I felt cold, like it was always midwinter. The year I became sixteen, a year before I came here, I listened to you and went to a school that offered brush-up courses in English so that I could get into the United States. I didn't want to learn English, but I did it for you, to make you happy. In my class there was a boy called Liu Xiong. He was very handsome, and he...loved me very much. I liked him too. We studied English together, went to restaurants together, and together...went to his home. Afterwards, I became pregnant."

"What?" Qiming glared.

"Ningning!" Yan cried and clutched her husband's shoulder.

"What are you yelling for?" Ningning detested her parents for the shock they displayed. "Now that you know, you get excited, you yell. But where were you then?" Ningning asked accusingly.

Qiming and Yan were speechless. They lowered their eyes. Brushing aside her tears, Ningning continued, "It hurt terribly when I was on that abortion table. I cried out for both of you. I cried: Mommy, Mommy, where are you? Daddy, Daddy, why don't you come and take me away? Do you know how much I needed both of you then? How much I wanted you to be there and pat me on the head? Even if it meant being scolded?"

Yan wept broken-heartedly. The veins on Qiming's forehead throbbed.

"What happened to that...that bastard?" he asked.

Ningning lit a cigarette with shaking fingers and took several deep puffs at it.

Qiming didn't try to stop her this time. "Tell me, where is he now?"

"He's a thug. He was arrested later by the police because he got involved with other girls." Ningning said this in a flat, casual tone, as though she were talking about a complete stranger.

Qiming wanted to go up to this good-for-nothing daughter of his and slap her. But filled with a sense of his own guilt, he couldn't even look her in the eye.

"Since I've come to the United States," continued Ningning, "you've had nothing on your minds besides your factory, your business, and making money. You'd like to keep me locked up at home because that would solve all your problems. I wouldn't be a burden to you, and I could look after the house. You could go out and get richer, and at the same time boast about the nice, obedient little daughter you have at home. Don't you realize how selfish you've been?"

Ningning cried uncontrollably, each sob wracking her whole body. The ponytail at the back of her head quivered with the shaking of her shoulders. A long section of ash dropped from her cigarette onto the cream-white carpet. She ground it with her heel, leaving an ugly black mark on the unblemished carpet. That mark would probably never come out.

She drew in another lung full of smoke. "I'm a human being, too. I want my share of life. I want my friends and my own existence. Haven't I given up enough already for the sake of your accomplishments? Do I have to go on sacrificing myself now that I'm in the United States? Must I stay locked up at home like that dog for the sake of your status and reputation? Must I wag my tail and fawn on you for my three meals a day? No, Dad. No, Mom. I can't do it, and I'm not going to do it."

She had finished. She'd unloaded herself of all she'd wanted to say, and that gave her a certain sense of relief. She picked up the little dog and went upstairs to her bedroom, her ponytail bouncing behind her like a flickering black flame.

The living room seemed empty after Ningning had left. "The poor child," said Yan. She burst into tears again. Qiming clutched his head between his hands, not knowing what to say. After a while he heaved a deep sigh.

. . .

Ningning went back to her room and flopped onto the bed. She buried her head under the pillow to muffle her sobs. She cried, curled up in a shivering ball. Some time later she pushed aside the tear-soaked pillow and rolled around to face upward. She stared at the ceiling. Tears came again to her eyes and hung in two glistening lines on her cheeks.

What day was it today? Today's my birthday, she reflected. The expensive cosmetics around her eyes had smeared into dark patches, making the sockets look like those of a mummy. Lighting another cigarette, she recalled how James had brutalized her that afternoon, and what had happened to her the year she turned sixteen. Self-pity overcame her.

She hadn't wanted to hurt her parents. She realized how much her words must have pained them. The sight of their shock and grief had even aroused feelings of pity and sympathy in her, but that pity and sympathy had been mixed with a vengeful glee.

Why was born I into this family? she asked herself. Why am I so different from other kids? Is there truly a karma? If so, why is mine so bitter? In China everyone envied me, saying I was lucky to have my parents in the United States, lucky to be able to spend American dollars and have so many foreign-made things. Why, then, did I always get this feeling of being abandoned?

Ningning asked herself these questions, venting her grievances through her recollections. They don't know that I went to the Fragrant Hill Park that day, all by myself, riding my bike. It was winter and snowing hard, and the park was empty, all except for the trees on the hill and myself. I climbed to the top of the hill. I don't know how many times I fell. Up there, on top of the hill, with the north wind blowing around me, I cried and cried and cried. I was so scared that someone might see me crying like an idiot at the top of Fragrant Hill. And I hoped so much that my Dad and Mom would somehow come all the way from the United States and hear me crying.

Dad! Mom! It's you who made me different, who gave me those American dollars that brought me so much trouble. Out in the streets I was a juicy piece of meat to those young wolf-men. I didn't know whether they were after me or my money. At the movies and at dances I became a sweet-smelling flower and attracted swarms of human bees and butterflies. I had no way of telling what was attracting them, me or you—my parents in the United States.

Because of those U.S. dollars you sent me I lost any sense of good and bad and right and wrong. I fell in the mud and couldn't get up anymore. Now you're always pushing me to study hard. You ought to know that in junior middle school I didn't have a single day where I could go to class and do my homework in peace. Every time you wrote, you urged me to concentrate on my English and said that Chinese wouldn't be much use.

You kept on telling me I'd come to the United States soon. Soon, soon, maybe tomorrow, maybe next week. How did you expect me to settle down and study? If you want to know, my mind has been anywhere but on my studies these last years. I get a headache every time I see a book.

Even now you give examples, telling me that a certain guy with an M.A. is running a restaurant, or someone with a PhD. is ironing sweaters. You say that a lot of book-learning doesn't make a person rich, and even if somebody does get a good education and earns fifty, sixty thousand a year, he still has to tighten his belt to make payments on a house and a car.

I've wanted to learn to do business, but you think I'm too young and green and will get duped or ripped off. Before I even get started on anything you tell me I'm dumb, stupid. Just what am I going to do with my life? Where's my future? It isn't me who hasn't learned to live in the United States, it's you who haven't learned to live with me.

Things can't go on like this, thought Ningning. I must find work and make some money to earn my own keep. I'll talk to them about it tomorrow morning.

After a while she undressed and fell asleep. Meanwhile, Qiming and Yan were lying in bed, wrapped in their own thoughts. No matter how they looked at the problem they weren't able to find a solution. The night was long, but they couldn't sleep.

- 14 -

Early the next morning Qiming dimly heard the chiming of the clock downstairs. He sat up in bed, then got up and went to the bathroom. He'd acquired the habit of taking a bath in the morning, like many Americans do. He took a morning bath less for the sake of hygiene and cleanliness than to clear his mind, to wash away the night's sludge and to let the soothing water wake up his brain and brace his lethargic body.

While he was in his bath, Qiming decided he should have a serious talk with his daughter. Yes, he was confident she would understand him; he, too, should try to understand his daughter. He felt much more relaxed after the bath. Drying himself with a large towel, he came out of the bathroom.

"Qiming!"

Who was calling him?

"Qiming!" It was Yan. Her voice, shrill and alarmed, told him something was wrong. Winding the bath towel around his waist, he rushed out of his bedroom.

Yan was stumbling down the stairs, ghostly pale. "Ningning, Ningning..." she cried.

Brushing her aside, Qiming raced up the staircase to Ningning's bedroom. The door was open, the room empty. Qiming looked in the other room. She wasn't there. Nor was she in the study. Or in the living room. Or on the balcony. Or in the kitchen.

Qiming searched the house from top to bottom, shouting his daughter's name. There was no reply.

Yan ran up to him, clutching a sheet of paper she'd found. "Look, Qiming! She left this!"

Qiming snatched the piece of paper and swept his eyes over it.

Dear Dad and Mom,

I'm leaving. Forgive me for not saying goodbye to you. I don't want to wake you up, because I know you are very tired on account of the factory and me. That's why I'm being so quiet.

I'm sorry I said a lot of things last night that must have made you angry or hurt you. Please forget what I said. Actually, I didn't want to make you angry. I love you both.

Dad and Mom! I've grown up. In the United States, young people my age want to leave home and make their own living. But you always want to keep me at home. This is bad for me, and for you, too.

As Dad says, one has to learn to think for oneself before one can grow up. I'm going out now to try my luck, just as you did. I'm leaving now. Don't worry too much about me.

I love you, truly.
Your Ningning.

P.S. It's 5 a.m.

On the reverse side of the sheet of paper was a hurried scrawl.

Mom, Dad: Two things. I've bought headache pills for Dad. They're beside the fridge. I haven't taken all the clothes Mom gave me. Wear them yourself, Mom. It's cold in New York.

So long! Ningning.

Qiming reeled as though he'd been punched in the head. He was sweating again, and moisture was trickling from his hair which hadn't had a chance to dry out. The little dog he and Yan had just bought sat in a corner with its tongue hanging out, eyeing its new owners' strange behavior with suspicion.

"I'll report this to the police!" said Qiming.

"To the police?" echoed Yan.

"Yes, at once."

He snatched up the phone and dialed 911. His call went through at once. As briefly as possible, Qiming explained in English what had happened and asked the police to find Ningning for him.

The police officer's cold reply came back over the line. "I'm afraid we can't help you in this matter."

"Why not?"

"She's eighteen years old."

"So what if she's eighteen?"

"According to the law you may not keep your daughter, an eighteen-year-old girl, shut up at home. Legally, she's an adult. So, unfortunately for you, you've been violating the law."

"Me?"

"Right. So if you have nothing else to report I have other..."

Angrily and with no regard for courtesy, Qiming hung up. "Fucking law!" he swore. He called up all of Ningning's friends, at least all the ones he knew about. Nobody knew where she was.

"Maybe she'll give us a call," said Yan. "Let's wait a bit."

Qiming put down the receiver. He sat down, then got up, only to sit down again. He was as nervous as a caged leopard.

Finally the phone rang. Yan reached it first. "I'll take it," she said. She snatched up the receiver. "Hello!" The voice wasn't Ningning's.

"This is Xiumei! Come quickly to the factory. Something serious has happened. Yes, come at once!"

. . .

Xiumei saw Qiming and Yan coming through the door and went forward to meet them. "See here, Boss," she said to Qiming. "I reminded you last week that we'd used the wrong wool on the shoulders of batch 334. But you said to deliver them anyway. Now look at that!" She pointed at twenty or more cartons stacked up inside the factory gate. "They've been returned?" Qiming realized the gravity of the situation.

"All of them!"

Xiumei's face was red with emotion and she breathed heavily. Qiming flew at once into a rage. "So you're blaming me for these returns! Haven't I told you again and again to be more careful?"

None of those present dared utter a sound.

"Did I tell you to use the wrong wool?" Qiming strode around the workshop, venting all his resentment. "So the knitters were careless. But what were the ironers doing? And you packers, are you a bunch of freeloaders? Where the hell were all of you? I'll give it to you straight from the shoulder. This batch of returns is costing us sixty-eight thousand dollars all told. And don't think I've got the money to foot the bill. I don't have a red cent to plug holes with! If you want to get paid, if you want to eat, the only way is to redo these sweaters in two days and send them back to the client. Otherwise we'll all go hungry. And when that happens don't try to lay the blame on me!"

As Qiming spoke, his voice grew louder and more high-pitched, and his words sharper. He wasn't leaving any "face" for anyone.

Yan merely stood and listened. She knew very well that her husband's frustrations had mostly to do with Ningning. But the employees didn't know that and kept their eyes on the ground.

"We're all of us Chinese," he said. "It's hard for a Chinese living abroad to find work and make a few bucks. And you ought to know that I can't afford to have clients sending back whole batches of goods. Those of you who are game will do overtime and night shifts the next two days to get this job done. If not, then we won't waste any words. You get out and I'll see you to the door."

Ending his fiery speech, he turned on his heel and went to his office. The windows rattled as he slammed the door. The workers laid down whatever they had been working on and looked at each other. None of them had ever seen Qiming throw such a tantrum. Flabbergasted, they remained mute and motionless.

Yan knew what role she had to take now. With a short laugh she turned to the workers. "That's the kind of temper he's got. He has to get things off his chest, and once he's done it he's O.K. again. So don't any of you take it to heart. On the other hand, you can't blame him for blowing up like that. Anyone would get excited if his rice bowl, his livelihood, was in danger!"

After these conciliatory remarks she got down to business. "These sweaters have been rejected, but that doesn't mean we have to knit them all over again. All we have to do is change the wool on the shoulders by opening up the shoulder section and knitting the front strip inward from the sides. I know we can get it done in two days. Let's all put in an extra bit of effort, and I'll look at it as a personal favor to me!" She sat down, took a sweater and began to work on it.

The workers couldn't very well say anything after what Yan had said, and they silently went to work on the sweaters. In the office, Qiming sat with his head in his hands, not knowing what to think and not thinking anything.

After a long while Yan came in. "I'll take charge of the factory," she said to Qiming. "Go and look for her."

Qiming nodded.

He went to Ningning's school. The teachers told him they hadn't seen her for two weeks already. He also went to the police department. The officers shrugged and spread out their hands, indicating that they couldn't intervene in this matter. These not-unexpected results only aggravated Qiming's sense of frustration. He got in his car and dialed Ah Chun's number.

"You want to see me about something?"

"Yes."

"Is it important?"

"Very."

"Then come. I'll be waiting for you."

Qiming had, in the last few years, developed the habit of going to Ah Chun when he encountered problems he found hard to solve or when he had frustrations he couldn't shake off. In the dulcet tones of her voice he found calm seas for the storm-tossed ship of his soul and a haven from all his worries and anxieties.

"The problem lies in yourself," said Ah Chun. She stood before him balancing a snifter half-filled with a brandy that gave off golden glints.

"In myself?"

"Yes. You're making a mountain out of a molehill." Raising the snifter and taking a sip from it, she quietly continued: "You yourself decided to bring her here from China, and you set your mind on pushing her into society, didn't you? So why are you making a fuss about it?"

"But she..."

"I know what you're thinking about." Ah Chun smiled thinly. "Smoking, swearing, marijuana, sex. But, so what? That's society. You should have foreseen such things when you decided to let her go into society."

"But these things are too...too hard to accept!"

Ah Chun set the snifter down on the coffee table beside her. "Remember," she said. "You're living in the United Sates now. On the surface this country looks chaotic, but it has its own regularities and laws, its own rules of the game, all of them quite strict. Its code of ethics can only operate within these rules. One can't live in a vacuum, so how can you ask your daughter to live in the United States and at the same time hold onto traditional Chinese values? Wouldn't that be abnormal?"

"But I'm afraid," he said anxiously. "Afraid that something will happen to her now that she's left us, something completely unforeseen."

"Would you foresee everything about her if she hadn't left? Had you foreseen that she would smoke marijuana? That she would become pregnant and have an abortion in China?"

Qiming had nothing to say.

"The unforeseen didn't happen just yesterday. You only happened to find out about it yesterday."

"I'm scared."

"Of what? There are other, bigger things that should scare you." Before Qiming could say anything she continued to speak, walking away from the table and pacing back and forth, glass in hand. "It's true no books have been written on the subject, since there's no market for them and no profit to be made, and the number of Chinese immigrants in the United States is too small. No one shows real concern for them or makes studies of them."

She walked to the window and looked up at the sky. "The education of immigrants and their children is a very complex subject. Even adults experience suffering and a cultural impact that touches their very souls, to say nothing of children. Americans call it culture shock. An immigrant is like a person who is having a severed limb joined back onto him, bone to bone, nerve to nerve, and skin to skin, at the cost of excruciating pain. You can spot people for whom this rejoining has been a slipshod affair. Their gait, their movements, their expressions are so lacking in harmony and grace."

Qiming listened spellbound. The cigarette butt he was holding burned his fingers. He quickly stubbed it out, then lit another cigarette.

"As for their children, especially young people under twenty, they are completely confused by their new environment. They can't distinguish between right and wrong any more. The standards are all different. The old values can't be relied upon any more and have to be exchanged for new ones, like putting on a new set of clothes. Most of these youngsters don't even recognize themselves any more."

"Do they feel comfortable with themselves?"

"Feel comfortable?" Ah Chun snorted. "How can they? They resist all of this instinctively, and at the same time unconsciously absorb everything this new society brings them. All at once they become nothing at all. They can't become Americans, nor are they Chinese any longer. Their new life is utterly strange to them, yet they've left their old life-style on the other side of the ocean."

Qiming looked at Ah Chun with respect.

"They join gangs, the Huaching Gang, the Black Dragons, the Demon Shadows. And now there's the Vietnam Gang. They engage in murder, robbery and prostitution, in all these things which are the bane of American society. And their parents? They can only look on helplessly as their children fall into criminal ways, these children who were once so docile and well-behaved. The parents must work day in and day out to make a living. They have no time to educate their children. They lack the ability to teach and discipline them, since they don't know as much English or as much about American society as even their own children. Or they simply don't have the energy to do so. So what can they do besides watch their children turn into demons?"

"Then what can we do about it?"

"Nothing."

"Nothing at all?"

"There's little we can do for these young people. Because this is history, an irresistible historical process."

"But..."

"As far as specific persons are concerned, there are things you must do, of course."

"What things?"

"Take precautions."

"Precautions?"

"Yes." Ah Chun spoke with experience. "You should guard against certain people around Ningning, against people lurking behind the scenes. They of course know you're a businessman and that you have money on hand. They may take action against you. Moreover..."

"Yes?"

"There's another possibility. They may take Ningning as a hostage to extort large sums of money from you."

Qiming listened carefully, nodding repeatedly. The truth is, he was nervous. And it was because he was nervous that he listened so carefully to Ah Chun. She was an immigrant of many years and her experience was worth its weight in gold.

"Actually," said Ah Chun, "you're minding things that are none of your business."

"Minding things that are none of my business?!"

"Yes," Ah Chun affirmed. "American law is based on people's rights. Ningning is eighteen years old, so you no longer have the right to interfere in her affairs."

"Me? Interfering in her affairs?"

"Yes."

"But she isn't an adult yet, she doesn't know how to take care of herself!"

"Starting next year, a major change will take place in your tax matters. Ningning's expenses will no longer be listed on your tax returns. And she'll no longer be covered by any of your insurance policies. Her name will be deleted from your family roster."

"But I don't want that."

"All that will happen whether you like it or not. That's the law."

"The law..." muttered Qiming to himself. What enormous weight that simple word carried!

"You came to the United States on your own decision, nobody asked you to come. And since you're here you must obey the country's laws. You might as well get used to the idea that, here, you can't have family relations according to the traditional Chinese concept."

"Does that mean none of the traditional Chinese concepts apply here?"

"Well, not exactly. There's a Chinese saying: Let the children take care of themselves; any soil provides a final resting place. I believe soil is soil, whether it's in the Eastern or the Western hemisphere. It makes no difference where a person is buried after he dies."

Ah Chun finished off her brandy. The snifter hid her face and it was impossible to see or guess what her expression was like behind the glass. Qiming also took a gulp of brandy.

"It's time you went," said Ah Chun.

"Are you chasing me away?"

"No. But it isn't right to leave your wife alone in charge of the entire factory, especially at such a time."

"How's your restaurant coming along?" asked Qiming, changing the subject.

Ah Chun sighed. "It's a mess. The accounts are in absolute chaos."

"Partnerships don't agree with your temperament."

"You think I should buy my partners out? Where'll I find the money? Those two bastards would like to sell their shares, but they want a hundred thousand in cash for the first installment. They're deliberately putting me on the spot."

"Ah Chun," said Qiming as he opened the door to go out.

"Without you in my life I don't know how I'd keep on going."

"Don't talk nonsense!" She pushed him into his car.

A few days later Ah Chun received a check for one hundred thousand dollars. On the check was signed a name she knew well—Wang Qiming. For a long time she stood looking at the vigorous strokes of the signature.

- 15 -

Jerry, the dog Qiming had bought for Ningning, was getting bigger. Qiming had been told that this type of dog weighed only about seven or eight pounds when it reached maturity, but its hair could grow to a length of ten inches. It was white all over; its coat didn't contain a single hair of another color. The only spots of color on it were its black nose and its pink lolling tongue. This dog was purely a household pet, a plaything.

There was no question that Jerry had a superb lineage. On his birth registration card it was written that his blood line could be traced back six or seven generations within the same family. No one could doubt this fact, because the card carried the breeder's signature, the seller's signature and the dog's serial number as well as seals affixed by the relevant government institutions. And this because it was the United States.

Everyone knows about the status of dogs in American society. But Qiming and Yan only found out how much importance dogs are accorded after Jerry came to their home. Before that, when Qiming had bought the dog, he had had to fill in a stack of forms. He had filled in his name as the buyer, his address and telephone number, and most important of all, his social security number under the dog's name. Thereafter he and the dog were inseparably tied together, on the forms at least.

Qiming's original intention in getting a dog was to keep Ningning tied up at home, to draw her interest and keep her from running around outside. It hadn't turned out that way. The one he'd tried to tie down hadn't stayed. But now the dog was here to stay.

The dog was no end of trouble. In Qiming's words, instead of buying a pet he'd brought a holy little terror into the house. Every week he got at least two or three letters regarding Jerry. Some were from animal protection societies asking him to write out reports on Jerry's recent condition; others were from Jerry's veterinarian notifying Qiming that he should bring Jerry on such and such a day to have him inoculated; still others were from the dog beautician saying it was time Jerry had his coat trimmed. The most ridiculous were those from dog clubs: written as though the author were a dog, they contained invitations to Jerry to come to parties; and please note, evening dress required!

Since Yan hadn't learned to drive a car, it was Qiming who had to hurry here and there with the shaggy little monster, running himself ragged, wanting to laugh and swear at the same time. The biggest headache of all, after the dog came, was when both Qiming and Yan had to go on a trip together. That called for a lengthy conference.

Take Jerry along? What with his food and his clothes and his cage and his toys—his things would amount to more than both Qiming's and Yan's luggage put together.

Leave him at home? They couldn't just lock the door and go; they could be prosecuted if Jerry started to bark and no one was there to attend to him. The only alternative was to send him to a dog hostel, where one night's lodgings cost a good deal more than a hotel for human beings.

They finally decided to put Jerry in a dog hostel. Although the expense was enough to make a person gasp, they could at least put their minds at ease and use all their time to deal with human affairs.

In the six months that passed since Ningning had disappeared, Yan turned into a real dog fanatic. She loved Jerry most, she had the most concern for him, she understood him best. She got up half an hour earlier in the mornings to walk the dog. When they came back to the house she started to get his breakfast ready without stopping to take a minute's rest. Then she hunkered down beside Jerry to talk to him.

"Jerry," she'd say. "Mommy's going to work, to make money for you. Stay at home and don't be naughty. If you're good, mommy will take you out next week and buy you a new toy. How do you like that? So long. Say bye-bye to mommy."

Coming home in the evenings, no matter how tired she was she'd lie down on the carpet and play with Jerry for a half hour before getting around to cooking dinner. Seeing her like this, Qiming would shake his head. But he didn't dare say anything. He realized that she was placing on the dog all the love and longing she felt for Ningning.

One day Jerry went bananas playing in the sitting room, and before he could run out into the garden he'd peed on the white carpet. Qiming caught him and gave him a little kick. Yan happened to be coming down the stairs and saw this. She started to scream, accusing Qiming of being inhuman and a no-good sonovabitch. She ran to Jerry and took him in her arms. "Don't be scared, Jerry. Don't pay any attention to him. He's no good. All he does is blow his top and swear and hit people. Tell mommy, did he hurt you?"

She got some paper napkins, intending to soak up Jerry's urine. She'd squatted down and was just about to wipe the carpet, when she caught sight of the dark patch Ningning's cigarette ash had made the night before she went away. With shaking fingers Yan touched the dark patch. Dropping the paper napkins, she picked Jerry up and ran upstairs.

Qiming had watched all of this without saying a word. He lay on the couch, pursing his lips and blowing smoke rings at the ceiling. After a while the rims of his eyes became red. In the silence of the room he could hear Yan sobbing upstairs and talking to Jerry.

"Does it hurt, Jerry? Tell Mommy. Don't be angry. He has a bad temper. But Mommy will look after you."

Qiming rubbed his palm, yokel fashion, across the tears on his face.

Jerry really lived up to all the love and care Yan was giving him. The moment Yan came home he would be close on her heels, following her like a bodyguard. As if he was using a magic mirror, this little dog could sense emotions hidden in Yan's heart, emotions Qiming didn't know and couldn't even guess were there.

After Ningning left Yan would often sit by herself, staring blankly into space. Jerry would run over to her and bark a few times, then he'd take his toy bone and drop it in her lap to break her out of her trance. When Yan looked worried or cried, he'd jump onto her lap and lick her face and neck until she smiled. Then he'd hop down and go to sleep beside her feet. At night Jerry slept on Yan's bed, the warmth of his body helping her to sleep more soundly.

When a nightmare frightened Yan out of her sleep, Jerry would spring to his feet, prick up his ears and listen wide-eyed for any sign of movement around them. This breed of dog was always among the top winners at annual competitions in the United States, not only on account of its adorable appearance, but chiefly because its IQ was much higher than that of other types of dogs. This dog was almost human, they thought.

Because Ningning had left, and Yan and the dog had become inseparable, Qiming and Yan had slept apart for more than half a year. Qiming would catch some sleep here and there like a guerrilla fighter, in the sitting room, upstairs in the spare bedroom, or sometimes at the office. One night, when his loneliness became more than he could bear, he crept into the big bedroom where Yan slept. He walked up to the bed and touched Yan's shoulder. Yan gave a start and woke up.

Jerry immediately sprang up, put his paws protectively on Yan's shoulder and barked and bared his teeth at Qiming. Qiming stepped back, feeling both angry and amused.

"Jerry! Don't growl," Yan said soothingly to the little dog. "This is your daddy." Only then did Jerry quiet down.

Qiming was given the right to lie on the bed only after he became the dog's daddy.

Another six months passed. Jerry had grown a little more and had reached the size this type of dog usually reaches. He was prettier than ever, with long hair that fell to the ground and that flounced up and down when he ran. When he sat still at the head of the bed an outsider would have taken him for a toy dog. And so when Jerry had grown up and become a "big dog," Qiming was allowed to move back into the big bedroom. Sex with Yan was a haphazard affair at best, but at least they talked and laughed together and life was back to normal.

As time passed changes took place in Qiming, too. One morning as he was sitting at breakfast and reading his newspaper, he couldn't make out the words on the paper. Craning his neck backward, he held the newspaper as far forward as he could. He couldn't read the words. He blinked his eyes. The letters still weren't clear.

"Yan!" he called out. "One day my eyes are okay and the next day I need glasses. It's really weird!"

"Nervous people need glasses earlier than other people," said Yan, glancing at him.

"Where's the connection? What does a guy's temperament have to do with glasses? That's really funny!" But even as he said this, he knew he was getting undeniably older, and that people who worry age more quickly. And that was the truth. From then on he wore a pair of glasses with a thick black frame.

With these glasses on, and with the little paunch he was developing, he began to look more and more like a duck, especially when he was walking. But one shouldn't sneer at this duck-like gait. It was useful. When the workers at the factory saw him they'd say jokingly, "Hey! Walking like that he looks even more like a big *laoban*!"

Qiming didn't say anything when he heard such comments, but he felt quite pleased and his waddle became more pronounced. Yes, that duck's waddle was useful. Especially when he was talking business with clients. That, and the glasses which he wore even when he wasn't reading anything and didn't need to put them on.

The Yanks really lapped up that kind of thing. The more Qiming swayed and waddled and put on his glasses whether he needed them or not, the richer they believed him to be. And they were willing to place large orders with him. Whether or not this last had anything to do with his waddle and his glasses is hard to prove today. Whatever the case, business became better and better for him and he bought a new car for himself and some more jewelry and precious stones for Yan.

Yan changed, too. Her hair became blacker and more shiny. Although one or two more wrinkles creased the corners of her eyes and a double chin hung over her collar, the shiny black hair gave people the impression of a lively woman.

That hair didn't fool any perceptive woman, who knew at first sight it was dyed. But the women at the factory knew the art of flattery, and kept on telling Yan the older she got the younger she looked. This made Yan pay even more attention to her appearance. She spent more time in front of her mirror every day. When she and Qiming were going out, she would still be upstairs even after Qiming had started the car and was looking impatiently at his watch, stamping his feet, walking in circles or honking the horn.

She would not be hurried. Sitting at her dressing table, she would take her time putting the last touches on her face, and then with agonizing slowness walk down the stairs, open the door, lock it behind her and get in the car. When she was in the car, Qiming would say with a grin, "You old witch!"

And Yan would return the compliment with, "You old crow bait!"

Both of them were getting older. But were they really old? They were only in their forties. Actually, in the United States, a person at such an age isn't seen as getting old. In the business world especially, he is regarded as just getting off to a start. Qiming's business partners, almost all of them in their sixties and seventies, would pat his shoulder after each round of business talks and say: "Be good, boy!"

No, he wasn't getting old. Not at all. If he seemed older it was only because he was putting it on. "I can afford to," he said to himself. "We had only fifty dollars between us when we got off the plane eight years ago. Today we're worth more than a million dollars."

Put it on? Why not? He put on a lot of things. He swanked, showed off his money, put on airs, and all the while his waddle got worse.

He often went to restaurants and nightclubs with bigwigs from the Chinese chambers of commerce, spending hundreds of dollars an evening. Before leaving he'd simply toss a credit card on the table and wipe his greasy lips while he waited to sign his name.

On weekends his house became a mahjong den. With not just a single table, but three or four, and each win running into hundreds of dollars, and each loss as well. But he thought nothing of it. "It's all part of the game." he'd say. "A person needs some fun."

One could see that he'd really changed, changed so much he hardly knew himself any more. He knew his own name, of course, but to what category did he belong now? On that he was vague and unclear.

Was he a fat cat? You got to be kidding! There were plenty of people richer than he was. On that score he was quite clear.

Still, he walked around with his nose up in the air, smug and self-satisfied. People around him praised him, saying how capable he was, how intelligent he was. His reputation soared. Hostesses in nightclubs called him the new Robin Hood. New York tycoons described him as up-and-coming. The Chinese media wrote him up as a prodigy among the newer immigrants.

All this, of course, fed his vanity. No one could have resisted such flattery. He became conceited, arrogant, haughty, overbearing.

Even Yan was getting to be quite proud. She bought so many new clothes, especially evening dresses, her wardrobe couldn't hold any more. But still she'd go every weekend to famous stores to select new fashions. She had her own reasons: people looked down on you if you went twice to the same place wearing the same clothes. She had long ago replaced the old Longine on her wrist with an eighteen-carat gold Rolex.

She often prodded Qiming to buy a new car. "I say, why don't you get a Mercedes? Driving around in an American car doesn't suit your status."

There was a subtle change in her way of walking, too. You could say she was slower, or getting sluggish, but that wasn't it. In Beijing they'd say she was always "holding it," holding a pose, trying to look dignified.

And why did she "hold it?" She did it because she felt her status called for that. If she didn't, she'd fall in other people's estimation, or as Ningning would say, her "share" would "drop." She was always busy. Besides managing the factory, she went weekends to Weight Watchers, saw masseurs, got facials and went to do aerobics. Put it this way: she'd try any gimmick invented to get money out of people, and she happily took her dollars to them. It was only when she was alone with Qiming that she showed something of her old self.

"I really wonder how Ningning is getting along," she said one night as she was removing her make-up.

"She could have everything in life, but she doesn't want it," replied Qiming, unknotting his expensive tie. "That's her tough luck."

He felt depressed when his daughter was mentioned, but he didn't want to think about her since the wounds she had left in him still rankled.

"She should at least give us a call," said Yan, pursuing her train of thought.

"There are lots of things she should do. On the other hand, should she have done any of the things she's already done?" Qiming felt unhappy whenever he remembered the way his daughter had flown at him. He'd never forgotten her accusations, and that perhaps because they were justified.

"Don't you worry about our daughter, Qiming?" asked Yan, turning around to face him.

"Worry?" He lit a cigarette. "What's the use of worrying? Let the children take care of themselves, any soil provides a resting place..." He stopped abruptly. Who had spoken those words? Ah Chun!

The thought of Ah Chun further complicated his mental processes. He shook his head as if to get rid of his confused state of mind. "Don't worry!" he said at last. Then, as if that would settle everything, he added: "It isn't that I don't worry about her. But what's the use of worrying all the time?"

"I'm afraid that she..."

"What?"

"That she'll get into trouble."

"She's been in enough trouble as it is. Look at it this way. She's nineteen years old and an adult. The United States being what it is, we're not allowed to trouble ourselves on her account." Here, he added a sentence in English: "It's none of our business."

"Do you think anything has happened to her?"

"It's nearly a year since she left. If anything had happened we'd have read about it in the papers." But he too was seized with anxiety. He ground out his cigarette. "Nothing...I hope...has happened to her."

- 16 -

It was in early August that two uninvited guests came to Qiming's home. Yan was frying soybean paste for noodles when the doorbell rang. She turned down the gas flame and went to open the door. It was a man and a woman.

"May I ask..." she began, wary but polite.

"May we come in?" said the man, his face wreathed in smiles. Without waiting to be invited in, he stuck his foot in the doorway.

Qiming put down the newspaper he'd been reading and got up to meet the visitors. He saw a short, fat man in his sixties, bald but with sparse gray hair rimming the shiny dome of his head. Thick, round glasses were perched on his bridgeless, button-like nose. Everything about him was round—his head, his jowls, and the big belly that his charcoal-gray suit could hardly cover. Even the sound of his voice was round—and unctuous.

"Wang Laoban, I've heard much about you," the man said glibly. "My humble name is also Wang. There are many Wangs in China, but since there are so few in the United States we should consider ourselves relatives of a sort, don't you think?"

These opening remarks were enough to tell Qiming that the man was an old pro and a slick talker. But he knew from his experience in the business world that snubbing a person for no good reason is taboo in business dealings. So he only nodded courteously.

"I have long known you by reputation, but have never come to visit you," continued the man. "So today I have come to redeem myself. I would have called to make an appointment, but I knew you are a busy man. I therefore dispensed with this formality. I crave your indulgence for my breaking in on you like this and for coming uninvited."

"Please don't stand on ceremony," replied Qiming. The man irritated him, but he had to make a show of courtesy.

"However," said the man, changing his tack and apparently about to come to the subject. "It is for your sake that I have committed this rude intrusion. For what reason? I turned on my computer this morning and received a shock. You are in great danger!"

Qiming was amused by this sudden alarmist turn. Unconcerned, he smiled briefly. "May I know your..."

The visitor pushed up the precariously perched spectacles, and the woman at once handed Qiming a business card. The two actions were so well coordinated that Qiming suspected the man's pushing up his spectacles to be a prearranged signal. He disliked these visitors.

Taking the visiting card, he read:

Metropolitan Insurance Co.
WANG TANG DI
General Representative for Chinese Residents

Qiming respectfully put away the card and turned his attention back to the visitors.

"You said just now that I was in danger. I don't quite understand."

At this point, Yan finished whatever she was doing. Switching off the suction fan over the kitchen range, she entered the living room.

"It's serious, very serious. However, dangerous as the matter is, you needn't worry. With your humble servant here to handle your affairs you have absolutely no reason to be concerned." After all this palaver, the man still wasn't coming to the point.

Qiming knew he was trying to build up suspense. All insurance companies used the same trick to get you willy-nilly to buy life insurance. So he wasn't particularly affected by the man's sensation mongering.

"Your present life insurance policy was purchased five years ago, but according to our information your policy doesn't gear in with your status and adjustments must be made at once."

"Doesn't gear in? One would think you were talking about machinery. Adjustments? What needs adjusting?"

"One thing at a time! I'm surprised you know so little about such things. But that, after all, is my fault. However, it's still not too late." He took a sip of tea, getting ready to launch into another long sales pitch.

Qiming was beginning to feel sorry for himself. His stomach had been rumbling for some time already in expectation of the noodles with soy sauce that should have been slipping down his gullet.

"All right, then!" he said. "To cut matters short, you tell me what adjustments are needed and how much more money I have to pay, and I'll write you out a check. How's that?"

The fat man beamed with pleasure. "The moment I saw you I knew you were a straightforward person. But there are some hows and whys I have to explain to you first. Anyone with eyes can see that you've prospered these last few years. Just look at this grand, spacious house! And the furnishings—so luxurious, so sumptuous, so elegant! Mrs. Wang, I only have to look at you to know that you have good fortune. Your features tell me at once that you were born to have wealth and position."

Fearing that the man was getting away from the subject again, Qiming quickly interrupted him. "Can you tell me how much more I have to pay?"

"Yes, just a minute." The man leafed through his notebook. "According to your present financial status...your monthly payment should come to...three thousand six hundred forty-two dollars and twenty-three cents."

Yan lost her cool. "That much?"

"That much! Mrs. Wang, everyone would like to pay that much. Not everyone can do it. If one has a lot of property, one of course buys a lot of insurance. Not every woman in this world has such a good husband as you have!"

Qiming hadn't expected he would have to pay so much insurance every month.

"Why do I need so much insurance?" he asked.

"To begin with, you bought only three hundred thousand dollars' worth of insurance five years ago. Can you tell me your life is worth only that much? Of course not. Today you are worth two million. Secondly, your business requires you to travel by car and by plane all the year round, hence your probability of having an accident is higher than the average. Assuming you have an accident and die, you'll have no more worries, but you shall be leaving your wife only three hundred thousand dollars. Will that be enough to support her for the rest of her life? Of course not. Since she'll have such a large estate to maintain, those three hundred thou- sand will last her three and a half years on the outside."

"If something does happen to me," said Qiming, bullheadedly, "my wife can always sell my property and lay her hands on some money."

"Hold it!" The fat man suddenly interrupted Qiming. "That's precisely why I'm here today, why I say you are in danger, and that's also my third point. It is evident that you know nothing about American laws on property and inheritance taxation."

"True. I don't know much about such things."

"Let's first take the tax law on the buying and selling of property. When you bought this house you only made a down payment, and the greater part of the payment was made with a bank loan. Am I right? You felt you had made a profit after you had bought the house. But you should know that the IRS will take fifty-eight percent of any profit you make. Deduct the bank loan, and how much do you have left? You might even have to dig in your own pockets if there's a downturn in the economy and real estate values drop. And even assuming the economy stays strong and you don't lose anything, you'll have very little money left over."

He spoke with great conviction, raising his voice more and more and spraying flecks of saliva. He took out a handkerchief, mopped up the beads of perspiration on his round pate, and continued:

"And that isn't all. There's the law on inheritance, and that's even worse. Imagine that one day you have an accident and depart from this world. The day the hearse takes you to the cemetery, the IRS will show up and demand a heavy tax from your wife. This tax is the inheritance tax, and under the regulations your wife will have to pay sixty-nine percent of the value of all property under your name. Adding lawyers' fees, that will come to about seventy percent. Even if your wife sells all the property and throws in the three hundred thousand from your insurance, she won't have enough to pay that tax! Now you know the terrible danger you're in. Your wife will be left homeless and penniless."

Qiming and Yan had never been told such things. They now listened round-eyed to the man and didn't interrupt him any more. Seeing that the time was getting ripe, the fat man laid it on even thicker.

"Many women of rank and position wander from place to place after their husbands die to avoid creditors. Their children become vagrants overnight. Some take their own lives, others are sent to poor people's homes to live on government hand-outs. It's really pitiful, heart-rending! And the reason for their plight is that they failed to buy life insurance."

The man's last sentence was too blatant and nearly wiped out the impression of sincerity he'd managed to create.

"And what if I don't die?" asked Qiming, vexed.

"That's impossible," said the man with aggravating insistence. "Absolutely impossible. Everyone dies, sooner or later. That's certain."

These words rubbed Qiming the wrong way, but respect for the man's calling prevented him from flaring up and calling the old fellow a bastard. Yan, too, was a bit peeved. "What if we die together?" she asked.

"Yes, like the hero and the heroine in *The Butterfly Lovers,*" Qiming chimed in.

"No, no," replied the man with a worldly-wise smile. "It's hardly possible."

"But what if it does happen?"

"In that case, the government will take over all your property three hundred days after your decease and auction it off as municipal property."

Qiming fell silent. He'd heard of such things.

Seeing that he'd made a point, the man decided to strike while the iron was hot. "Would you be willing to see all your hard-earned property returned to the United States? Would you have the heart to leave your wife alone in the world without any means of support?"

"What, in your opinion, should I do?"

"Make an adjustment."

"How?"

"By increasing your premium from three hundred thousand to two million dollars."

"Four thousand a month! That, for me, is a lot of money."

"You're a smart businessman and I don't have to spell everything out. If those four thousand go onto your company's accounts, you'll save on taxes and at the same time secure your property. So why not do it?"

"Good!" Qiming nodded. He'd made up his mind. He got up to get his check book.

Guessing Qiming's intention, the man said at once: "It won't be necessary for you to make out monthly checks. Just tell us the number of your bank account, and my company will transfer the money. That will save you a lot of trouble."

Qiming didn't say anything, but he admired the way those insurance people did business: They didn't leave a guy any loophole or excuse. He told the man his account number and signed his name. Thanking Qiming again and again, the fat man got to his feet and bowed so deeply he nearly bumped his shiny head on the table.

When he and the woman had left, Qiming remarked to Yan, "From now on I'll have another ancestor to kowtow to. Every month I'll have to burn joss sticks to the insurance company."

"You didn't have to buy that new policy."

"I did it for you," said Qiming, slurping down his noodles. "How would you live if I really died before you did?"

"Swellhead! You don't really think I couldn't live without you, do you?"

"No, it's the other way around. I can't live without you."

"You talk more sweetly than you sing."

Although Yan spoke like this, she was actually thinking the same thing as most women in the United States do: that she'd have to depend on her husband for the rest of her life, since relying on the second generation to support her in her old age was like believing stories from the Arabian Nights. Why do people in America always think about what'll happen after they get old? The reason is simple. The United States doesn't look after the aged.

July 4th is American National Day. Qiming and Yan had scheduled their activities for the day long before it came. There was a restaurant in New York called The Only Place, which specialized in Beijing-style snacks. It was, actually, the only place that sold Beijing-style snacks in this city, and Yan and Qiming had decided to have breakfast there. The owner of The Only Place, a man named He, had come from Taiwan. Nevertheless, he was a genuine Beijinger and spoke like one.

Qiming liked to come here, not only to treat his taste buds to Beijing snacks, but also for the kick of talking with someone in the Beijing dialect. His ears were full of foreign sounds since he'd come to the United States, and it felt good to hear some pure Beijing patois.

"Hey! What'll it be today, Wang Taitai, Wang Laoban? Stove buns and crullers with sweet soy milk? Or millet mush, lima bean cakes and honeyed dough ears?" Proprietor He's crisp Beijing accent was to Qiming like a breath of fresh, clean air.

"Let's switch to something else today," replied Qiming. "We'll have a portion of pan-fried meat rolls and two sets of sesame bun sandwiches with sliced brown beef, plus two bowls of millet porridge and a dish of shredded turnip pickles with some sesame oil."

He was placing his order not for the food itself, but for the feel of the words rolling off his tongue. In all of New York, this was "the only place" he could show off what a true Beijinger he was.

"This is National Day, isn't it?" Qiming sat down at a table and went on shooting the breeze with the proprietor. "How come there are so few people around?"

"That's the way it is. If things go on like this, I'll have to wrap up this place sooner or later." Proprietor He poured out his woes to Qiming. "Let me tell you, I made a bum move when I set up this joint, and now I'm paying through the nose for it. The Yanks don't come here, they say the food's no good. Neither do those Cantonese. They don't cotton to our Beijing snacks. Taiwanese only go places where it stinks of fish. And there aren't a whole lot of Beijingers here from the mainland. I spent close to two hundred grand fixing this place up to look like a second Tiananmen, but people just stand out there gawking and hardly anybody comes in to eat. What can I do about it? Eh?" He sighed.

"Sit tight and wait. Who knows, maybe in six months or a year your luck will change. Maybe by that time people will get to like Beijing snacks and your business will take off."

"Don't try to make me feel better. I'm not the same as you. You're a big boss and you've got enough dough to stick it out. Not me. I squeezed those two hundred grand out between my teeth. Now I've blown the lot and I don't have a cent left."

Qiming was about to say something else, but Yan poked him in the ribs, hinting that the man felt bad enough without having to listen to any more guff.

Seeing that the conversation had dried up, Proprietor He shouted, "Xiao Li! Bring up the order! Don't keep Wang Laoban waiting too long!"

A short young fellow wearing a grimy apron came out of the kitchen at a trot and put two bowls of millet porridge on the table.

Qiming looked up. "Hey! You're Xiao Li, aren't you? How come you're still in restaurants after all these years?" He was surprised, not at seeing Xiao Li, but over the fate of this Master in Biology.

"Not everyone's got your luck. One in ten thousand, maybe. What would I do if I didn't work in restaurants?"

"How've you been lately?" Qiming stood up and grasped Xiao Li's hand. Yan got up too.

"So-so. Still muddling along as usual." He was obviously embarrassed and had the hangdog look of a man faced by someone much more successful than himself.

"Sit with us a while," Yan said courteously, trying to put Xiao Li at ease. "Let's chat and have something to eat."

A shout came from the kitchen. "Xiao Li! Stop dragging your feet out there. There's plenty of work waiting for you in here!"

Hurriedly freeing his hand, Xiao Li said goodbye and rushed back to the kitchen. A moment later he was heard yelling in his Zhejiang accent. "Who the hell d'you think you are, screaming like that? I started working restaurants long before you came to the U.S.!"

That afternoon, as they were taking a walk in Central Park, the morning's events were brought up again. Yan was giving Qiming some advice. "Don't think that because you have some money now you can be careless about what you say and about other people's self-respect. You're liable to hurt people's feelings."

"I didn't mean to do it."

"I feel really sorry for him. Working all these years in restaurants and not being able to pull himself out!"

"Huh! There are plenty of others worse off than him. People who've made it like us are as rare as phoenix feathers and unicorn horns."

"Well, well! Just listen to the guy!"

"I wasn't talking about myself. What I meant was, I have a good wife!"

"You're getting to be a real bum!"

They went on talking as they walked through the park. The grass was covered with sunbathers, with men in brief shorts and women in bikinis, sprawling in every position and making the park look like a market for live flesh.

There would be a fireworks display that evening, and people were coming in droves to look for a vantage point and stake out their positions. Qiming and Yan came to the edge of the lake. Although it was midsummer, a breeze blowing over the lake's surface felt very pleasant as they walked slowly, hand in hand. A small crowd blocked their way.

Qiming was already in his forties, but he was still as curious as a boy and liked to squeeze into a crowd to see what was going on. Yan waited for him on the edge of the crowd.

Soon, Qiming pushed his way out again, his face beaded with perspiration. "What a coincidence," he said delightedly to his wife. "Just look who's in there—Chen Fen!"

Yan peered over some shoulders and saw a casually dressed painter. But for the life of her she couldn't recall where she'd heard the familiar-sounding name, Chen Fen. Laying down his paint brush, the painter walked out of the crowd and hugged Qiming tightly.

"Qiming!"

"Chen Fen!"

As Qiming embraced Chen Fen, he kept throwing reminders at Yan. "Seven years ago...the jalopy...the American sun...that poem..."

"Oh yes! The *Ode to the Sun*." Yan had remembered at last.

"I was told long ago that you two had hit it big." Chen Fen said this very emotionally. "I planned to look you up but I couldn't find your phone number."

"And how are you doing?"

"So-so." Like Xiao Li, Chen Fen sounded bitter when he talked about himself.

"Still painting?"

"Yes, still painting. I've been painting at the same spot in Central Park all these years and I've never moved. Painting these Yanks for a few bucks a throw."

"Do you get many clients?"

"In this business you depend on the weather, like the peasants in northern Shaanxi province but the other way around. You hope for dry weather, and it had better be dry, or else nobody comes to be painted and you have no business."

"And when it rains?"

"When it rains or snows you've had it. You stay at home and snooze the time away."

Only then did Qiming and Yan remark that Chen Fen's face was darker and thinner. As they were speaking, someone sat down on the stool in front of Chen Fen's easel.

"Hey! I've got a customer. I'll talk to you later."

Chen Fen hurried back to his easel. Qiming and Yan decided to take their leave, so as not to affect Chen Fen's business.

After Qiming had left his card on Chen Fen's open paint box and made a date for Chen Fen to call him up the following week, they walked quickly away. Neither of them spoke another word as they walked along the lake bank. They were thinking how lucky they were.

- 17 -

A fireworks display was put on in New York on the evening of July 4th. There was nothing special about it if one had seen the large-scale spectaculars in Beijing on October First. So Qiming proposed to Yan that they go home and get to bed early, and since Yan had no objection they drove back to their house.

The sedan entered the garage and the automatic, remote-controlled door lowered itself to the ground. Qiming was just about to go in the house when Yan clutched his arm.

"What is it?" Qiming asked.

"There's somebody in the living room," whispered Yan, shivering.

He stopped in his tracks and looked toward the house. Sure enough, shadows were flitting across the living room window.

"Burglars!" exclaimed Qiming, keeping his voice low. But he didn't dare stop them. The burglars in New York were a vicious lot and carried guns. Reckless people who tried to catch them often died at their hands.

"Quick! Let's call 911." He pulled his wife's arm, trying to make her hurry.

But Yan wouldn't move. Instead, she murmured, "Jerry! Jerry!"

"We have to call the police quickly if we want to save Jerry!" Only then did Yan follow Qiming.

This being a holiday, none of their neighbors were home and they couldn't find a telephone. The frantic couple ran two full blocks to a public pay phone. 911 answered immediately, and the dispatcher said they'd be there immediately. The two returned and stood under a large tree some distance from their house. By the light of the fireworks they watched for signs of movement in their home. The street was very quiet. No cars passed.

Shivering, Yan kept muttering "Jerry! Jerry!"

Afraid that the light from the fireworks was too bright and the burglars might see them, Qiming pulled Yan behind the tree and stood there trembling as hard as she was.

Suddenly, shadows jumped out of one of the windows, one, two, three, four... Altogether four big men, all of them holding large and small sacks. A small van appeared and silently stopped in front of their house. The four men swiftly threw the sacks into the back of the van and jumped in themselves, and the van was gone.

"The motherfuckers!" swore Qiming.

The police came just after the burglars had left. When the two police officers had verified Qiming's identity as owner of the house they ordered him to open the door.

"The burglars are getting away. Aren't you going after them?"

"Open the door!"

Helplessly Qiming unlocked the door and, like a museum guide, took the officers around the house. He had never imagined that burglars would be so destructive. Everything in the living room had been shoved aside or overturned. The video camera, the video cassette player, the CD sound system and the karaoke were gone; the color TV, perhaps too heavy to carry, was still there but left lying in the middle of the living room floor. The bedrooms were no better. Clothes, letters, empty jewelry cases and purses lay all over the floor. Even Yan's bras and panties had been thrown about.

When Jerry caught sight of Yan he jumped into her arms like a frightened child, trembling and shrinking into a ball. Yan patted him. "Don't be scared, don't be scared," she said. "You poor boy, mommy's come back!" Actually, she was trembling harder than the dog.

The police began to take pictures and look for fingerprints. They obviously didn't take cases like this one very seriously. As they worked they talked and laughed and discussed the coming mayoral elections in New York.

Qiming was very much disturbed by their lack of concern for his plight. And so, when an officer began to question him about the circumstances, he said loudly, "I would have shot them if I'd had a gun!"

"You can't do that." The officer shook his head. "If you shoot and kill someone, you'd be breaking the law and we'd probably arrest you first of all."

"Then what should I do in such a situation? Help them carry off my things?"

"The best is to let them go, as you did today." The policeman's advice was most discouraging.

"Let them go? Perhaps I should have gotten them a taxi too!"

"As far as I am aware they had their own transportation. Right?" said the officer humorously. He looked at Qiming, this naive Chinaman, with curiosity.

"But why should I be so polite and accommodating to burglars?"

"Why don't you improve the anti-burglary equipment in your house?" countered the officer. "By the looks of things, you can afford to do so."

The police officers appeared to have completed their tasks. They asked Qiming to sign a form, then saluted and left. The police car drove away, leaving silence in the house.

"They want us to take precautions ourselves! What's the use of having policemen?" complained Qiming, looking amid the disorder for a place to sit down.

"What is this, anyway? Things that you've worked so hard to get, gone just like that?" Yan was feeling bad about her jewelry. Such nice jewelry! Too good for that pack of thieves!

"D'you know, they say losing some money wards off other disasters?" Seeing that Yan was feeling really sorry for herself, he tried to console her. "Don't take it so hard. I'll get some more for you."

"But that means spending more money! It's years already since I've been collecting that jewelry!"

"If you don't buy things, you have to pay taxes anyway. The municipal government takes your money and gives it as relief to people like those burglars. So they're simply saving the government trouble by taking it straight from your house."

"Still joking, at a time like this!"

"I'm not joking. This is something I've learned about the United States. You mustn't expect to put everything you earn into your own pockets. You've got to hand some of it over."

"But I don't want to hand it over that way!"

"You feel you've been shortchanged, don't you? Actually you haven't. Not so long as you haven't lost your life, and you can thank your lucky stars."

"But what about the future? Can you guarantee it won't happen again?"

This was a reminder to Qiming. "You're right. We'll have to think about some precautions."

Once Qiming had made up his mind, he got down to work. In less than two weeks big changes had taken place in their house. All windows, large and small, upstairs and downstairs, had been fitted with steel bars as thick as your finger. The front, back and side doors had been replaced with heavy iron ones that clanged when you went in or out of the house.

Infrared monitors had been put up around the house, and anything that passed in front of the doors, whether cars or people or even a cat or a mouse, automatically turned on lights so bright and dazzling you could hardly keep your eyes open.

He also put in an alarm system. This device was linked up with the police station. Once the two had left the house and switched on the current, any person who so much as touched the house would set off an alarm bell and simultaneously cause a red light to flash at the police station, and the police would arrive in less than three minutes.

All good and fine. Now the house was like a prison, or a fortress. Everything had been installed. Qiming and Yan were sitting on the couch and Qiming was staring into space, when suddenly he burst out laughing.

"What's so funny?" asked Yan.

"When you're poor, you want to have money. And once you've got it, you make your house look like a prison and play at being a convict."

"Why do they do it? People come to the United States to find freedom, don't they?"

"When you don't have any money, you're a stooge and not one person in a thousand pays any attention to you. But as soon as you get rich a million people are waiting to rob, burglarize and destroy you. So where can you hide? In a prison! It makes one wonder what's better: To be poor, or to be rich? Can anyone explain that to me?"

"Nobody can."

. . .

Another week passed. On Sunday Qiming went out to play mahjong. Yan stayed at home and since she had nothing to do she was getting quite bored. The bars on the windows made her feel claustrophobic, so she went out into the garden with Jerry and sat on the grass.

The lawn, recently mowed by the gardener, was neat and trim and gave off the sweet smell of cut grass. Yan liked the smell. She lay down with her face to the sky. Then she shut her eyes and let the sunshine play on her eyelids, creating a red glow in her vision. She wasn't thinking of anything. She had emptied her brain of all thoughts to give her mind a rest, and to give herself a moment's peace.

A car braked near her with a screech. The sound, loud and harsh, was very much out of keeping with the sunshine and the grass. She sat up and looked around. A black sports car was standing on her driveway. Ningning's car! She got to her feet and stared at it. A clean-featured boy got out, went to the other side of the car and opened the door. A girl came out.

It was Ningning! She was outlandishly made up and her ponytail was gone. In its place was a tuft of hair jutting straight over her forehead and another one at least eight inches long dangling down her face and covering half of her left eye.

A miniskirt that couldn't have been any shorter clung to her hips, leaving the bottom half of her buttocks uncovered. A tiny vest hugged her already mature breasts; her belly was, of course, unabashedly bare. If it hadn't been for her face which looked so much like Qiming's, Yan would hardly have believed that this was her own daughter, Ningning.

Yan stood still, prevented from moving by a tangle of conflicting feelings—astonishment, longing, resentment, numbness. She didn't know how she should speak to Ningning or what to say. Her lips quivered as though she would say something but no words came. She moved her feet, wanting to go forward and hug her daughter but somehow feeling that Ningning was far away, as though on the other side of a wide river.

"Mom!" said Ningning, stepping forward.

That one word touched Yan to the quick. She wiped her eyes and said softly, "Ningning, you've come back." Then her tears gushed forth.

"Mom, this is my friend James."

"Hi!" James briefly raised his right hand in what passed for a greeting.

"Do we have any soft drinks? We're dying of thirst."

"Yes. Come in and get some."

Yan showed Ningning and James into the house. Jerry looked at the two strangers and began to bark.

"Jerry, don't you remember me?" Ningning tried to pick Jerry up but the dog evaded her and barked all the more loudly.

"Don't touch the beast!" said James. "Careful he doesn't bite you!"

Jerry whirled around as if he'd understood James' insult and bit one of his gym shoes. Without the slightest hesitation James drew back his foot and kicked Jerry.

"Beat it!" he snarled.

Yan snatched Jerry up and gave James a reproachful glance. Then she went upstairs to shut Jerry up in her room.

James took a swig from a soft drink bottle and snapped his fingers at a picture standing on the piano, one of Ningning playing the violin when she was seven years old.

"What's that?" he asked.

"Me playing the violin," Ningning told him.

"You must be sick! What d'you learn that stuff for? You want to learn how to make money."

Yan came downstairs again and took Ningning's hand.

"Come home to stay, child," she said. "I miss you."

"Mom, I need some money." She ignored Yan's plea.

"Your dad misses you too. Come back."

"Didn't you hear me, Mom? I need some money."

"Money?" Yan frowned.

"That's right, Mom."

"How much do you want?"

"I don't want it. I'm borrowing it."

"Borrowing money?"

"What I'm saying is, we'll return it to you," said Ningning.

"What do you want it for?"

"To do business."

"What kind of business?"

"Never you mind, Mom."

"But I must know if I'm going to lend you the money."

"You want to know what kind of business?"

"That's right."

"Sorry. I don't know."

"You don't know! Then I can't lend it to you."

"Mom!" Ningning took her mother aside and spoke softly in her ear.

"James is a good guy, do you understand?"

"A good guy?"

"Yes. He's helped me a lot, this last year."

"He helped you?"

"That's right. I wouldn't be alive today if he hadn't."

"Did anything happen to you?"

"No. Nothing's happened. What I'm saying is, he's a real good guy. He has a big business deal lined up and he needs money. Mom, help him just this once, won't you?"

"How can I lend you any money when you don't even know what kind of business it is?"

"Mom! I really don't know. But I can promise you he's a good guy and he'll make good on the deal, and he'll return the money to you."

"Ask him what kind of business it is."

"All right. Hey, James! what kind of business are you in?"

"Big business. It'll get me a lot of money." James had one leg up on the other knee and spoke very cockily.

"Did you get that, Mom? It's big business. Do it for my sake and lend me the money!"

"How much?"

"Only a hundred thousand dollars."

"One hundred thousand!"

"Why, is that a lot?"

"You'll have to talk to your dad!"

Ningning stole a glance at James, who stuck out five fingers. "Fifty thousand, then." Ningning had quick reflexes.

"Fifty thousand is still a large figure. You must wait for your dad."

"OK, then let's go!"

James stood up. Taking Ningning by the waist, he started to leave.

Yan followed them to the door. "You should wait for your dad," she said to Ningning.

"Never mind!"

Ningning walked away without looking back. Yan could hear James telling Ningning, "Your Mom's a crack-pot!"

With screaming tires the black sports car zoomed out of the driveway.

- 18 -

Qiming and Yan closed their account books at the end of another year and smiled at one another. They'd made a profit again. After deducting all costs, overheads and taxes they had cleared several hundred thousand dollars.

As they looked at one another, however, they were also a bit worried. Where would they put all that money?

In the bank, at eight percent interest?

Only fools do that. In stocks? Too risky. You don't fool around with those things. In a restaurant? They didn't know the first thing about the food business. Eating it, yes; but making it, hardly. And if you aren't a pro in the business you're liable to go on the rocks. The longer Qiming thought about it, the more he felt that the safest thing to do was to put it in real estate.

A house doesn't run away, nor does land. They'll always be sitting there nice and solid. And if things don't work out and you have to sell, you don't lose too much on the deal.

These days, he'd had his eye on a new commercial building. The location wasn't too bad and the building itself was fine. Qiming kept going to look at it, like he'd look at a pretty girl. According to the rough reckonings he made on his pocket calculator the worst thing that could happen was that he'd break even. He'd heard all kinds of stories about such-and-such a person striking it rich in real estate, or such-and-such a person buying a commercial building for a few hundred thousand and seeing it turn into a property worth millions in less than no time. If you see a house you like, get it fast.

Yan didn't like the idea. "You're never satisfied," she said. "You're always hankering after the birds in the bush."

"But we can't keep that money sitting around or just look at it as if it were a pretty picture," he protested.

"You have three hundred thousand in cash, and you want to buy a building worth more than two million? You must be nuts."

"I'm not one of those old Chinese immigrants who'll take out only five dollars when they have ten. You never get rich if you're always scared and stick to small business."

"But isn't it too risky?"

"In business you've got to take risks. Nobody's going to bring things to you on a platter," said Qiming. "We're in the United States now. If we don't take risks we'll be back where we started."

"But you can only pay ten percent of the price of that building. No bank is going to lend you that much money."

"I've already asked around. My lawyer tells me that with my business and my credit history I can get a loan without any problem."

"I still say you'd better give it more thought," said Yan.

"What thought? This is an opportunity. If we don't grab it, if we let it get away for others to get rich on, nobody will cry but us."

"But how will you be able to keep your present business going if you don't have anything left for working funds?"

"Sure I will," replied Qiming. "Business has been good these last two years, and we've only to keep up our deliveries for the cash to roll in. Forget about working funds. We won't have any problems."

No problems? Really no problems?

Qiming was, after all, a business novice who'd been in the States less than ten years. Even though he was clever, resourceful and shrewd, he didn't know much about the American economy and its regularities and cycles—when it would be up or down or strong or weak. Canny old businessmen were tightening up their finances—shortening their lines of defense, so to speak—in readiness for the economic slump that was in the offing. They knew that when economic development peaked out another slump was due to come.

Things had worked out too easily for Qiming in the United States, and he was too sure of himself. Acting purely on an impulse, he got a loan and bought the building. He had no idea that there'd soon be a storm that would give him a good soaking. The very next day after he signed the purchase contract he started to fill in registration forms and contact acquaintances who might be able to help him lease the building out.

He had to rent that building out quickly. If he didn't, it would burn him as though he were holding a red hot poker. Every month he would be paying the bank almost ten thousand dollars on his loan. That wouldn't be a problem if he rented out the building. It just meant taking a bit less profit. What if it didn't get rented out? Then he'd have to pay for the loan out of his pocket. And supposing that building got stuck in his hands, it wouldn't take long, a few months at most, for the thing to drag him down. And then the bank would come and take it back. All of it.

One week passed. Two weeks passed. Three weeks!

Never mind renting the building, not a single person showed up even to ask about the price.

Worrying, wasn't it! But what good did it do to worry! Qiming walked into the empty building and wandered about aimlessly. The walls of the new building were still a bit damp and gave off a musty smell. His footsteps rang loudly in the empty corridors. The heating hadn't been turned on since there were no tenants, and a cold draft chilled him to the marrow. Turning up the collar of his overcoat, he went to a window and looked out.

Few pedestrians or cars were to be seen on the street. Children were playing in a primary school on the other side of the street, and the kind of noise that only schools produce floated to his ears. Qiming vaguely understood that he'd made a mistake. He drove back to his office and drafted another renting notice.

COMMERCIAL BUILDING FOR RENT

For rent: 10,000 square feet of floor space. Excellent location. New, fully-equipped building. First story faces 18th Street. Has large shopping area suitable for stores, restaurants, beauty parlors, grocery stores and other small and medium-sized businesses. Moderate rentals. Second story has offices with southern exposure, well-illuminated and equipped with heating and air conditioning. Available for rent to law, accountancy, insurance, real estate and other firms at low rates. Apartments on third story. Basement may bė used as warehouse. Limited area available. First come first served. Tel.: 718-463-5381. Ask for Wang Qiming.

Qiming made a number of copies and faxed them to the major local papers. He felt somewhat more at ease after he'd done this.

For the next several days he sat in his office without budging, his eyes riveted on the two white telephones. He stared at them all day until his eyes began to smart. If he wasn't able to rent out the building he'd be out of pocket for four hundred dollars per day, and four hundred a day was no small figure.

Who wouldn't be worried?

He'd already used up all his working funds and the end of the month was just around the corner. Banks were hard-hearted taskmasters. They made you pay interest for every day your payments were late. The first month you failed to pay up, they immediately sent you a yellow warning slip. The second month it was red slip. And if they didn't see your money by the third month they'd repossess the building. Qiming broke out in a cold sweat at the thought of this. He ran around in circles like an ant on a hot frying pan.

What else could he do but run around in circles?

This time, Yan didn't pour any oil on the flames. She merely advised him to be patient, to wait a bit longer. Now and then he did get a couple of phone calls, but either the location wasn't suitable or the price wasn't right. And before Qiming could offer a lower price the other side would hang up. Then things really became serious.

One Monday, the New York stock exchange took a header and stock prices plummeted. Black Monday. Right after that, the papers and the TV reported the folding up of large and small enterprises. News programs were full of such items as the sale of the Rockefeller Center and the financial problems of real estate tycoon Donald Trump.

Qiming, who never read anything apart from the entertainment pages and China reports, now put on his reading glasses and spent hours poring over the financial columns. All he found was bad news. Restaurant auctions. Government takeovers of factories. Even the high-and-mighty automobile industries and airline companies were going bankrupt one after another. Thousands upon thousands of unsold and unsalable cars stood in endless rows on the huge wharfs of Port Elizabeth.

Everywhere, mountains of home electrical appliances were put on sale. Large discounts were given even for such things as milk, bread and meat products. Bosses' faces became ashen, and people walking on the streets didn't smile anymore.

One day, Qiming went to the office of his old business partner Antonio. Antonio, too, had prospered. The little display room he'd once rented couldn't hold a candle to this large and luxurious office suite.

The two cups of coffee on the desk were already cold, but no one had touched them. Smoking wasn't allowed. Qiming was automatically flipping a book of matches over and over in his hand.

Antonio walked back and forth, wearing an ambiguous expression on his face. The atmosphere in the office was very oppressive.

It was Antonio who broke the silence at last. "You know, too, that the market is in a depressed state just now," he said. "And there's nothing we can do."

"I know that."

"It's hard to do business. I'm having a difficult time."

"But I can't make any profit with the price you're offering. Not a cent. What'll I exist on?"

Antonio winked one of his blue eyes.

"Don't play games, Mr. Wang," he said gently. "You can make some money. Yes, you can. Only, you'll make less than before. A little less."

"I'd like to..."

"Please continue."

"To add two dollars to the price of each piece."

"We've worked together seven years, Mr. Wang. Seven years is a long time. I know you, and you know me. If you don't take this order, I'll have to go to another contractor. Orders aren't easy to find, these days."

Antonio's tones weren't any harder than usual, but the threat in them was at once evident.

Qiming reflected a moment, then made up his mind. "All right, I accept your price. But you must let me have at least two thousand pieces. Those are my terms. If not, I won't take the order."

Antonio did some mental arithmetic, then smiled. "You're in luck," he said. "I can give you that many."

"Is it a deal, then?"

"It's a deal!" Antonio looked pleased. "Sign here."

Qiming reckoned that he could still make a profit, even if the price was low, by doing more work. Forget about profits, you weren't doing badly in these times if you didn't show a loss—and if you could find work to do. With a big order like this he could meet his expenses. Even if he failed to rent out the building, he could make up the deficit with the profit on this order and just about break even. He told the good news to Yan. She, however, was aghast.

"Two thousand pieces in thirty days!" she exclaimed. "You must be joking!"

"If I hadn't taken the order, there are plenty of others who would. Making some profit is always better than not having anything to do."

"We don't have enough workers."

"Hire more. There are lots of unemployed workers. People are easier to find than work nowadays."

"But we don't know what kind of work the new workers will be capable of doing," said Yan. "Management will be difficult with more people, and with so little time we won't be able to ensure quality. What'll we do if there are too many defectives and the client refuses to pay? Besides, we won't have enough money for salaries and to buy wool even if we sell our three houses!"

Yan had a point there. He was taking a big risk. But he'd already come this far. There was nothing he could do but to go ahead with the job.

That commercial building was costing him four hundred dollars every day! "We'll have to get this order out even if we die trying. Otherwise we're at a dead end."

"But..." Yan was hesitant.

"No buts. If you don't want to do it, I will. I'm not afraid of suffering or dying even though you may be!" That's the kind of person he was. He could become very unreasonable when he was angry.

Seeing that Qiming had gone into a bullish mood and was set on doing the job, Yan realized she couldn't change his mind. "What say we sell that commercial building?" She kept her voice down, trying to discuss things with him.

"Well, well! How clever of you! Who the hell sells property in such times, unless he's crazy or a fool? Haven't you noticed that prices for real estate are falling by the day? Never since the world was created have they ever dropped so low. It's absolutely weird. That lousy real estate broker must have seen that something like this was coming up, so he dumped that building that nobody wants on me. The bastard suckered me, that's what!" Utterly depressed, Qiming broke into curses: "I fuck his grandmother!"

Hiring people was easy, just as Qiming had predicted. The moment his help wanted ad appeared in the papers, they swarmed in on the factory, filling the workshop and the grounds.

Qiming couldn't help feeling somewhat self-satisfied when he saw all these people and reflected that they'd all be listening to him. With his overcoat draped over his shoulders, he stood at the door of his office and began to speak with the studied restraint of a typical boss.

"Welcome to all of you!" He cleared his voice. "You all must know that business is bad this year. I've accepted an order although the payment is low. I did it so that you would have work to do and earn some money. Since the payment is low, however, you'll all have to help me take up the slack."

None of the workers spoke. They were waiting for what would follow. For the most important part.

"Times are difficult, and so I'll have to adjust your wages downward a bit. Two fifty less for each sweater, and three dollars less for each outfit. Those of you who want the work can come forward to draw your wool and patterns. If any of you don't want the job, you're free to refuse it. I'll make up the money to you when business picks up next year."

To hear him talking, you'd think all he'd said was so honest and straightforward, and said so unwillingly. But the older workers sensed they were being cheated somehow. The whole thing smelled like a rip-off. The workers standing at the back of the crowd began to shuffle and mutter among themselves.

"That guy's got a black heart all right! He's exploiting us, that's what!"

"It adds up to less than four dollars an hour. Nothing doing!"

"Might as well take it. After all, it's the same everywhere this year. You can't blame him."

"I'm taking the job. Anything's better than sitting around doing nothing."

Qiming watched the workers debating among themselves. Although he was too far to hear their exact words he knew what they were saying.

"As I've said," he raised his voice. "Those of you who want the work can ask Xiumei or Shen Ping for wool. Those who don't want the job are free to leave."

Qiming took such a tough line because he figured that very few of them would refuse his offer. Making his way through the crowd, he left the factory. He'd guessed right. Not one of the workers walked away; all went to get some wool.

When all the workers had drawn their wool, Xiumei said to Shen Ping: "I don't know what's come over him. He ought to know that with the rates and deadline he's accepted, things are sure to go wrong."

"I agree with you," said Shen Ping. "Nobody's going to do the work properly at low rates like these. I bet there'll be a whole lot of defectives, and he'll be stuck with them this time. I can't feel sorry for him. But I do feel sorry for his wife."

Yan had already taken off her expensive overcoat and her Rolex, and had pitched into the job with the other workers. Perspiration streaked her make-up, but she didn't have time to repair it. She'd known before what it was to bear hardships; and she was ready to do it again. And she didn't complain about it.

In line with the old division of work between them, Yan managed the factory while Qiming looked after the business side. Now, he walked out the factory, looked at his watch and got into his car. He was going to see Ah Chun, but first he gave her a call. He was hoping to find some comfort with Ah Chun, and moreover that she would let him have thirty or forty thousand dollars if she could spare it.

The car passed through Manhattan and the Holland Tunnel into New Jersey. Another half hour's drive on Highway 19 brought Qiming to Ah Chun's new Hunan Garden.

He was still quite far from the restaurant when he saw Ah Chun standing at the door and waving to him. She looked elegant and distinguished in her black ermine coat. Stepping hard on the accelerator, he sped up to her.

He had hardly stopped the car when Ah Chun opened a door to get in. "Is it cold!" she said as she sat down, shivering, beside Qiming. She thrust her icy hands under his collar.

"Hey! Take them out!" He yelped, laughing.

She merely giggled and pushed her hands deeper.

Qiming pulled her hands down against his chest and warmed them with the heat from his body. Slipping forward, she raised her face to his.

"I've missed you a lot," said Qiming, kissing her.

"In trouble again? I know you wouldn't come to me without a reason."

Qiming smiled. He lowered his head to kiss her again, but she turned her face away saying, "Not here!"

She pointed toward the restaurant. "Let's go."

"Where to?"

"Let's elope!"

"What!"

"Frightened you, didn't I!" She sat up and took off her coat, revealing a thin, close-fitting sweater.

The warmth in the car, after the cold air outside, brought a rosy flush to Ah Chun's cheeks and made her look especially spirited and lovely.

"Well, where do you want to go?" asked Qiming.

"To Atlantic City."

"To gamble?"

"To try my luck."

Since it was only a two-hour drive from Ah Chun's restaurant, Qiming agreed and started the car. The sedan flew at sixty-five miles per hour along the pencil-straight highway leading to Atlantic City. As the car was new and the road surface well maintained, the ride felt smooth and comfortable. Qiming drove with one hand and with the other held Ah Chun's hand. Naughtily, she tickled his palm with her fingers.

"We'll get in a crash," smiled Qiming.

"Then we'll die together," she replied coquettishly.

"I don't know what to make of you, Ah Chun. First you want to elope, then you want to die together with me. You're like a cloud, a patch of mist that a person can't touch or lay hold of."

"Huh! I'm not a schoolgirl any more. That stuff from Ch'iung Yao[1] doesn't send me."

Qiming wondered why he felt so much younger when he was with Ah Chun. He seemed to go back twenty years to the time he was a young boy; his words and actions were not at all like those of a mature man.

"All right," said Ah Chun, "Today I'll give you a chance to unburden yourself. Say whatever you want to say. I won't interrupt."

So saying, she kicked off her shoes and placed her silk-stockinged feet on top of the dashboard. Her thin skirt rode up, revealing white thighs. It wasn't a weekend and very few cars were to be seen on the highway to Atlantic City. They seemed to be sailing in a solitary boat on a vast, lonely ocean.

Qiming ordered his thoughts and tried not to look like a nervous youngster. "Ah Chun," he said. "I love you."

Ah Chun's only response was to wiggle her toes inside the silk stockings.

"It's true. I love you. I've always wanted, dreamed of having a woman like you. You're intelligent, beautiful, capable, virtuous, reasonable, understanding."

Ah Chun giggled. "Can't you think of any better words?" she asked.

"It's true, Ah Chun. You don't think I'm deceiving you, do you?"

---

[1] A Taiwanese authoress whose romantic novelettes are very popular with teenagers.

"Even if you were, what you're saying is nice to listen to. Women all like to be flattered, and I'm no exception. Go on talking!"

"Can't you be serious?"

"Of course I can. I like to be serious."

"I first met you nearly ten years ago, the day after I landed in the United States. Since then you've been enormously helpful to me, both materially and spiritually. I owe everything I am today to your help."

"Ah Chun, I sympathize with your personal situation, but at the same time I'm afraid you'll marry someone else some day and go far away from me. I can't bear to think of that, because I can't do without you. Maybe you think I'm selfish, but I don't care. If one day you meet another man, I'll do everything possible to break up your relationship. And if you marry him, I'll come at night to your house and steal you out of your bed."

Ah Chun tightened her grip on his hand and leaned her head against his shoulder. At such times a woman's intelligence level probably goes down to zero. She suddenly lost control of herself and turned in her seat to hug and kiss him. Wildly, she kissed his face, nose, mouth, eyes. Qiming's line of vision was cut off.

The car swerved drunkenly first one way and then the other on the highway.

"Do you really want us to die together?" he almost shouted.

Ah Chun ignored his warning.

"Let's die! Let's die!" she murmured as she continued to kiss him.

Qiming stopped the car on the shoulder of the highway, letting other cars zoom past them. They fell into an ardent embrace, kissing frenziedly, caressing each other. In broad daylight, on the exposed shoulder of the highway, they tumbled onto the narrow back seat of the car.

"I love you," he said, panting.

"I love you, too."

"I need you."

"I need you, too."

No other words interrupted their frantic kisses. The car's tires flattened rhythmically under the lightly bouncing chassis.

- 19 -

Caesar,s Palace sits in gilded glory on the banks of the Atlantic Ocean. The throngs of people and cars passing in and around the area and the atmosphere of prosperity make it seem somehow insulated from the recession.

New Yorkers like to gamble. Actually, the Chinese are even greater gamblers, and world-famous as such. As you look around the casino, half the faces you see are Asian, and you can tell without asking that eight or nine out of every ten of these people are either Chinese or Korean. The Chinese are very much at home in the casino; they seem to be more comfortable here than in their own houses.

Special attention is shown to Chinese by the casino's manager, and even the bikini-clad girl attendants are extra cordial and hospitable to people with Asian features. That's because everyone here knows that the Chinese gamble big, and they hand out generous tips at the gaming tables without batting an eye.

These Chinese—proprietors, employees, chefs, women clothing workers—come from their restaurants and garment sweatshops to give their hard-earned money back to the United States. Old Chinese immigrants, some who have toiled all their lives, hand in all their paychecks at the gaming table. Ask them why they do it, and they smile at you and say: "It's like making small deposits in the bank and then taking out a lump sum. Sooner or later I'll get it all back."

Qiming and Ah Chun, both using their own credit cards, bought 2,500 dollars worth of chips and went to a table to play twenty-one—what the Americans call black-jack. It wasn't too different from the game called Ten-and-a-Half Qiming used to play in Beijing, except that here the number of winning points was twenty-one. The house was the bank. That was the rule and there was no getting around it. Ten people sat at each table.

As soon as Ah Chun sat down she began to place her bets. Each time she put down three or four ten-dollar chips, which meant winning or losing thirty or forty bucks a go.

Since this was the first time Qiming was playing blackjack, he stood behind Ah Chun to see when she asked for cards and when she stopped. Anybody catches on if he looks at the game for ten minutes, and Qiming was sharper than most people. After watching for less than ten minutes, he was itching to go. So he sat at the table and put down four chips.

Forty dollars. Not much, but not too little either for a beginner.

Ah Chun flashed a smile at him. "Take it easy," she whispered. "Go slow."

Qiming winked at her. In the time it took him to light up a cigarette the four chips had become ten. He'd won with a full twenty-one points at the very first go. Before he could say anything the dealer had pushed six chips toward him.

He was lucky. By the time he'd gathered up the chips the dealer had already finished dealing. Qiming took a drag from his cigarette, and while he was blowing the smoke out again the ten chips had turned into twenty-five chips. He'd again made twenty-one points.

Lucky. Fantastically lucky! Qiming was ecstatic. In just a few minutes his original capital of forty dollars had gone up to two hundred and fifty dollars! Who'd have thought it possible! Where else could one make so much money in such a short time?

"Go slow, play small!"

Who was talking to him? He looked around and saw it was Ah Chun.

"Go slow," she quietly advised him. "Play small."

He listened to her. Raking in his two hundred or more chips, he put four of them back. He'd started up again with a forty-dollar bet. Very soon he had a pile of chips in front of him, so many he couldn't count them.

He noticed that Ah Chun's bets were getting bigger. He, too, increased his bets.

Ah Chun took a few quick puffs at her cigarette, then put down twenty chips. Qiming promptly followed suit. No luck! After counting up the points the dealer swept away their chips.

Qiming glanced at Ah Chun. She still looked very calm. Taking a quick drag from her cigarette, she placed forty chips on the table. He did the same.

Qiming was a bit nervous. His heart was thumping. The first card was dealt. Ah Chun got a king. Qiming was just after her with a queen. The dealer had an eight. The crucial second cards were turned up. Amazing! Both Ah Chun and Qiming had aces.

"Great!" Ah Chun couldn't help crying out. Funny thing is, nothing can stop a streak of gambling luck. By three o'clock in the afternoon, both had taken in more than ten thousand dollars.

Qiming was tickled pink. Everything else was forgotten—the empty commercial building, the order being rushed out at the factory, all forgotten.

Pretty attendants bought them cigarettes and drinks, and the manager came to congratulate them on their success. Shaking hands with them, he said, "You're a lucky couple." He gave them two vouchers, one for a full course dinner and the other for a luxurious suite, both free.

Ah Chun and Qiming exchanged their chips for cash, which they carefully put away in their pockets. Then they went to the dining area where they had their fill of steak and lobster. They also drank more than half a bottle of champagne.

"We were quite lucky today," said Ah Chun, wiping her lips with a napkin. "But remember, don't come to this place too often. Now and then is all right, but you're a goner if you make a habit of it. Plenty of people who do it go bankrupt and sell everything they own."

Qiming nodded. "Don't worry, I won't come very often."

"Gambling is purely a matter of luck. Today we played small. If we'd gone for big stakes we could have won a hundred or two hundred thousand dollars. A nervy person who rides his luck might even have made half a million or a million."

Qiming's eyes glistened.

"But never gamble greedily, or too long. Learn control. People who can't control themselves are always losers, and those are the people casinos like best. Why do you think they're giving us free food and lodgings? They want us to go on gambling."

"They don't like it if you take your money and leave?"

"Of course not."

"Then let's play a bit longer." Qiming hadn't had enough yet.

"No," Ah Chun said firmly.

"But with the luck we've been having we might win a lot more. A person doesn't always have such luck."

Ah Chun was, after all, a gambler herself. She looked at her watch; it wasn't even three o'clock yet. "On one condition, then," she said. "We put away the money we started with and don't touch it."

Qiming nodded happily. The two went back to their old table. This time around, Ah Chun went for really big stakes, each time betting a thousand dollars. Qiming wasn't to be outdone. So let it be a thousand! In any case the money was coming out of his earlier winnings.

But when your luck goes away, it's gone. Their cards were nothing to look at and got worse with each deal. Either they were too small or they busted before the dealer's did. Their piles of chips shrank, layer by layer, and when you're betting a thousand a throw, ten grand gives you only ten chances. In nothing flat they had only three thousand left. Qiming was seeing red, and even Ah Chun lost her cool. The more they lost, the harder it was to stop and the crazier they got. They both staked their last three thousand—six thousand in all—and put them in the same square.

The dealer calmly dealt his cards. The first was a nine. Not too bad. The dealer had a six, smaller than theirs. The next card they got was an eight, making a total of seventeen points. This figure, neither high nor low, was a difficult one to cope with. If they asked for another card and got anything bigger than a four, the six thousand dollars would go down the drain. Seeing that the dealer also had a poor card—a ten, Ah Chun made a sign that she wasn't taking any more cards.

The dealer now had sixteen points. Since he had less than seventeen, the rules required him to take another card. This was the crucial moment and both Qiming and Ah Chun waited tensely for his third card. The dealer deliberately took his time dealing the last card. Time seemed to stop.

Unhurriedly, the dealer turned over the card. Qiming and Ah Chun were dumbstruck. From where did he get such goddamn luck! He actually had a five, bringing his total to exactly twenty-one points. The dealer swept his hand over the table and their six thousand dollars were gone.

"Shit!" exclaimed Ah Chun.

Qiming said nothing, but thought to himself, "The motherfucker!"

Neither Qiming nor Ah Chun said much on the way home. They'd expended too much energy at the casino and now felt washed out. Qiming was driving on the slow lane. Ah Chun leaned against his shoulder and gazed blankly at the pencil-straight road in front of them.

"Well, we can't complain," said Qiming to liven up the atmosphere a bit. "We didn't lose anything at least, and we had a good time with a free meal and free games thrown in. But we'd certainly have lost our money if you hadn't put those controls on it."

"Gambling is controllable."

"Then what isn't?"

"One's feelings."

Qiming hadn't expected this.

"I love you very much," continued Ah Chun. "You don't know it, but actually I miss you much more than you miss me."

"Don't be so sure."

"I'm quite sure. You have a wife and a family. I don't have anything. I'm always alone, always lonely. I know our relation is more a matter of necessity than of love. In actual fact..."

"You shouldn't talk that way," protested Qiming.

"In actual fact," said Ah Chun, ignoring the interruption, "our relation is merely a union of two lonesome people, a meeting of two lonely souls. It isn't all real love. There's a large element of necessity in it."

"No, Ah Chun. I really love you."

"Really? Would you be able to leave Yan for me? Would you have the heart to put her in a state where she'd be unable to survive? Of course not. You and I are mature people. We cannot deceive ourselves."

"Deceive ourselves?"

"You can't, and neither can I. I'd feel like a criminal if I broke up your marriage, because that would be like killing Yan. Moreover, assuming we did get married, I'd face the same fate as Yan, wouldn't I?"

"What do you mean?"

"Do I have to spell it out? I've learned my lesson. I know very well what goes on in men's hearts, in the hearts of men who have money, in the hearts of American men, and in the hearts of rich men in America."

"But I..."

"But you're different, is that it?" said Ah Chun, not letting him speak. "You're different from those men because you come from mainland China where the education one gets is different, where one grows up in a simple environment and one's mental make-up is less sophisticated. Is that what you want to say? Well, you're wrong. The fact is, you've become the same as them. Don't you realize enormous changes have taken place in you?"

"The changes..."

"In spite of it all, I can't control my feelings. No force can stop me from missing you. I need you."

"Just as I need you. But I don't see that there's such a big gap between love and necessity..."

"A love that doesn't have an outcome is perhaps sweeter than one that does."

Qiming took Ah Chun back to the restaurant, then drove home with his foot hard on the accelerator. He'd already gone into the house when he remembered that Yan was still at the factory. He immediately gave her a call.

"I have to work tonight," shouted Yan over the line. "Fix yourself something to eat. It looks like we'll have to work late every day after the first batch goes out."

"But you have to get some sleep at least. Tell Xiumei to stand in for you for a while."

"I can't. We're both needed here." Yan hung up.

Qiming dropped on the couch and lay thinking for a long time.

...

The commercial building stood as before, cold and deserted. No one came to rent or ask about it, or even made an inquiry over the phone. Frequent calls did come from the wool factory, however—three or four calls a day, all on the same subject. Payments.

But these were dealt with without too much trouble. What worried Qiming most was that the workers, who got their wages on a biweekly basis, were due to be paid soon. He was very much aware of the importance of paying them promptly. If ever they didn't get their pay they'd drop whatever they were doing and walk out on you without so much as a beg-your-pardon. Then you'd be left with a hodgepodge of half-finished garments and not enough time to get them fixed up.

Qiming was really anxious now. He didn't have a single dollar in working funds and was counting on this delivery for the money to meet payroll. He glanced at the calendar, although he didn't need to look at it to know that the delivery had to go out today for the cash to come in. He didn't care how much there'd be, as long as it covered the wages.

His mailbox was stuffed with statements on his loan interest, which was snowballing at a frightening rate. He knew only too well what it meant to go bankrupt. As soon as you did, the IRS would come to close down your factory. Nor would the workers let you off; they'd be quite capable of taking or dismantling anything large or small that could be exchanged for cash.

And when that happened, the sight of the empty workshop and the scraps of paper and wool lying around on the floor would be enough to make a grown man cry. And nobody would give a damn about you!

Qiming got so worked up thinking such thoughts he couldn't sit at home any longer and hotfooted it to the factory.

"Faster! Faster! Today's a weekend." He chased around the workshop, urging everyone to get cracking. The workers could see that Wang Laoban was having a bad case of nerves, and they pitched in with all they had.

Yan worked so hard to get the delivery ready by three in the afternoon she was staggering on her feet and looked ready to break down. This delivery had really taken it out of her. She was two sizes smaller around the waist, she'd lost so much weight. She hadn't gone home once to sleep over the last ten days. At night, when she really couldn't take any more, she'd go to Qiming's office to lie down on a bench and close her eyes for a while. And she didn't have any time for regular meals, either. She kept a few cookies in her pockets and took out a couple whenever she felt hungry.

It was after two in the afternoon now. Qiming looked at his watch. "Can we make it?"

Yan was counting the items. "Yes, we can," she replied. She was quite positive about that, even though her voice was faint and she seemed to have difficulty concentrating.

Watching her pale face, Qiming sensed a sudden compassion as well as a certain ardor. He felt that she was his guardian angel. He wanted to hold her in his arms and tell her about all the remorse and pain and love he had in his heart.

Exactly three o'clock. Yan saw to it that the goods were promptly loaded. Qiming started the car and drove off. Only then did Yan allow herself to relax. She wiped the sweat on her forehead with the back of her hand, then called Xiumei.

"What is it, Yan?" Xiumei, too, was so tired she was swaying on her feet.

Yan handed her a wad of bills. "Go to a good Chinese restaurant and order enough food for everyone. All of us must have a good meal and get some rest."

"Sure," said Xiumei.

"And don't forget to buy something to drink."

"I won't."

That evening the workers had a great time at the restaurant, eating, laughing and talking. All agreed it was a pleasure to work with Yan and that it didn't matter that the work was tiring sometimes because one felt good.

Yan hardly listened to such praise. She kept her wine glass pressed to her forehead. And she actually dozed off sitting at the table, something she'd never done before.

- 20 -

Qiming drove the fully loaded car at a speed of seventy-five miles an hour. Although the car, was only a year old, it couldn't handle heavy loads at such crazy speeds and the engine was making funny noises.

Things always turn out all right in the end, he thought. Now that they had managed to get this delivery out on time, the first move was to settle the salary problem and forget everything else. Two weeks later, when the entire order was completed and all the money was in, he'd make the payments on the bank loan. He'd be a few days late on those payments but that didn't matter too much. At most he'd have to pay a small penalty. His luck was holding out. These thoughts put Qiming in a good mood and he started to whistle a tune.

After the goods had been checked out and put away, Qiming went to Antonio's office to get his check. But things didn't go as smoothly as he had imagined they would. Antonio's words gave him a shock.

"My dear Mr. Wang," Antonio was being unusually formal today. "There's one thing I have to make clear to you. The American economy is in very bad shape right now and the big stores that take my goods aren't paying on time. I'm being victimized. I can't get enough money."

"Enough money? What for?"

"For paying you."

"You mean..."

"I can only pay you a quarter of what I owe you." Antonio spread his hands helplessly. "I'll make up the full sum to you when I get my money back."

Qiming was furious. Ignoring their eight-year friendship and future business prospects, he jumped up and started to shout. "You bastard! If you don't pay me all my money today, you won't get another sweater out of me!"

"Very well." Anyone could see that Antonio was much more experienced than Qiming, and more level-headed. "I'm not paying you a single cent today."

"I'll...sue you!"

Antonio wasn't bothered by such threats. "Go ahead and sue me," he said, still smiling. "But I must remind you that I can sue you, too, for breach of contract, since you first threatened to withhold deliveries. Don't forget your signature is on the contract."

He's a hard one, thought Qiming. He doesn't pay me, and he wants to sue me. The son of a bitch. But Qiming realized it was no use taking a tough line, and he'd have to change tactics. Don't pick any bones with him, he told himself, it won't do you any good. Best avoid a head-on confrontation.

Qiming changed his tone. "I think we still have to work together," he said. "Maybe we should meet each other halfway, to get both of us over our difficulties. That's the thing that counts most."

Seeing that Qiming had backed down, Antonio showed signs of relenting and looking for a compromise. After a lot of wangling and haggling he agreed to pay a third of the money, or forty thousand dollars.

Back in his car, Qiming yelled and swore for several minutes before calming down. Forty thousand. That wouldn't solve all his problems but he could at least pay some of the workers who needed money most. He'd have to beg the regulars to bear with him another two weeks. He'd get them to help him out even if he had to eat humble pie. As for the bank and the wool factory, well, they'd just have to wait.

As he drove off, Qiming muttered curses at Antonio. All these years Qiming had given the guy plenty of assistance and helped him make a good deal of money. Antonio had come a long way since the days he'd rented that shabby showroom and that measly little apartment. His showroom today was like an exhibition hall and his villa was a fucking palace! After all I, Qiming, have done for him, he turns around and kicks me in the teeth.

Suddenly a thought flashed through Qiming's mind. Yes, that was a good idea! From his car he called up the factory. He heard Yan's weary tones in the receiver. "Did you get it?" asked Yan.

"Half of it."

"What? Only half of the money?"

"Well, maybe less than a half."

"But how will we pay the workers?"

"I'll find some way. Yes, I know I can."

"Suit yourself."

Yan had hung up. Qiming drove onto the highway. It was getting dark and the trees on both sides were black shadows. He turned on the headlights to see better. The light beam swept across a road sign. On it was the legend: ATLANTIC CITY

Right, that was where he was going. To gamble. To win some money and pay back his debts. He was taking a risk, of course, a terrible risk. Still he had to give it a try. He had no other choice. To calm his nerves he slid the tape Ah Chun had given him into the cassette player and listened to the music. It was that country song:

> If you love him
> Send him to New York,
> 'Cause that's where Heaven is.
> If you hate him
> Send him to New York,
> 'Cause that's where Hell is...

He'd learned the song by heart and now he hummed along with the singer. The melody filled him with bitter-sweet memories. He sang the song over and over again. Less than two hours later an aura of light appeared over the shore of the Atlantic. The glow grew brighter until the entire night sky took on a pale white color. Atlantic City.

As it was a Saturday, Caesar's casino was chock-full of weekend gamblers. A mass of bobbing heads, cigarette smoke, noise and commotion filled the entire establishment. Qiming made straight for the gambling area and without a second thought sat down at a table. He bought ten thousand dollars' worth of chips at a single go. You could see a sort of wild recklessness in his manner. He asked a girl attendant for a glass of brandy and took a gulp from it. Then, without daring to think about the desperate encounter that lay ahead, he took the plunge.

He placed his bet.

The very first one was for a thousand dollars. People around the table looked at him. Apart from surprise, you could read in their eyes envy of his money and admiration at the big way he was gambling. The round ended. He had won. One thousand had become two thousand.

Qiming was feeling more sure of himself now. He didn't take back the two thousand but bet the whole amount. The second time he made a "blackjack." He now had five thousand.

His hand was shaking a bit. He wanted to stop for a while. He seemed to hear Ah Chun telling him to play small and go slow. He waggled his hand at the dealer, indicating that he'd skip the next round. But it just happened that the dealer blew his cards this time and had to pay up all around. Excited shouts broke from all the players at the table. "Hell," thought Qiming. "I missed that chance. Shouldn't have chickened out."

When the dealer's got a run of bad luck, then's your chance to get rich. This time he bet five thousand dollars. But unluckily for Qiming, the dealer collected just one more point than he did and the five thousand went to the other side of the table.

Qiming was sweating. Too reckless this time. Steady, steady, he told himself. He went on betting a thousand at a time. This was less risky, but for the next ten rounds the chips passed backward and forward without anyone winning or losing. The game had gotten into a rut. Qiming glanced at his watch; it was already midnight. He didn't have much more time.

Play for big stakes if you want to win big money. What was that old Chinese saying? Spare the kid and catch no wolves. What the fuck! Give it a go! He bet ten thousand dollars, and had a feeling that it wasn't those chips he was staking, it was his own life. His chest tightened into a knot. Holding his breath, he stared at the cards on the table.

Turn them up.

"The old whore!" Qiming had mumbled the curse in Chinese, so no one understood what he'd said. He had lost.

Qiming nearly blacked out. He couldn't see anything apart from the chips the dealer was gathering up from the table. As he did so, the dealer smiled and said: "I'm sorry." It was enough to make a man blow his stack.

Qiming saw red. It seemed to him that a fire was burning at the base of his skull and heating his brains until they were ready to bubble. Lose? He couldn't afford to. How would he pay the workers and the bank? He had to win back his capital.

He hesitated a moment, then bet twenty thousand. Where had his luck gone?! The dealer turned over the cards and swept up the chips. "I'm sorry!" Again that blasted hypocrisy!

What to do? Leave? The last ten thousand would be safe then. But that meant leaving the other thirty thousand to these oily bastards. Qiming sprang to his feet. Gasping like a wounded bull or a police dog straining against its leash, Qiming shook all the money he had left out of his pockets. Without counting it, he scooped it up with trembling fingers and dumped it on the gaming table. Eyes bloodshot, and with veins bulging on his forehead, he riveted his stare on the cards the dealer was skimming off the deck.

His first card: a ten. The dealer's was a seven. "This time I've got you!" thought Qiming.

The next card came. He had a..."Ten!" shouted Qiming, but turning it over he saw a five.

The dealer stopped to give Qiming time to think. He had to take the gamble. With fifteen points he was dead if he didn't take a card. Squashing his cigarette he shouted "Again!"

He turned the card over. A seven. Twenty-two points. He'd blown it. He was wiped out.

He didn't curse or swear. Nor did he moan and groan. He just walked quietly through the crowds and out of the casino. He never said a word, as though he were a deaf-mute. He kept his head down like a beaten boxer.

Only when he was sitting in his car did he utter a single word. "Motherfucker!"

Who was he cursing? Maybe himself.

He started the car and was about to step on the accelerator, when he saw that the fuel indicator was close to the zero mark. He'd been in too much of a hurry on the trip out and had forgotten to fill the tank. But he had no more money now, not even a bit of loose change. He opened his wallet. There were a number of credit cards in it, but he'd used up all the credit on them. Luckily he had a gas card.

It was snowing again. He didn't dare drive very fast. The tape recorder was still playing the same country music. Listening to the lyrics, he thought they were very good. They might have been written specially for him.

New York. You're Heaven in Hell, you're also Hell in Heaven. And you might say I'm a little demon who's just about done for. He kept on reproaching himself.

The falling snow made the whole sky white. He was driving slowly. At this rate he figured it would take him four or five hours to get home. Some time around daybreak, perhaps. Damn it all, he thought, is everything I've built up since coming to New York really going up in smoke? Why is fate treating me like this?

New York! New York! You took me from nil and turned me into something. Are you going to send me back to nil again?

Qiming bitterly regretted going to the casino. How could he have goofed so badly as to go to Atlantic City!

He'd at least have those forty thousand if he hadn't gone there to gamble. Those forty thousand would have kept the workers off his back for a while. But now nothing was left.

You shouldn't have gambled! You're a son of a bitch, he told himself. You must have been out of your mind, going into something that could only make you lose the shirt off your back! Nobody's ever seen a person who's gotten rich gambling.

He stopped the car by the side of the highway and leaned his head against the steering wheel to get a moment's rest. Snow beat against the windshield, soon obscuring half of it. Qiming raised his head and switched on the wipers. The snow collapsed and fell from the windshield. Looking into the darkness before him, Qiming smiled in spite of himself. He shouldn't have gambled?

Everywhere you went people gambled, didn't they? Coming to New York had been like stepping into a big gambling establishment. Large gambling houses stood right in front your eyes. Huge racecourses weren't much farther away. The lotteries in every street and alley with results appearing daily on TV, the sweepstakes offices on every other street for everything from horse racing to football, basketball, baseball and boxing, the numbers in cigarette packs and under the bottle caps of the soft drinks you drank every day—that was gambling, too, wasn't it?

Was there any place where people didn't gamble? Was it possible not to gamble? Take your own business. Every time you made an investment or put money into a project, your feelings were the same as when you were betting your money at a gambling table, weren't they? Only nobody was there to call out: "Gentlemen, place your bets!"

And when your business opponents had you up against the wall with no escape, and were taking all your possessions away, their expressions were almost the same as that of the dealer who had swept up your chips. The only difference was, a businessman wouldn't say "I'm sorry." They never apologized for such things. No one did. Victors never deigned to apologize to the defeated. I wouldn't either, if I won.

With such thoughts in his mind, Qiming started his car again. Crunching over the snow that lay thickly on the ground, the sedan rolled back onto the highway. Yes, people gambled everywhere, and he was only a newcomer, a small-time gambler in the big gambling house called New York.

All at once, Ah Chun's words returned to him. She had said: "You'll lose sooner or later to the dealer if you play too long." He glanced at his watch. It was already five in the morning. Looking out of the windshield he realized he wasn't very far from Ah Chun's restaurant. He punched her number on his car phone. "Hello," she answered sleepily.

"Is this Ah Chun?"

"Yes."

"It's Qiming."

"Qiming? Where are you?"

He himself didn't quite know where he was. He told her the whole story of what had happened, and he felt better after this confession.

"You must be crazy!" said Ah Chun. "You're a bullheaded, blundering fool. First of all, you shouldn't have taken that order at such a low price. Secondly, you shouldn't have let your client default on so much of his payment. It was even more foolish to have gone to Atlantic City. And you mustn't think of selling that building now!"

"But I don't know what I should do."

"You're such a brainless fool! A spineless, good-for-nothing idiot! There's no way I can help you!"

"Ah Chun!"

"Do as you see fit!"

The line went dead. A feeling of hopelessness engulfed Qiming. He put down the receiver and drove on slowly. A few minutes later the phone rang. Picking up the receiver, he heard Ah Chun's voice again.

"I simply don't know what to say to you! Go home and get some sleep. I'll be waiting for you at the Queens

Boulevard Nightclub at nine tomorrow evening. Goodbye!"

- 21 -

Ningning lay under the dirty gray blanket, curled up in a ball. The floor of the damp, dark basement room was strewn with a jumble of dented tin cans, empty wine bottles and old newspapers. Cigarette butts and remnants of cookies littered the top of the wooden box beside the bed.

Ningning's teeth were chattering and a humming sound came from her nose. Her low moans were less audible than the squeaking of the rats in the walls. Stretching out a hand, she pulled the blanket over her head. If her shivering hadn't caused the blanket to tremble slightly it would have been difficult to say whether the blanket covered a living person or a corpse.

Above the basement rose a large building of a dozen or more stories, and facing the building was a trunk road with twin lanes. The building and the noisy city over her head completely smothered her moans. And even if people had heard them, few would have done anything to help her.

All day, from early morning, she'd been lying in the basement, suffering and hanging in as best she could. In the evening the door was kicked open. James walked in. He took off his leather jacket, then picked up a bottle of whiskey and took several gulps from it.

Wiping his mouth with the back of his hand, he squatted down in front of the box beside the bed. He found a dirty syringe and shakily took from his pocket a small glass phial filled with a transparent liquid. Biting off the tip of the phial, he thrust in the needle of the syringe and drew out some of the liquid.

Then, holding the syringe between his teeth, he took Ningning's left arm from under the blanket. The white skin around the veins was spotted with tiny needle marks.

James wound a rubber tube around Ningning's arm. Then he spat on the inside of her elbow and slapped it a few times. The veins quickly swelled up. He took the syringe from his mouth and stuck the needle in Ningning's arm. Without hurrying, he pushed down the plunger. The colorless, transparent liquid flowed through the needle into Ningning's veins, heart, brain.

Ningning lay motionless under the blanket. James pulled out the needle. Two or three minutes later the blanket began to move and Ningning's head slowly emerged from under it.

She sat up and rubbed her eyes woozily with the back of her hand. The blanket slipped down, revealing her well-formed little breasts. They were sagging slightly and all her ribs were clearly visible.

Ningning coughed, then threw a jacket over her shoulders and went to the washroom. James began to make preparations for injecting himself. There was the rushing sound of a toilet being flushed and Ningning came out again. She seemed to have recovered some of her girlish verve.

She noticed that James was having some difficulty doing the injection on himself. Kneeling down beside him, she took the syringe. But he apparently found her efforts at inserting the needle too slow, clumsy and painful. He shoved her aside. Ningning went back to the bed and lay down on, facing upward and completely naked.

When James had finished injecting himself he stretched lazily and approached the bed. He took off his clothes and threw himself upon Ningning, covering her body with his own. As the drug took effect they lost all control over themselves and began to rut like animals, doing things even animals wouldn't do.

After a while James said he was hungry. They dressed and went out, James grabbing his leather jacket. He lifted her onto the back seat of a motorcycle parked outside the building. Ningning's sports car had long since been exchanged for cocaine.

"Where are we going?" inquired Ningning.

"To the Queens nightclub," replied James. "Some guys are waiting for me there."

The motorcycle threaded through the stream of traffic. Ningning's hair, blown by the wind, floated up behind her. It was already ten thirty in the evening when James and Ningning together with some friends swept into the Queens Boulevard Nightclub.

Like all fashionable nightclubs, the interior was so dark as to be almost pitch-black; the only light was provided by a small flickering candle on each table. A band was making frenetic, ear-splitting noises. The pounding rhythms almost jarred people off their feet.

Peeling off their coats and jackets, James, Ningning, and their company rushed toward the dance floor. Perhaps because they'd been drinking or because they were still high on drugs they danced tirelessly, writhing and gyrating like clockwork figures with tightly wound springs. Their wild capers sent the entire dance floor into a seething frenzy. Even the musicians were goaded to greater efforts.

Qiming and Ah Chun were seated unobtrusively in a corner of the nightclub. An earnest and agitated discussion was going on between them; but because the music was too loud they had to raise their voices and continually make signs with their hands.

It was too difficult to talk this way. Ah Chun couldn't stand the noise any longer. Taking Qiming by the hand, she led him out of the ballroom to a small smoking lounge. It was deserted except for a pair of lovers necking and locked in a tight hug. The sound of the music was not too loud here.

"Then what exactly should I do?" asked Qiming. Obviously various proposals of his had already been vetoed by Ah Chun and he was becoming exasperated.

"Whatever you do, don't sue them!"

"Why not?"

"You'll be paying lawyers' fees for nothing."

"But why?"

"Listen to me. If ever you sue them, they'll at once declare you bankrupt. Then they can legally get your factory closed down and legally refuse to pay you anything. That's an old trick of theirs, and the one who'll suffer in the end is you."

"But what'll I do if Antonio defaults on the entire payment for the final delivery next week?"

"You can only keep on asking for it and wait patiently."

"Don't I have any other options?"

"Not for the time being. You must keep on getting at him and squeeze as much out of him as you can. But it's important you don't let him feel that you intend to sue him."

"But my lawyer tells me I must sue."

"What did he say?"

"He said the Yanks make a point of ripping off timid Chinese businessmen who don't know anything about commercial laws."

"You can't believe what lawyers tell you!" Ah Chun was very positive. "They don't carry daggers, but they're a bunch of brigands. Your lawyer would like nothing better than to see you sue Antonio. Where would his fees come from if you didn't? How much is he charging you?"

"Fifty percent."

"What did I tell you! Even assuming you win the case, you'll only get back fifty percent of your money. But you'd also have to first make a down payment, am I right?"

"Yes."

"Furthermore, it isn't rare for a business case like this one to drag on eight or ten years after it goes to court. And when it's settled you'll get back next to nothing—at best ten percent of the money owed you."

"By what rights?"

"By the law on legal bankruptcies. All will be legal and aboveboard. You can appeal but it won't get you anywhere."

"But that's unreasonable and unfair! Under such laws, refusing to pay up and ripping people off becomes legal, doesn't it?"

"It isn't the time now to discuss the law."

Ah Chun noticed that the cigarette between Qiming's fingers was shaking.

"Don't worry, Qiming. You have one alternative."

"What's that?"

"Declare bankruptcy."

"What kind of alternative is that!"

"It is one. If you do that, you can legally decline to pay your workers' wages, legally decline to pay the wool factory, and legally get your enterprise's debts canceled."

"But that would be ripping people off!"

"You're being ripped off yourself!" Ah Chun was annoyed by his Oriental sense of morality.

"I don't have the heart..."

"To rip others off, so you sit around and wait for others to rip you off! Forget your Chinese moral concepts. This is the United States, this is New York. Either you hold on to your Chinese ethics and get done in, or you rip others off, in which case you survive, make money and live well. The choice is yours."

Ah Chun stopped speaking. She puffed viciously at her cigarette, staring at this basically naive and honest Chinese in front of her and hating him as a mother hates a feckless son. Qiming, on his part, felt deeply ashamed of his own weakness and incompetence.

A fateful struggle was at this moment going on within him, a trial of strength between the Qiming of the past and the Qiming of the future. He sat, his head lowered, for a full five minutes. Ah Chun waited patiently, puffing at her cigarette.

Finally Qiming looked up at Ah Chun and asked, "There is no choice in this matter, is there?"

Ah Chun couldn't bear to look any longer at Qiming struggling so painfully with himself.

"You're getting too worked up," she said. "Let's go and relax a bit." She took him by the arm and led him back to the ballroom. The band was playing a soft dance tune. "Come on!" Ah Chun propelled him toward the dance floor.

"No."

"Why not? Forget everything else." They began a slow fox-trot, clasped tightly in one another's arms.

Only a few couples were on the floor; this kind of music was too classical for New York. Qiming held Ah Chun's body close to his own and pressed his cheek against hers. He felt less tense now. Gradually his worries and anxieties were forgotten, dissipated by the soft music and leisurely dance movements.

He had no idea that at this very moment his daughter was behind him and staring at him, trying to see who he was.

Ningning had been sitting and drinking at a table close to the dance pit. She was feeling tired, and anyway, she didn't like this old-fashioned music and was glad of the opportunity to sit down a while and moisten her parched throat. She'd been looking casually around, when her eyes were attracted by a familiar looking back. That hairdo, that bearing, those broad shoulders and back...

But it couldn't be. Her father wouldn't come here. Besides, the woman wasn't her mother. She turned around, clinked glasses with James and took a drink. But an unaccountable urge made her look back. The longer she stared at the man, the more it looked like him. To satisfy her curiosity and answer the questions in her mind, she hopped down onto the dance floor. It was him!

She at once returned to her seat, her pretty mouth convulsed with agitation, hatred and resentment. Qiming and Ah Chun, immersed in their own bliss, hadn't noticed her presence. The music stopped and they went back hand in hand to their table.

An indefinable rage gripped Ningning, making her body burn and her scalp tingle. She jumped up and made straight for Qiming's table. The brass and rhythm sections of the band went back to their earlier frenzy.

Ningning plumped herself down at the table, staring fixedly at Qiming as if to verify the accuracy of her observations.

Qiming was startled by this sudden and uninvited appearance. He wondered who the person was who could be so crude and discourteous. Turning to look, he received a shock.

"Dad!"

Ningning sounded as though she had seen a ghost.

"Ningning! What are you doing here?"

"You ask me!" Ningning's voice was quivering. "I'm asking you. What are you doing here?"

She looked daggers at Ah Chun.

"If I see you touching my Dad again," she said fiercely, "I'll kill you!"

Ah Chun of course knew what was unfolding before her eyes. "We're friends," she said with a pleasant smile. "There's nothing between us."

Qiming raised a hand to prevent any further remarks from Ningning. "Be polite, Ningning," he said weakly.

"Polite!" The word stung her to the quick. "I've never learned how to be polite!"

Ah Chun had no reply to that.

Nor did Qiming know what to say.

Crying, Ningning threw up her chin and made an obscene, insulting gesture at Ah Chun.

"Fuck you!" she shouted. Then, whirling around, she ran toward the exit. James and his companions hooted and jeered. Qiming hurried after Ningning.

Ah Chun walked up to the young people and scolded them, calling them a pack of cold-blooded beasts. Their only reaction to that was more catcalling.

Qiming hurried across the ballroom, but when he got to the entrance of the nightclub Ningning was nowhere to be seen. With a quick word of farewell to Ah Chun, who had hastened after him, Qiming got in his car and drove off.

Qiming drove at high speed along Highway 495. But he didn't go home at once. His thoughts were in a turmoil and his body felt feverish. The temperature was below zero outside the car but he opened the window anyway. The icy wind slashed at his face like a knife blade. Rubbing his burning cheeks, he reflected that his fortunes had really hit rock bottom.

More than a year had passed since he'd last seen Ningning, and when he did meet her it had had to happen so suddenly, and in such damning circumstances! He must explain things to his daughter and clarify everything. Maybe she'd forgive him.

Qiming groaned. When a guy was down on his luck everything hit him at the same time, as though someone had planned it that way. It was sickening. There was that commercial building he'd bought and couldn't get rid of any more, the bank's almost daily demands for loan payments, Antonio's refusal to pay him for goods deliveries, and that asinine decision to go gambling which had resulted in his being cleaned out.

He glanced out of the side window. With all the rotten breaks he'd been getting it would almost be worth his while to give the steering wheel a twist and be done with it all. At the speed he was driving it should be quite easy. Perhaps even painless.

But in the end Qiming didn't do anything of the kind. Instead, he drove home. A sense of guilt came over him when he saw the house.

As soon as the car stopped, he heard the sound of an argument going on. He stood still and listened. One of the persons was Yan, the other was his daughter Ningning.

"Don't you believe me, Mom?" Ningning was saying.

"No, I don't!" That was Yan.

"But I saw them with my own eyes. I was only that far from them—him and that woman."

"If you hate your father, Ningning, there are other ways you can show it."

"You're too kindhearted, Mom!"

"This isn't a matter of being kindhearted or not."

"Yes, it is! While you're working your fingers to the bone, he goes out and whoops it up. You're right, I don't like him. But I'm not lying, Mom!"

"What proof can you show me? I can't believe it simply because you say it is so. I know him. He's not that kind of person. He's a good husband and a good father."

"He's a two-timer, Mom. And you're going to suffer because of it."

"Please don't say such things about him, Ningning. You should know that he has enough worries as it is, what with the factory in such a mess and business so difficult. I beg you, don't add to his troubles."

"I'm no good, Mom. I didn't listen to you, I left home, I haven't gone to college. I know I'm bad. But in spite of all that I still have a conscience. I can't bear to watch him take advantage of you."

"He isn't taking advantage of me. He's a good man."

"He's a hooligan!"

A sharp crack rang out as Yan slapped Ningning's face. This was the first time Yan had ever struck anyone, let alone Ningning. That blow had been an instinctive reaction to protect her husband's reputation.

She was aghast at what she'd done. As though demented, she grabbed Ningning and shook her, crying, "Ningning, Ningning! Try to understand me! I...I cannot believe you. I'm so afraid, afraid that if what you said is true...No, Ningning! It isn't possible. You were mistaken. You must have been mistaken."

"Mom!" Ningning hugged her mother and broke into tears.

At this point Qiming opened the door. He walked stiffly into the room and, seeming not to notice that his daughter was at home, went to the couch and sat down. Ningning shook off her mother's arms.

"Mom," she said icily. "I'm going."

"Wait!" exclaimed Qiming. "I have something to say to you."

Ningning stopped and reflected a moment. "O.K., let's talk."

"Ningning!" Qiming lit a cigarette to conceal the shaking of his hands. "I hope you'll come home. I beg you to."

"That's none of your business."

"No, you're wrong. I'll make it my business."

"You have no right to do so."

Qiming did his best to sound amiable, or at least not to lose his temper. "I have the right to do so, child. You should know that I'm concerned about you..."

"What do you think you are?"

"I'm your father."

"Oh, give me a fucking break!"

"Ningning!" cried Yan. "You mustn't talk to your father like that!"

"O.K., now I understand. I'd better go."

Ningning turned around and headed for the door. Qiming stood up and tried to stop her. He put out his arm but Ningning unceremoniously shoved it aside.

"Wait a minute, Ningning!"

"No! No!"

"Ningning!"

"I hate you. I hate you both! I hate this home! I hate this family!"

Weeping and shouting, she ran out of the house. She was shaking her fist at the house even after she'd gone out into the street.

Ningning left just like that. Neither Qiming nor Yan followed her. They knew it was no use. When their daughter's curses could no longer be heard, they began to take notice of one another's existence.

He knew what she was about to say. She, too, knew what was on his mind.

"Qiming."

"Uh?"

"Is it true what Ningning said?"

So softly and timidly had she spoken that her voice had been almost inaudible; she had asked the question, afraid to do so, and fearing the answer she might get.

Qiming knelt beside her and took her hands in his. "Yan," he said. "Listen to me..."

"I only want an answer. Yes, or no?"

"Listen to me..."

"Yes or no?"

Yan gazed at him expectantly. The truth is, she was hoping he would deny everything, even hoping that he would lie to her. But as Qiming looked at her tired, thin body and pallid face, he hadn't the heart to lie to her. He gave a slight nod.

"You mean, yes?" she asked with disbelief.

He nodded again.

"My god!"

She hadn't spoken loudly; it had sounded almost like an ordinary figure of speech. But there'd been a hoarse, bleak desperation in her voice. Qiming recoiled at the sound. He didn't dare approach her again.

Yan sat a little longer, then shook her head like a dead body coming to life. She got up and went upstairs, moving her legs as though they were made of wood.

Qiming didn't follow her. He was curled up on the couch with his arms around his knees, shaking his head in utter misery and weeping soundlessly.

- 22 -

Some time later, Qiming woke up from his painful daze. He heard someone talking. Upstairs, yes, it was upstairs.

At first he thought he was mistaken. Struggling out of his apathy, he listened hard. Yes, someone was talking. It was Yan. Her voice was gentle and placid, as though she were having a heart-to-heart conversation. But with whom?

"It's cold outside, really cold. You mustn't go out. Mummy doesn't want you to catch cold. And don't go to sleep. Mummy wants to talk with you. Are you hungry? I'll open a can of food for you, all right?"

Hell! It was Jerry she was talking to! Qiming shivered, not so much because Yan was talking to the dog; it was her unusual tone of voice, so gentle and placid, that made his flesh creep.

"Jerry, are you angry? Mummy isn't a good person. Mummy hit someone. She slapped your sister Ningning. Poor Ningning, she didn't deserve that. But she's a naughty girl. She doesn't come home, and that's bad of her. She's too busy running around to come and see Mummy. Jerry's a good boy. He doesn't go out. He stays with Mummy."

Qiming jumped up, intending to go upstairs and tell Yan not to talk like that. But he stopped himself. He felt he had no right to say anything to her. Sitting down again, he listened silently.

She was still talking to Jerry. "Mummy misses her home, her old home in China. But how can she take you there? You're a foreign dog, an American dog, and the people at home won't like you. They won't let you into the house. Poor Jerry, we're both unwanted. Jerry, Mummy learned to play the violin when she was eight years old and went to the music school attached to the Conservatory when she was thirteen. The Cultural Revolution started before she graduated. Mummy's been a Red Guard, but she never hit anyone. Later she was packed off to the countryside. Life was really hard there. When she was twenty she was assigned to the ensemble. A few years later she got married, and then there was Ningning. But life's been even harder for Mummy since she came to the United States ten years ago. You've seen that yourself, Jerry. My Jerry knows Mummy better than anyone else, doesn't he? People are bad. They prey on other people, they bully and cheat and hit and swear at people. My Jerry is better than they are. He doesn't do such things."

As Qiming listened to Yan saying things that could only come from a broken heart, he began to weep.

"People are heartless. There's no use being good to them, they'll only turn around and cheat on you. They don't have consciences. My Jerry has a conscience, doesn't he? When you grow big you'll get back at those bad people for me. You'll bite their feet, their legs and their necks, won't you?

"It doesn't matter if we can't go back to our old home. I'll take you away and I'll work as a maid or baby sitter. Oh, that's right. People don't let maids bring dogs with them. But never mind. The two of us can rent a basement apartment. Mummy will knit sweaters and earn some money. We'll save it up and Mummy will buy you toys, take you to the best beauty parlors and the best doctors. Jerry, Mummy will always keep you with her, Mummy knows you have a conscience and will never leave her.

"If Mummy dies, don't cry, don't fuss, don't look for me. I'll find a good family before I die and they'll take care of you. But you must behave yourself with them."

Yan had begun to sob. "Remember, Jerry. You mustn't come to look for me. It's too dangerous for you to run around by yourself on the streets. There are lots of bad people there. They'll cheat you, swindle you, eat you up. If Mummy doesn't die and gets rich, she'll buy you a big house and find a wife for you, and the two of you will have a lot of little Jerries. Won't that be nice?"

Instead of crying Yan was laughing lightheartedly now. The sound of that crazy laughter made shivers run up and down Qiming's spine. Yan talked all night long with the dog. Qiming listened to her mumbling, crying and laughing upstairs. At some point—he didn't know when—he dropped off to sleep.

He was awakened the next morning by Jerry's barking. Running up the stairs to Yan's room, he found her lying unconscious on the carpet. The dog barked angrily at him. Rushing downstairs again, he called an ambulance and took her to New York's First Hospital.

There he paced up and down in front of the emergency ward.

The resident physician came out. Qiming asked him about Yan's condition. "She's all right." The resident spoke wearily and coldly. "She's suffering from excessive mental stress and over exhaustion and needs a period of rest."

"For how long?"

"Two weeks or so."

"Thank you."

Qiming immediately drove home, opened a can of dog food and emptied the contents into Jerry's bowl. Then he washed himself up and, without taking a moment's rest, went straight to the factory.

It was as bleak and deserted as a burial ground. The workers had left. Of course, since they hadn't been paid. Piles of half-completed sweaters lay around; stacks of boxes filled with unused wool almost reached the ceiling. Rows of machines stood motionless with half-knitted garments dangling from them. The silence was scary. Qiming yearned for the earlier scenes of busy activity here. But now all was as quiet as death. The only sound he could hear was the thumping of his own heart.

A telephone rang in his office. He went in and reached for the receiver. But he drew his hand back without touching it. Another telephone began to ring. He knew who was calling. It was some creditor or worker who wanted to press him for a payment or for wages. He walked out of the office and closed the door behind him. Let those damned phones ring.

Leaving the factory, he got in his car and drove toward home. He wanted to run out on his debts, to quit New York and go for a spin in Europe. But his thoughts went back again to Yan lying pale and thin in the hospital, and to the dog who was waiting alone at home and who had more of a conscience than human beings. Jerry. What a nice name.

He drove up to his house. Jerry's anger at him seemed to have evaporated, and the moment he saw Qiming he jumped around and wagged his tail. Qiming picked the dog up. Tears welled up in his eyes. The dog raised its muzzle to Qiming's face and snuffled as though to console him, then licked away his tears with its soft, moist tongue.

Qiming was touched by this show of affection and concern. He hugged the dog, and as Yan had done began to talk to Jerry—to this dog who knew human nature better than human beings themselves.

"Have you missed Daddy, Jerry?" asked Qiming, gently and placidly. "Mummy's in the hospital. But don't worry, she's all right."

Jerry gave two little barks in reply.

"You're a good boy, our good boy. Nobody's more faithful than you are. I bet no one can beat you for loyalty and devotion, especially not a human being. I've been unfair to you, Jerry. All this time you've been with us I didn't notice your good qualities. It's only now that I've found you, Jerry. You aren't offended, are you?

"I'm worn out. I've been done in by those people. Who are they? They aren't bad guys. They're the same as I am, and they're doing these things to survive. You mustn't think they're bad people. Everyone does the same thing, and there's nothing unreasonable about it. The thing is, Jerry, I'm tired. I don't have any more strength. I must relax. That's right, Jerry! I'd like to have a drink. Is that okay with you?" He got up, took a bottle of whiskey from the sideboard and uncorked it.

"Want some, Jerry?" he said as he sat down again and began drinking. "You know, Jerry, I still have a trick or two up my sleeve. I can't hold a candle to you, but I'm fairly intelligent as far as human beings go. Yes, I know what to do."

He called up his bank and asked for another loan, offering his two houses as collateral. The bank employee was very polite. "Mr. Wang, allow me to check the documentation on these two houses before giving you a reply."

"Yes, that seems reasonable." Qiming hung up to wait for the answer.

He took another drink. "You see, Jerry? We're saved now. And who's saving us? We ourselves! I've got what it takes to get us out of this fix. I'll get help. The bank will bail me out. My credit has always been unassailable. They'll help me for sure, now that I'm in a tight spot."

Maybe because he was tired or had had too much whiskey, Qiming was feeling a bit dizzy. He was debating with himself whether or not to take a nap when the phone rang. It was the bank employee.

"Mr. Wang, your loan won't be very large. We can't lend you any money on the house you bought the year before last. Its value has gone down considerably and is continuing to fall. Besides, your down payment on it is quite inconsistent with current market prices." He sounded very polite but very cold-blooded. "As for your other house, the old one, we propose to lend you twenty-five thousand dollars on it."

"How much?"

"Twenty-five thousand dollars. If you agree to that, come in and sign for it tomorrow morning."

"Twenty-five thousand! What good will that do me? I need two hundred and fifty thousand at the very least!"

"In that case we can't help you. I'm very sorry."

Qiming helplessly put down the receiver. Those American banks were too clever. When you had money they came to help you and were willing to lend their money, knowing you were able to pay them back. But once you were strapped for cash and needed to borrow some, they dropped you cold and simply looked on as you tried to keep your head above water.

Finished! He was at the end of his rope. He picked up the bottle and tipped it over his glass. Nothing came out. He gave the empty bottle a push. It fell off the table onto the floor without breaking and rolled up to Jerry's feet. Jerry gave a few barks.

Lack of sleep, the relentless tension of the past few days and the effects of the alcohol made it impossible for him to think any more. He lay down on the couch and almost at once fell fast asleep. A parched feeling in his mouth woke him up in the middle of the night. He looked at the big grandfather clock standing against the wall.

It was three o'clock. He stood up unsteadily and went to get some water. Just at this moment the phone began to ring. "Don't answer!" he told himself. "It must be those workers playing a practical joke, purposely preventing me from sleeping or getting some peace of mind."

Wearily he returned to the couch. He intended to ignore that pesky ringing. But the phone kept on ringing, insistently. All right! Answer it! He remembered a line from the Peking Opera *Taking Tiger Mountain by Strategem*. How did it go? "You want money? I haven't got any. Food? It's all been taken away. My life? That you can have!"

He picked up the receiver. "Wang Qiming speaking."

"Are you Mr. Wang?"

"Yes."

"Excuse me for disturbing you at such a late hour."

The person at the other end was speaking Chinese with slight Cantonese overtones. But the accent was neither fish nor fowl, and Qiming couldn't tell whether a Chinese or an American was talking. "Go on, please. Who's speaking?"

"That doesn't matter."

"What's the meaning of this? Why an anonymous call?"

"Let's not talk about this. It's irrelevant."

"Then what do you want to talk about, calling at three in the morning?"

"Your daughter."

"Ningning?" He felt as though someone had taken his heart in a vise-like grip.

"Yes, that's her name."

"Where is she?"

"She's fine. She wants to see you. And I think you want to see her, too."

"Tell me where she is."

"She's with me. You know, I'm short on cash."

Qiming knew now what kind of person he was dealing with. "How much do you want?"

"Five hundred thousand."

"This is kidnapping!"

"You're real smart!"

"I'll get the police. They'll arrest you."

"No you won't. You wouldn't be that stupid. If you do that, you'll see your daughter again, but she won't see you."

"You lousy bastard!"

"Cut the crap! Are you paying up or not? I'm hanging up now."

"Wait a minute!"

Beads of sweat broke out on Qiming's forehead. He looked helplessly around but found nothing that could offer him any inspiration. "Look here," he said into the receiver. "I can't get that much money together at the moment."

"Let's not be so shy about it. Everybody in New York's Chinese commercial circles knows how much you're good for."

"But I have problems right now!"

"Bullshit! Bring the dough if you want her alive. Do you want that?"

"Yes! Yes!"

"I'll let her say a few words to you, in case you think I'm conning you!"

Ningning's voice came on the line. "Dad! Don't give them the money! Don't..."

The sound of someone being slapped came over the receiver, then a man said savagely, "Okay. Have you made up your mind?"

"Yes. I'll pay."

"That's the spirit! One hour from now, under the highway culvert to the left of Queens Cemetery. I want cash, used bills. Remember, don't play any games, or you'll get yours at the same time!"

There was a click and the phone went dead.

- 23 -

Qiming went upstairs to his bedroom and took a briefcase out of the wardrobe. Carrying it downstairs to the living room, he lined it with bundles of cut newspapers. On top of this he spread a layer of paper bills, a few hundred dollars. This was the last of his money.

He closed the lid and locked it. Jerry sat on the couch, watching him.

He then went to his desk and opened a drawer. Taking out an Italian-made revolver, he checked each of the chambers: seven bullets. They gleamed with a cold, sinister light. He snapped the cylinder back into position and pushed on the safety, then slipped the gun into the pocket of his overcoat.

Everything was ready. He looked at his watch. Thirty more minutes. He took a deep breath and touched the gun, then picked up the briefcase and walked out of the house. The night was as dark as a cave. Hardly any cars were to be seen on the highway.

He drove toward the appointed spot, his face expressionless and his mind a blank. He would rescue Ningning even if he died in the attempt. The headlights of occasional cars cruising in the opposite direction swept across the hood of his car and over his wooden features.

The car stopped beside the highway, near the long, dark tunnel of the culvert. On the other side of the culvert was the cemetery. The night was absolutely still, a waning moon hung distantly in the sky. Qiming got out of the car with the briefcase and loitered near the mouth of the culvert. He reckoned that the hour was up, but no one was in sight.

He sensed that he was shivering, perhaps from the cold, or perhaps because he was too tense. Crouching down, he kept his eyes glued to the culvert and his ears alert for sounds, like a cat lurking beside a rat hole.

A voice spoke inside the culvert. "Put down the money."

It was the voice on the phone and it echoed in the tunnel.

"I want to see my daughter first," Qiming said firmly.

"Put down the money and take ten steps back!" came the order.

Qiming could hear footsteps inside the tunnel. He ignored the order. Instead, he took two steps forward.

"You heard me. Put the money down."

Qiming still didn't lay down the briefcase.

"Put the money down and take ten steps back, or else I'll shoot."

"I won't put the money down unless I see my daughter."

"I'll count ten," replied the voice in the tunnel. "If you don't put down the money I'll kill your daughter."

"How do I know if my daughter's here," Qiming shouted furiously. "Ningning! Ningning!"

"One, two, three, four..."

Qiming stood undecided. But when the count reached six he unwillingly dropped the briefcase on the ground. Someone in the tunnel walked forward.

"That's more like it!"

The kidnapper was coming out. Qiming began to panic; he couldn't let the guy find out about the money.

Kill the bastard! But he didn't know how many of them there were, and Ningning was still in their hands.

He put his hand in his pocket. Suddenly, there was the sound of someone falling in the tunnel, followed by Ningning's shouts.

"Dad! Dad! Never mind me! Don't give it to them! Don't..."

Two shots rang out.

More sounds of hurried footsteps mixed with cursing. Throwing caution to the winds, Qiming drew out his gun and rushed into the tunnel.

"Ningning! Ningning!"

He would kill those sons of bitches! He ran several steps in pursuit, then stumbled over something soft and yielding. In the darkness he heard his daughter moaning. Bending down, he groped around. "Ningning! Ningning!" he shouted. "Where are you?"

Suddenly, he touched Ningning's breast, then her face. He fell on his knees. His hand was sticky with warm blood, Ningning's blood. He crouched down by her ear.

"Ningning, Ningning," he called softly. "This is your dad. I've come for you. I've come to get you."

Ningning's voice came to his very faintly. "Dad."

"Yes, Ningning."

"Dad... I..."

"What do you want?"

"I want...to go home."

"Yes, Daddy's come to take you home."

"No. To our...old home."

Hot tears rose in his eyes. He picked his daughter up in his arms and staggered out of the tunnel. He could feel the blood pulsing out of the two bullet holes in her chest. Her blood covered his coat, soaked his trousers.

"Dad!"

"I hear you, Ningning!"

"Send me...back to our old home..."

"Right away! As soon as..."

Qiming felt his daughter's body shudder and then stiffen. By the light of the lamps along the highway he could see her ashen face. Her eyes were closed, never to open again.

Qiming stood stock-still for a moment. Then he turned toward the dark mouth of the culvert and screamed in despair.

"I fuck your ancestors!" His curses echoed for a long time in the empty culvert.

Carrying Ningning's body, Qiming got into the car. On the highway, lights now and then flitted across his face and over that of his dead daughter. Qiming cradled Ningning's head on his lap and wept.

"Ningning, Ningning! Sleep for a while. We'll be going home soon, to our old home..."

. .

It was only two in the afternoon but the sky was already as dark as it normally is at dusk. The cars on the highway had to turn on their headlights. A wind was rising. Heavy, black clouds bore down on New York's skyscrapers and soon the top stories were shrouded in impenetrable mist.

The wind strengthened. It whirled up old newspapers from the ground and swept them across deserted sidewalks or plastered them against street lamps where they flapped noisily. Some of the papers lurched forward along the walls like elderly people on unsteady legs.

Drivers stepped harder on their accelerators, realizing that a storm was imminent and hoping to get home before it broke.

A blast of thunder pealed overhead. Qiming in his new car had just emerged from the tunnel when the rain began to fall in Niagara-like torrents drumming heavily on the roof of the car.

The wipers operated at top speed, flinging rain from the windshield. But the roadway ahead, obscured behind curtains of water, was hardly visible. The wheels threw up sprays of water like the bow waves of a speedboat. Accumulated rainwater lay in sheets on the ground, making it difficult to control the car, which kept swerving. But Qiming didn't slow down. He kept his foot pressed hard on the accelerator.

The car charged forward at high speed, battling and struggling with the storm. The violent bucking and swerving caused a bouquet of white flowers on the dashboard to fall on the floor. Keeping his left hand on the steering wheel and his eyes on the road ahead, Qiming bent down to grope for the bouquet with his other hand.

He found the flowers and was about to put them back on the dashboard when he suddenly saw a pair of brake lights flash in front of his car. It was already too late to hit the brakes. He spun his steering wheel to the left. At once the central divider of the highway came straight at the nose of his car. He spun the wheel back to the right. His car shot past the other car, scraping the concrete divider and raising a shower of sparks.

The body of his new car was scored from end to end with deep scratches that would probably never be entirely removed. With complete indifference, Qiming accelerated again and the damaged car flew through the barrier of rain.

The cemetery, where generally few people came, had no visitors at all this day because of the weather. As he opened the car door and stepped out, the rain beat down so heavily he could hardly raise his head. Bending over and hugging the bouquet of flowers to his breast, he searched for his daughter's grave. He couldn't find it. The driving rain made keeping his eyes open difficult and blurred the lettering on the tombstones.

Lightning split the sky. Guided perhaps by the lightning, his eyes lit on Ningning's tombstone. Its apparition, as abrupt as Ningning's appearances when she had been alive, almost took Qiming by surprise.

He stood in front of his daughter's tombstone. On it he read:

CATHY WANG
FEBRUARY 1969-DECEMBER 1988

He gazed at the letters as though he were seeking his daughter's face in them. With shaking hands he placed the bouquet at the foot of the tombstone. The delicate petals of the flowers were instantly beaten down by wind and rain into the grass at his feet. Thunder rumbled in long, hundred-gun salvoes.

He had a feeling that the skin had been flayed from his back and stretched over a drum and that heavy sticks were pounding it. His whole body quivered. With his arm and the back of this hand he wiped his face, hardly knowing whether the moisture was rainwater or tears. He wanted to look once more at the white flowers but by now they had been torn apart by the rain.

"Ningning."

His voice was so low only he could have heard it, but he was sure Ningning would hear it too.

"Daddy has come to see you."

He paused a little while. "I was wrong, Ningning! And I was unfair to you."

He slipped to his knees and pressed his head against the tombstone. His shoulders shook. Weeping, speaking in broken, incoherent bursts, he talked and talked to his daughter, confident that wherever she was she would hear his repenting words. Suddenly he saw a petal from one of the flowers. Picking it up carefully, he pressed it to his lips.

"I was wrong, Ningning. I really was!"

But where had he been wrong? Was he wrong because he had hit her? Or because he let her have her independence? Or because he let her have it too soon? Should or shouldn't he have gone to that infernal culvert?

Maybe he shouldn't have brought her to New York. Or maybe he shouldn't even have come himself! Where exactly had he been wrong? Qiming wasn't clear himself. All he could do was pour out everything he had in his heart; the right and the wrong, the clear and the unclear.

Ningning would understand.

. . .

When Qiming got home he changed into dry clothes. If he remembered correctly, the CAAC flight from China was arriving exactly two hours from now. He had to meet someone at the airport.

Just as he was leaving the house the phone rang. He decided not to answer it. But the ringing continued as he locked the doors. Changing his mind, he unlocked the doors again and went to the phone. It was Antonio. He told Qiming that his financial situation had improved somewhat and that he would soon pay what he owed for the deliveries.

"Once more my apologies," said Antonio. "I hope we will work together with greater success in the future."

"Thank you," replied Qiming coldly.

"When can we discuss our next deal?" Antonio sounded quite warm and enthusiastic.

"Not now. I have to meet someone from China at the airport. I'm sorry."

"Then I mustn't hold you up. We'll talk later. By the way, is it a Chinese boy you're meeting?"

"Yes."

"I hope he'll be as fortunate as you."

"That's possible."

Hanging up, Qiming went out again and drove off toward JFK Airport. The rain had stopped. The car sped along the highway, which had been washed clean by the rain. In the distance, lights were coming on in Manhattan's tall building. Those lights looked especially bright today.

The spires of two of New York's most famous buildings, the Empire State Building and St. Patrick's Cathedral, pointed dagger-like at the sky. Their upside-down reflections appeared on the puddles of rainwater on the roadway. Qiming felt a sudden pain, as if those daggers had been plunged into his chest.

He arrived at the airport in good time. The CAAC flight had just arrived at the landing port and passengers from mainland China were pouring out of the baggage claim exit. Their eyes reflected undisguised curiosity and wonder.

"Qiming! Buddy!"

Qiming looked around and saw Deng Wei with a large suitcase on his shoulder and carrying a bag in one hand. Qiming went toward him.

Deng Wei put down the suitcase and bag and gave Qiming a bear hug. He was agitated and close to tears.

"I don't know how to thank you, buddy. Without you, I'd never have made it out!"

"Let's get going, Deng Wei." Qiming was in no mood to smile but he forced himself to do so. He'd have looked more cheerful if he'd cried instead.

"Qiming, where's Yan?"

"She's too busy!"

"That shouldn't keep her from coming to meet a buddy. If she's being uppity, don't try to stop me when I tell her where to get off!"

"Let's go."

"And where's Ningning? Actually, she's the one I've missed most. You wouldn't know how close to me she was after you left. Guess what? She even called me Daddy. That kid will be happier to see me than she was when she saw you. I've brought her some honeyed noodles. She likes them."

Qiming quickly averted his face.

Deng Wei kept on chattering excitedly as they walked along. "I never thought we'd get together again in New York! Remember that night ten years ago just before you came here? The four of us eating cabbage hearts and drinking Maotai? I bet you've forgotten that, you little punk!"

Qiming raised the suitcase to hide his eyes which were streaming with tears.

Deng Wei kept on talking. "And guess what? The guys at the ensemble are talking like mad about you and Yan, how you've hit it big in America. The big laoban, the rich businessman, the great success story. They're all green with envy."

They walked out of the airport, found Qiming's car and drove onto the highway.

"Hey, buddy!" said Deng Wei. "How much does a car like this cost? If you drove this car to Beijing, you'd really quake 'em down."

Ningning had used the same words the day she'd arrived in New York. Qiming winced with pain.

"Wow! Look at all those cars!" Deng Wei was gaping out of the window. "And the roads, so wide a smooth! Say, those are overpasses, aren't they? That's what I call modernization!"

Qiming didn't say anything, his eyes were fixed on the road ahead. Talk? What was there to talk about?

Deng Wei noticed his silence. "Hey, buddy! Why don't you say anything? Maybe you aren't happy to see me? Scared I'll give you trouble? Don't worry, buddy. I won't hassle you. If you can start out with nothing and become a millionaire, so can I. Just give me your prescription and I'll fill it out. Yes sirree!"

"It's no trouble," said Qiming. "I'm just not feeling well. Headache."

"You should've told me."

Deng Wei shut up after that. When they reached Manhattan, however, he couldn't keep quiet any longer.

"Wow! Just take a look at that! It's paradise!" He lowered the window and stared avidly at the sights. They drove through Manhattan and came to the Harlem district.

"Hey, buddy. Where are you taking me?" Deng Wei exclaimed. "What the hell is this place? How come there are such fucked-up places in New York? Hey, stop kidding. What are you stopping here for?"

The car stopped in from of the house Qiming had lived in when he first came to New York. Qiming got out and began to unload Deng Wei's luggage. Deng Wei was bewildered. "Hey, what's all this about?"

"I've taken your financial situation into consideration. The rent is relatively cheap here." He carried Deng Wei's things into the dark, dirty little building.

"What's this! You aren't leaving me here, are you?"

"No. The apartments on this story are too expensive. I've reserved one for you in the basement."

"Say, buddy. Are you pulling my leg, or what?"

Qiming showed Deng Wei to the basement apartment, then handed him an envelope. "Here's five hundred dollars. This, plus four hundred for the apartment's deposit and rent come to nine hundred dollars. Take the money. You can return it to me when you've made some money yourself."

Deng Wei merely gaped at him. Qiming looked at his watch.

"I have some urgent business," he said. "I've got to go." He opened the door and walked out.

Deng Wei's curses floated out of the tiny basement window. "It sure is weird! Why does a guy turn into such a fucker after he comes to the United States? This screwed-up place isn't fit for human beings!"

After depositing Deng Wei at the apartment Qiming drove back to the highway. He was going to see Yan. The night and the highway were pitch dark and he drove almost by instinct.

He turned on the tape recorder. The same old song came out of the speakers:

> If you love him
> Send him to New York,
> 'Cause that's where Heaven is.
> If you hate him
> Send him to New York,
> 'Cause that's where Hell is...

BEIJINGER IN NEW YORK

The bestselling novel in China is now available in an English translation. **BEIJINGER IN NEW YORK** tells the story of Wang Qiming, a poor musician who arrives with his wife in New York, full of hope for a new life. Numerous setbacks fail to discourage them, and it appears the American dream will become reality for them. But with their success comes tragedy, as their wealth comes at a high cost for their family life.

AUTHOR GLEN CAO

became a household name in China with the publication of this novel, serialization in a leading newspaper and the subsequent TV series based on the novel. The story here reflects and reinforces Chinese attitudes about the U.S., where material wealth may be gained, but at great personal sacrifice. With Chinese immigration to the U.S. a controversial topic, this translation of Cao's work is even more timely for American readers.

0-8351-2526-2 $14.95